# POWER'S GARDEN

# POWER'S GARDEN

A NOVEL BY

# DIANNE EBERTT BEEAFF

*Dianne Ebertt Beeaff*

FIL
Beeaff
7/11

## FIVE STAR PUBLICATIONS, INC.
### CHANDLER, ARIZONA

Linda F. Radke, President
Five Star Publications, Inc.
POB 6698
Chandler, AZ 85246-6698
480-940-8182

www.PowersGarden.com

Publisher's Cataloging-In-Publication Data

Library of Congress Cataloging-In-Publication Data

Beeaff, Dianne Ebertt.

Power's Garden : a novel / by Dianne Ebertt Beeaff. – 1st ed.

    p. cm.
ISBN-13: 978-1-58985-124-5
ISBN-10: 1-58985-124-2

1. Sheriffs – Fiction. 2. Mormons – Fiction. 3. Ranchers – Fiction.
4. Gunfights – Fiction. 5. Gila River Valley (N.M. and Ariz.) – Fiction. I. Title.

    PS3552.E319P68 2009
    813'.54–dc22

                    2009005026

Printed in the United States of America
PROJECT MANAGER: Sue DeFabis
EDITING BY: Jennifer Christensen
COVER DESIGN BY: Kris Taft-Miller
INTERIOR LAYOUT BY: Koren Publishing Services

10 9 8 7 6 5 4 3 2 1

*For Dan with love and gratitude*
*for always seeing me through.*

*"We see things
not as they are
but as we are."*

— G.T.W. Patrick

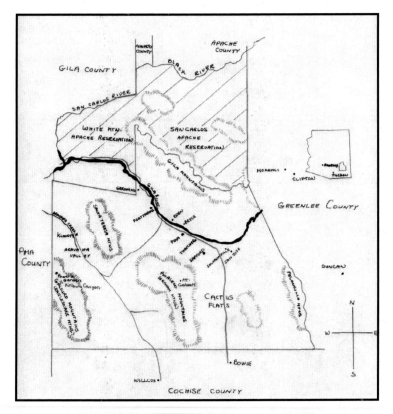

Upper Gila Valley, Graham County, 1918

# Prologue

In the early hours of February 10, 1918, four men surrounded an isolated cabin in Kielberg Canyon, nestled in the Galiuro Mountains of southeastern Arizona. In the gun battle that followed, four men died. Their deaths sparked the most intensive – and ultimately unjustified – manhunt in Arizona history.

The valley of the upper Gila River dominates Graham County in southeastern Arizona. The river passes through from the southeast on its way to the Salt, which in turn joins the Colorado further west. About thirty-five miles long, the upper Gila Valley opens from box canyons on either end. To the northeast lie the barren Gila Mountains, with the high Pinalenos rising twenty miles to the south. Beyond the

Pinalenos and bordering the Aravaipa Valley on the south-west lie the Galiuro Mountains.

Since the 1870s, the Church of Jesus Christ of Latter Day Saints has farmed the fertile upper Gila Valley, with the barren surrounding areas dominated by non-Mormon cattle ranchers. The men who rode into Kielberg Canyon that February morning were Deputy U.S. Marshal Robert Frank Haynes from Globe in Gila County, Frank McBride, the sheriff of Graham County from Safford in the Gila Valley, and two of his deputies – Martin R. Kempton and T.K. "Kane" Wootan, also from the Valley. All of the Graham County men belonged to the Mormon Church. Only Marshal Haynes survived.

Inside the Kielberg cabin were Thomas Jefferson Power, Sr. – who also died that February morning – his sons, Thomas Jefferson Power, Jr. and John Grant Power, and their hired hand, Tom Sisson. Jeff Power, Sr. had come from Texas in 1907, bringing with him his widowed mother and four young children – Tom, John, a third son, Charley, and his daughter, Ola May. The Power family worked cattle in and around Rattlesnake Spring Ranch, eight miles north of the Kielberg cabin. There, at a place still called Power's Garden, they had diverted Rattlesnake Creek for planting.

*Power's Garden* – the story of two families, one Mormon, one Texan – is told against the backdrop of both the Kielberg cabin shootout and the First World War. The tenuous, illusive and sometimes violent events unfolding in Arizona's Gila Valley throughout the early 20th century reflect a bitter ongoing culture clash, a division vividly and tragically expressed in Power's Garden in the winter of 1918. For tradition is not cut from one cloth, and what the people *believe* to have happened is at least as important as what actually did.

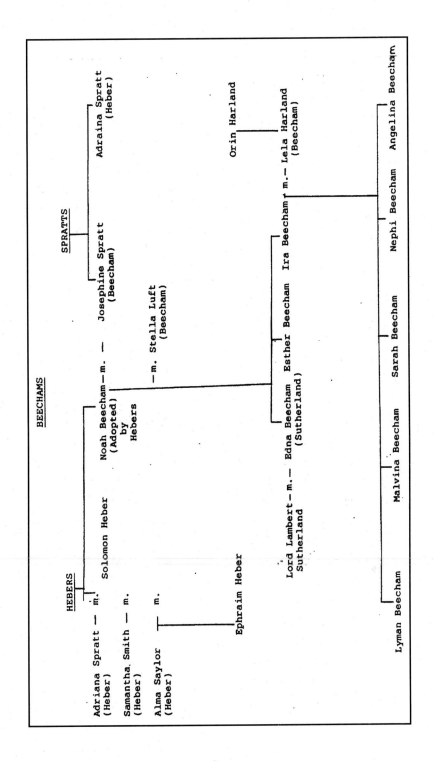

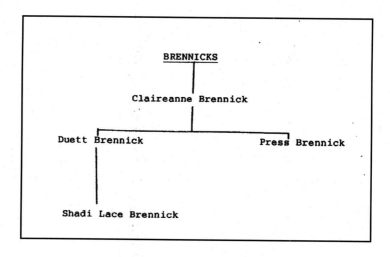

BRENNICKS

Claireanne Brennick

Duett Brennick                    Press Brennick

Shadi Lace Brennick

# BOOK ONE
# Mellie Beecham

# CHAPTER ONE

# Friday, November 16, 1917

"I won't have that Texas riffraff in this house!" Noah Beecham's bulk grazed the tabletop as he shuffled into the kitchen, his voice filling the room. He stopped and clapped his gnarled hands one atop the other on the crown of his walking stick and leaned on it heavily. "That which is lost can never be won again."

"Nothing's lost, Father Beecham," Mellie told her grandfather as she brushed aside the yellowing sun-bleached curtains that hung in the doorway of the bedroom that would soon be her mother's. Stepping inside, she crossed the small room to open the curtains at the west window. Failing sunlight dropped to the hardwood floor and glinted off the brass bed by the opposite wall, reflecting glimmering pink-tinged rays on the polished highboy in the northeast corner. Much like the room itself, the unmade bed was bare, except for a teetering collection of well-pressed cotton sheets that Mellie had just placed there. As she kneaded a particularly persistent lump in the thin mattress ticking, the stack of sheets slumped even further, the uppermost draping over the side of the bed, its hem nearly touching the floor.

"'And the wicked shall be cast out, thus saith the Lord!'" Noah added from the adjoining room.

Mellie sighed, flipped the fallen sheet roughly back onto the feather ticking with some annoyance, and smoothed the bodice of her shirtwaist, an off-white organdy fitted to her slim figure with a neat string of pin-tucks. Father Beecham had already pronounced the lace inserts in the sleeves as "frivolous." That he was clearly displeased gave Mellie a vague satisfaction. Adjusting the pins that held her sand-colored hair in a swirl over each ear, she stepped back into the kitchen.

"Do you hear me, Malvina?"

"Of course I do, Father Beecham." Mellie smiled past the silver rim of her grandfather's eyeglasses into deep sea-blue eyes – the sole trait it could be said she had inherited from the old man – and eased him gently into a kitchen chair. The wicker bottom snapped with his weight, and a musty odor seeped from his worn black homespun trousers. Without the splash of yellow silk in his lapel – lemon-yellow roses had been his first wife Josephine Spratt Beecham's favorite – Father Beecham's woolen suit and button-down vest would have seemed little more than a shroud.

"We need someone like Delfina," Mellie said as she lit the stove, recalling the cheerful face of Father Beecham's previous housekeeper. Orange rings began to glow from under the stove's iron plates as Mellie stoked the fire. "Papa's trusted me to find someone suitable to help out around the house now that Delfina's gone back to Tucson. We're to offer thirty dollars a month plus room and board." She reached for a shallow basket of clothing on top of the icebox beside the back door. "Mama will be out here at the farm for several weeks. At least until after the reunion on Sunday. And then there's Thanksgiving and Christmas. Someone should be in the house at all times, don't you think?"

Father Beecham rapped his cane on the speckled linoleum floor. "Someone from the Valley then," he said and propped his hands on the gold-tipped crown. "One of you fine Mormon girls not weary in well-doing. I don't trust this...what's this gentile woman's name?"

Mellie retreated to her mother's room again and transferred the contents of the basket into the highboy – black stockings, three slips, a pleated chemise and several cotton shirtwaists. Lela's frocks would soon fill the cherry-wood wardrobe behind her. "Duett Brennick. She's agreed to stay on. Miss Brennick and I met at the circus in Safford," she said with a slow half-smile. "She lost her husband in the mines a few years back."

"For the love of God, Malvina, have you no shame?" Father Beecham's voice shivered along Mellie's arms. "The Lord provides all things for which we have a true need. When I first came to the Valley of the Great Salt Lake with Solomon Heber and his family, having lost my own, there was great famine. We scoured the land for any weed at all, scarcely finding enough for one man's meal. But we prayed in great humility for something to eat. And in a short time Solomon came back with a basket of crisp greens. We were all amazed. They'd been planted before us, you see. Given by the hand of God. Only a miracle could have saved us then, and we recognized his blessing. The Lord provides whatever he deems our greatest good."

"Mama's greatest good is to have before her a friendly face and a competent hand, don't you think?" As Mellie re-entered the kitchen, a grating movement overhead snapped the upstairs silence. The sound moved closer, across the old wooden floorboards and down the front staircase. "If Nephi's around," she said, "he can help with Mama's blanket chest."

The old man shifted in his chair but said nothing more, and Mellie moved past him to the arched doorway of the dining room, expecting her younger brother to materialize out of the parlor's bare-walled gloom. Faint pulses from the mantle clock in the front library drifted in to creep along her arms as she waited.

Years ago, when all of the Beechams had lived at the farm together, the old house had been boisterous and agreeable, but those days were nearly forgotten. In the failing light, Mellie could just make out the parlor's long leather-topped desk, and she sighed with a fond recollection. She and her older brother, Lyman, had collected their lesson books there each morning before being hurried off to school.

The last time everyone had gathered here, though, was in the fall of 1905, when Mellie was just twelve. And it had been a somber occasion, a commemoration of Josephine's October death. By then, the Pima farm had already begun to sour and sag, and it had worsened in both structure and spirit with each passing year. Father Beecham homesteaded it now, as he had since Josephine's death.

"Nephi!" Mellie's voice bounded along the walls of the darkened house, in anticipation of her brother's appearance.

Instead, from across the dim parlor, a uniformed Ephraim Heber – Solomon Heber's youngest son by his third wife, the now-deceased Alma Saylor Heber – emerged from the shadows. A stifled groan escaped Mellie's lips as he stepped confidently into the room, readily accepting her unintended attention. "You're early, Ephraim," she said with no attempt to mask her disappointment. "Your postcard said you'd be on leave for two weeks over Christmas."

"Two weeks, yes…but not over Christmas." Something unsettling stirred in the back of Ephraim's coal-black eyes as he braced himself against the spindle-work archway of the kitchen pantry. In the faded light, his infantry uniform – a high-collared woolen jacket and wide-topped trousers – dulled to a brackish olive green. "You do my father and your grandfather much honor with the reunion you've arranged for Sunday, Malvina," he said, his menacingly handsome features softening. "I've just come from bringing Father Heber and Aunt Samantha's family into town." Ephraim's chilly gaze fell to the old man and then thawed a little with shared admiration of his father, Solomon Heber, and Solomon's second and only living wife, Samantha Smith Heber. "But I heard Father Beecham, and his point is well taken. We must direct our thoughts toward what is proper and good by God's Word, not by our own understanding."

Ignoring Ephraim's uninvited sermon, Mellie turned the conversation toward her fifteen-year-old sister, Sarah, Nephi's free-spirited twin. "Sarah's been a great help since Delfina left," she said, though this was not exactly true. Sarah's help had been sporadic at best but offered a welcome diversion. "Will you be here through Thanksgiving then?"

Ephraim glanced at Noah. "Looks like it. I'm headed overseas on my return to camp at the end of the month," he answered with a half-smile, his arms folded across his chest. "I suppose that's why my request for an early leave was approved."

"The Lord has told us these wars would come." Father

Beecham interjected, hauling himself from his chair and striking a match from the stove-top to light the oil lamp on the table. His bearded face flickered eerily in the circle of lamplight and left ghostly shadows dancing on the empty kitchen walls. "We must call upon our Divine Protector to defend us against our enemies, and our armies must rise up. Armies comprised of stalwart men like Ephraim here," Father Beecham acknowledged the young man with a forceful stab of his cane. "Such men are high-minded, honest and virtuous. They go with great honor to defend the liberties of mankind." The old man paused and gave Mellie a calculated stare. "A woman could have a lesser champion for her soul."

Mellie's jaw tightened and her eyes flickered from Ephraim to Father Beecham and back again. "Ephraim need not champion for me...or my soul," she said emphatically, aware that Father Beecham had already waved her objection aside.

"They call some of us in the camps 'slackers'," Ephraim said, the two men continuing as if Mellie had disappeared. He pronounced the word with intense loathing. "Slackers... because we didn't enlist back in April, when America first went to war. Slackers, because we were called up in the draft instead."

Father Beecham pounded his cane on the floor. "Those loafers down there by the border," he said, icy eyes darting around the room. "They're lawless brigands...and those boys from Texas skulking up there in Power's Garden... Outlaws the lot of them! Now *there* be your slackers. Crude, unprincipled, uneducated desperados just like their kinfolk. For such people, a free country means plain sinful license." He eyed Mellie again. "And it's one of these that my own granddaughter brings into this house."

Mellie went back to Lela's room and began to sort the bedclothes, shaking out the sheets with fuming gusto. "Could you bring Mama's blanket chest in from the auto, Ephraim?" she called out to the kitchen. "It'll be dark and cold soon. I'll fetch her in from the garden."

As the conversation between the two men grew less animated, Mellie paused in her work and watched her grandfather furtively through a narrowed opening in the curtained doorway. Two years of Saturdays after Josephine's death and five years before that, Mellie had walked the old man from the lane of the old Pima farmhouse on the edge of town to her father's Pima store for supper and a visit with the family. The duty had become a family tradition, a rite of passage for the children, and in February of 1910, when the twins, Sarah and Nephi, turned eight and were baptized into the Church, they had taken *their* turn. This past year, with Nephi having moved out to the farm, he and the old man had come in together, Ephraim Heber more often than not with them – at least until he'd been called to the Colors.

In December, Angelina, the youngest of the five Beecham children, would be baptized, and the duty would fall to her, poor child. Mellie didn't envy little Angel the newfound responsibility and hoped her baby sister would be spared their grandfather's tirades. As they'd made their way week after week through the wide Pima streets, Noah had frightened a young and impressionable Mellie with his coarse gray hair and frazzled beard. A grim, black tower of a man, he'd often speak only to demand some recitation or other from *The Book of Mormon or The Pearl of Great Price*, diverse collections of LDS scripture believed to have been translated by the founding Mormon prophet, Joseph Smith. Father Beecham was also known to lecture austerely on "living a life in the Lord," his lessons punctuated with endless tales of mysticism and miracles in the Valley of the Great Salt Lake that were far beyond a young child's comprehension. With time, though, Noah had lost much of his power to intimidate Mellie, and she found herself increasingly gratified by his discomfort. She hoped Angelina would fare as well.

Finished with the bedding, Mellie straightened, tugged the cord of the bare electric bulb overhead, and surveyed the room, now sharpened with light and new clarity. "A bit sparse, but adequate," she thought with some satisfaction. The brass bed was fluffed and inviting, the highboy topped with a flowery embroidered runner of her mother's own making. On the pinewood dressing table, Mellie had arranged an ivory-handled dresser set, along with a framed collection of family pictures, painstakingly developed at Lyman's photography studio in Safford.

Just left of the bed, an upended crate held a tight knot of beeswax candles, and Mellie had pushed two cane-bottomed chairs up against the west wall. An empty wardrobe was lost in the corner shadows, awaiting the room's upcoming occupancy. Pleased with her efforts, Mellie moved to close the thick mint-green window curtains adorning both windows, while all around the walls shadows shifted and swayed in the flickering light overhead.

Rejoining the men in the kitchen, Mellie drew a sharp breath when Ephraim placed a commanding hand at the small of her back. Undaunted, he flung open the outer door and maneuvered her outside, guiding her down the porch steps and across the yard as though she were a child.

Two women sat on the wooden bench at the end of the garden's stone-lined walkway. They were leaning toward each other warmly, deep in conversation in the gathering twilight. The nearest, her back to Mellie and Ephraim, gestured with animation, snatches of a sunny Texas drawl punctuating the air. A twinge of disapproval flickered across Ephraim's face, and Mellie suppressed a smile.

"Mellie dear," the other woman said with a welcoming wave. "And Ephraim," Lela Beecham's initial smile faded somewhat, but she was cordial. "How nice to see you again. Isn't the evening air peaceful? Miss Brennick, that is, Duett here, has been telling me the sweetest things about her little girl, Shadi Lace." Lela turned toward her daughter with outstretched arms. Slight and pale, she stood up with the embrace, her long graying hair swept from the sides of her thin face into a loose bun. The young woman beside her bent instinctively to retrieve an embroidered lap blanket that had escaped Lela's grasp and dropped to the ground below.

"Ephraim Heber," Mellie said. "This is Duett Brennick... Father Beecham's new housekeeper."

Ephraim stiffened and withdrew his arm from Mellie's waist. Duett Brennick, twenty-four and radiant, was clearly not the "fine Mormon girl not weary in well-doing" that both Ephraim and Father Beecham had envisioned and much preferred as a hired hand. Arrayed in a cotton shirt-waist, divided skirt and riding boots, Duett's form-fitting apparel shocked Ephraim's sense of propriety, and he acknowledged her with a disdainful nod. "My pleasure, I'm sure, Miss Brennick," he said icily.

"Mighty pleased I am to make *your* acquaintance, too, Mr. Heber," Duett answered, her brown eyes flashing beneath a fringe of thick, chestnut-colored hair.

Ephraim very nearly snapped to attention then, and Mellie flinched with the thought that he meant to salute the three of them. Clenching his chiseled jaw, Ephraim excused himself at once and went about his business.

# CHAPTER TWO

# Saturday, November 17, 1917

Lela Beecham's silky-fine hair spilled down the back of her chair, an upholstered balloon-backed favorite that she'd had delivered from the Pima store. Her room at the farm had also been furnished with a hand-carved blanket chest and her treasured Victrola, a luxury afforded her as an anniversary gift. At Lela's direction, Ephraim had placed the chest at the foot of the bed, and it now served as a tabletop for a butter-yellow cup of Father Beecham's hedge mustard tea.

Frequent childhood respiratory infections had weakened Lela's disposition, leaving her with a chronic bronchial condition that wracked her delicate frame with painful coughing fits. Hedge mustard tea was one of her father-in-law's favored cure-all remedies, though the bitter substance had as yet been of no great benefit to Lela, so far as Mellie could tell. Her mother's thin face paled more by the day, it seemed, her cheekbones framing sunken hollows, her water-blue eyes veiled with fatigue and shadowed below by darkened half-moons.

"I don't understand it, Mama," Mellie said. "After your conversion, you embraced the True Church fully, and yet Father Beecham treats you like you never really belong."

"Yes, Father Beecham is a man of…undeviating opinion," her mother answered knowingly. Lela's quiet laughter ignited another coughing spell, and Mellie reached for the tea, its pungent aroma making both women shudder.

Lela passed the teacup back to Mellie after a dutiful sip. "Your grandfather's sole interest is in living the law," she said. "He's held the world at arm's length here in the Valley for over thirty years. I suppose it's natural for him to be a bit skeptical of outsiders."

"But you're not an outsider, Mama," Mellie insisted, pulling a brush through the length of her mother's silver-sprinkled hair. "You're family! And besides, the Church controls so much of the Valley now. Water rights. Land. Father Beecham should be fellowshipping the newcomers, yet he's still so suspicious and afraid."

"I think he sees the Church losing ground in spiritual matters despite its seeming growth," Lela answered after some reflection. "A weakened spiritual influence means nothing to him if not an urgent and, I'm afraid, often frantic need for men like himself to defend the Faith. Not all of his words are issued in the spirit of goodwill by any means, I know. But he has a steady faith, and he does live the law." Lela paused and smiled faintly. "He's a very tired old man. And he's the only one who doesn't realize that yet."

Father Beecham's religious ardor had become increasingly puzzling for Mellie over the years. A dozen settlements dotted the Valley now, most of them Mormon. All of these, together with a string along the San Pedro River to the south and another along western New Mexico's portion of the Gila River, belonged to the St. Joseph Stake of the Church, an administrative unit akin to a Catholic diocese. Her grandfather's self-imposed isolation, even from members of his congregation, had left him with an acidic intolerance that seared both his soul and everyone around him.

"Father Beecham grew to manhood in Utah, in the very heart of Zion," Lela went on. "My father's poverty and 'rude manner of living,' as Father Beecham still likes to call it, left him with a strong sense of social superiority. I *am*, after all, one of those 'hot-tempered Southern converts' he so distrusts." She laughed again and reached for the tea. Lela's family had come from the backwoods of Arkansas in the late 1880s, so there was perhaps some truth to this, Mellie thought. After Lela's marriage, her father, Orin Harland, had continued to haul wood and water to Mormon homesteads in the Valley for over ten years. When artesian springs opened up an area to the south called Cactus Flats, Orin had readily moved to less arid ground.

From the eastern window, Mellie watched as Father Beecham paced the length of the orchard, stooping now and again to finger the dark soil. "Do you really think it's good for Nephi to be out here at the farm?" she asked her mother. "I mean with Father Beecham. And now with Ephraim back from training? Nephi's so frail and mystical, like Mother Josephine, and so easily influenced." In deep thought, Mellie stared after the old man. "The three of them seem like living parts of this house," she said. "They're like spindles on Father Beecham's old rocker in the library. Sometimes I can even see their faces in the yellow roses on the parlor wallpaper. I mean, Nephi's barely fifteen and they keep him spellbound, the two of them."

She shook her head and returned to her work. "You know, I remember when Nephi was just a little boy. The summer storms scared him so much he came into my room at night, and we'd sing away his fears. I told him all of that thunder was just for us – applause, you know. Like curtain call at the playhouse. We laughed and laughed, and he never once complained, even when he was sick for weeks on end with that lung trouble. He's changed so much these past years," Mellie lamented, her childhood memories overshadowed with worry.

"In the eyes of God, he's a man now, Malvina," Lela said softly. "Older and wiser."

"Oh, please." Mellie grimaced and looked to the ceiling. "Old is not a word I personally care to hear. It's usually followed with 'spinster.'"

Lela smiled. "Your trials are given to you to keep you humble, Mellie, so says the Faith. I gather Father Beecham has had Ephraim Heber on the auction block again."

"I'm twenty-four." Mellie sighed. "Is that so old? Father Beecham is determined that Ephraim and I will 'keep to the old ways as man and wife,' but when I marry, Mama, it will *not* be to Ephraim Heber. I haven't the will, the desire or the strength to endure him on earth, let alone share his 'glory' in the hereafter."

"You do have to follow your heart, Mellie." Lela chuckled. "And sometimes your heart leads you down a different path than you expected. A woman *may* find fulfillment through a husband and children, but she can still know the joy of work. Your calling now is in the classroom, Malvina. There's no shame in that. This is only your second year at the Academy in Thatcher, my dear. You still have time."

Over a comfortably shared silence, Lela took up her tea again. "What an inspiration your own school days were," she said wistfully. "The happiest of your life, as I recall. The work you're doing now can only enhance a future marriage."

"But is it selfish of me not to seek after marriage at all, Mama? All the spirits of heaven have to wait longer to be tested on earth, the Elders say, because of childless men and women like me."

"The family is the foundation of the Church, and a good home is God's great argument. That much is true. Women must prepare a new generation to better the world." Lela brushed her daughter's arm, the chill of ivory in her fingers. In spite of Father Beecham's prayers and ministrations, Lela's health had not improved. Her spirit, however, remained strong. "But remember, Malvina, when I used to challenge you children to find two blossoms or two leaves that were exactly alike? Or two pebbles in a stream? Could you ever do it?" Mellie shook her head. "Well, there it is. Variety is God's great handwork...Now, dear, when will the rest of the family be out for tomorrow's festivities?"

"Sarah's bringing Angelina from Primary at eleven. And then everyone but Lyman will be out straightaway with Papa. Nephi and Ephraim are outside now putting up the tables we borrowed from the Ward Hall." Mellie gathered in her mother's hair and, with the expertise of many years, bound it in a tight knot at the crown of Lela's head. "There now," she said. "You look lovely, Mama. Truly." Over the past several days, Lela's morning spells had diminished somewhat, but they had still taken a good deal out of her. "Let me help you lie down to rest."

Mellie supported Lela from behind as they stood, carefully guiding her mother to bed. Easing her onto the mattress, Mellie draped a small patchwork lap quilt over Lela's gathered skirts. "Duett has a wonderful meal planned, and Lyman's going to take photographs," Mellie said as she fluffed a pillow behind her mother's back. "I haven't had a chance to tell him that Ephraim's come home early, so we could have some, shall we say, unscheduled entertainment." She laughed and squeezed her mother's hand. "Rest a bit now. I'll be back in an hour or so." With a kiss to her mother's cheek, she left the room, closing the kitchen curtains behind her.

Despite the brilliant blue sky above, a chill had slipped into the evening air. Each November day had broken warmer than the last this year, but with little or no cloud cover, the nights dipped quickly back into the cold. In the kitchen, where Duett fluttered over the stove, Mellie went over a few last-minute details of the next day's reunion dinner and then went outside to oversee progress on seating arrangements. Near the orchard, Ephraim and Nephi had already arranged three collapsible tables and a stack of folding chairs, brought in from the Ward Amusement Hall down the road in Thatcher. One of these tables, the longest, stood framed against the orchard's hazy backdrop of winter fruit trees and the distant, barren hulk of the Gila Mountains. The other tables sat at either end, placed at right angles to the first.

The Beecham farmhouse squatted on the very edge of Pima, between the Safford road and the river. A steep mansard roof rose from all sides to the red brick central chimney, and bared mesquite trees bracketed a short flight of railed green steps that led up to an enclosed veranda trimmed in the same color. Just above the treetops, three evenly-spaced bedroom windows peaked over the slanted porch roof, each curtained in dull yellow lace. Parched straw-colored grasses sprinkled the back lot as far as the orchard and ran along all four sides of the house, except for a bald patch off the side porch, where Mellie's father, Ira, occasionally parked his Model T. Back toward town, across the yard to the southeast, a smatter of neighboring rooftops stood out among yellowing cottonwood trees, pale gray/green tamarisk and bare-limbed mesquites. In Pima, there was still water. Parched fields and a stale dustiness in the air were the only visible signs of a deepening drought that had closed in on the Valley since last summer.

Driving a borrowed black Packard, Ephraim and Nephi had just come in from Thatcher again, toting two short wooden benches. Nephi seemed preoccupied and somewhat hostile, so Mellie avoided the pair and settled herself on a step at the side entrance to the old house, pulling out notes for the upcoming program from her apron pocket. Ephraim's barked orders and Nephi's half-whispered replies accented the background as the furniture was unloaded. In time, her brother's meek voice disrupted Mellie's thoughts. "Malvina?" She looked up to see Nephi's pale face, his dusty blue eyes at once both pitiful and disturbing. One-third of the Host of Heaven had fallen from the grace of God in the spirit world, the Church taught. These fallen souls surrounded the earth, forever opposing and attempting to thwart the will of God. As a child, Mellie had been afraid one of these outcast spirits would possess her. That same haunted look suffused her brother's face.

"What is it, Nephi? Are you ill?"

"I've heard their voices, Mellie. I've heard the Three Nephites." Nephi sank to the step beside Mellie.

"Plain and precious things" lost in the Bible could be found in the Book of Mormon, the Church decreed. A history of the Nephite people was among these, a nation so favored that Christ had dwelt among them for a time in the

Americas. Of twelve apostles ordained by Christ in America, three had been allowed to live on the earth until his Second Coming, never tasting of death themselves. Poorly dressed, mild-mannered and well spoken, these three emissaries traveled the world, bestowing blessings on the faithful and healing the sick. They were old men with white beards who left no foot-prints in freshly fallen snow; who walked down a straight open road and disappeared; who brought miracles to Mormons in distress – a dollar in a shoe, a loaf of bread for a widow. Hundreds of accounts, both written and spoken of in hushed tones, circulated in the hills and valleys of Zion, the land of the Saints. But for some, the three Nephite vagabonds conjured up something more akin to terror. Mellie associated them with weed-grown cemeteries and shadowy willowed turns in the riverbed. "The Three Nephites?" she prompted.

"I heard them," Nephi said. "Like in a dream. They told me to follow the Word of God, so I opened the Bible and read in the book of Matthew, where Jesus says, 'Think not that I am come to send peace on earth. I came not to send peace but a sword.'"

Mellie's unease deepened. She had no idea what was on Nephi's mind, but he offered nothing more. The troubled lines on his face settled back into the small and vulnerable passivity she'd known throughout his childhood. "And so we have wars, like the one we're fighting now?" she asked. "Is that what you mean?"

Nephi shook his head. "No, it's not that exactly," he answered quietly. "The Lord sends the sword, but we must carry it. *Ephraim* must carry it." Nephi's voice intensified with emotion. "Will he be preserved?"

"What do you mean?" asked Mellie, still perplexed.

"Ephraim's faithful to the Church and he's faithful to

his country." Nephi swept a shag of sandy hair from his troubled eyes and tucked it under his cap. "This war *must* be just and honorable or Ephraim wouldn't go. And the Lord will sustain men who defend their freedom to worship, won't he?"

Nephi was sounding more like Father Beecham every day. The old man's fervor for the war had begun to mirror his scathing religious zeal, and Nephi was obviously enthralled. But beyond the Liberty Bonds and Meatless Tuesdays brought on by the conflict, Mellie had kept herself removed from it altogether. Even now, she could hardly give it her full attention. "I don't know how much of what we do is to defend ourselves or to preserve our right to worship God," she said. "But patriotism has to be more than a willingness to fight, don't you think?"

Nephi's forehead wrinkled, and he seemed about to speak again when Lyman's wagon lumbered up the lane and came to a creaking halt outside the barn. His response thwarted, Nephi turned his attention to Ephraim, who, at the foot of the side porch steps, had just begun to mend one of the slat-bottomed benches he'd unloaded from the Packard.

Lyman nimbly jumped off the far side of the wagon. As Mellie approached, he pulled a long, black necktie from the pocket of his tweed jacket, twisting it absentmindedly. "Ah, Mellie," he said with a smile. "Thought I'd bring the works out early and hitch a ride back to Safford with Pop later this afternoon. I can come out again tomorrow with Aunt Edna and take the wagon back after the reunion. Where's Nephi? He can turn out Punch and Judy here if he likes." He slapped the withers of the nearest mare.

Mellie planted her small hands on Lyman's shoulders. "No Jack Mormons tomorrow," she said. "Promise? No cigarettes…no whiskey…oh, and…" A broad mischievous smile lit her face. "Ephraim's back."

"So I see." Lyman said, nodding his head toward the porch. He looped the tie around his neck, swept a gray tweed cap from hair that matched his sister's and pressed it over his chest. "Ah, the noble warrior." He winked an ice-blue eye from behind egg-shaped wire-rimmed spectacles. "He's not been off blessing his bayonet has he?"

Mellie laughed, took Lyman's arm and steered him back toward the house. "Nephi's been talking strangely again," she said. "Something about the Three Nephites. He says he's heard them this time."

Lyman shoved his cap to the back of his head. His twenty-eight years dropped away and, for a moment, he looked younger than Nephi. "Nephi's strange because Ephraim's strange," he said as they reached the side porch steps. "And Ephraim's strange because Father Beecham's strange."

"Oh, I know. But he was telling me something just now, and I couldn't make much sense of it. Of any of them, for that matter."

Lyman frowned and opened the kitchen door. From Lela's bedroom, Duett swept into the room, a basin of water balanced on her right hip. She'd tensed momentarily but her face still glowed with confidence. The top several buttons of her shirtwaist were opened, and the smooth skin from the shadowed dip between her breasts to the hollow of her throat was beaded with sweat. This had not escaped Lyman's attention. "And you must be the charming Miss Brennick," he said gallantly.

Lyman tossed his hat to the table top, relieved Duett of the basin and dumped the contents into the porcelain sink beside the pantry. "Had I known you were in Safford for the circus last week, I'd have closed up the photo shop as fast as Mellie locked up the schoolhouse and gone myself."

# CHAPTER THREE

# Sunday, November 18, 1917

Sheltered under a broad sycamore tree at the edge of the orchard, Ira and Noah stood with Ephraim and his father, Solomon, behind the Pima farmhouse discussing current events. Gathered with them were Solomon's three sons by Samantha and a handful of other prominent men from the Valley's Mormon community. They would deliberate the war, religion, the weather, the alfalfa crop and winter wheat. Standing well apart, the Heber women – Samantha and her three daughters-in-law – were talking over an upcoming LDS Conference in Thatcher and preparations for a Thanksgiving masquerade to be held in Layton Hall. Assorted Heber grandchildren, dressed in their Sunday best, spun about in the sparse brown grass or went racing off into the orchard trees. Lyman, Sarah, and Nephi had each meandered off as well, and Edna Sutherland – Ira's younger sister – had stepped in to visit with Lela. Nearly ready to call the reunion to order, Mellie's anxiety had driven her to the solitude of the library to collect her thoughts.

Notwithstanding Duett's bustling in the kitchen, a death-like silence closed in on the old house. The swag velvet drapes in the library had been drawn over a layer of lace, and an electric lamp glowed on a tiny round tea-table by the east wall between two upholstered black chairs. The dim light shadowed Father Beecham's cherry-wood Bible-stand. Built-in wooden bookshelves, their dark upper surfaces covered in burlap, added to the room's general murkiness, with volumes like *Self-Help* and *Duty* staring out at Mellie from all around the shrouded room. Centered over the fireplace mantle like an apparition hung a portrait of Mellie's grandmother, Mother Josephine Beecham, a square-faced woman with dark braided hair and sorrowful, shadowed eyes. As a sort of epitaph, Father Beecham had placed a framed inscription under her picture that read:

> *"How happy in his low degree,*
> *How rich in humble poverty is he*
> *Who leads a quiet country life."*

Mellie had been half a year past her twelfth birthday that terrible October day in 1905 when Grandmother Josephine, who was Noah's first wife, had died. A distant and preoccupied woman of fifty-two then, Mother Beecham had left behind faint hints of a brittle but fervent love, of self-sacrifice and physical exhaustion, of melancholia and an unsettled mind. She'd lived all of her life "under the principle" – in a polygamous marriage – as was the custom of the early Church. The death in childbirth of her husband's second wife, Stella Luft Beecham, and the loss of her own baby daughter, Edna's twin sister, Esther, had brought Josephine inexorable grief that had altered the course of her life immeasurably. But whether it was these tragedies or some other torment that had ultimately claimed her spirit, no one could say. Josephine's last years had been lived in seclusion but for that fateful autumn day when she'd warily ventured out for church services, only to be struck down by one of Father Beecham's heavy supply wagons. Such an unfortunate death, and yet Josephine lived on – in this portrait that so much resembled Mellie herself, and in the ever-present yellow silk rose that decorated Father Beecham's lapel.

Noah's stifling library was Mellie's least favorite room in the old house, but with her grandfather's volatile nature and her own restless discontent, she craved a retreat that was secluded yet accessible. The mantle clock beat a steady rhythm in the still air, and several times, Mellie imagined she heard footsteps in the outer hall. But no one came. She hovered near the center of the room, unsettled by the slightest movement and yet unable, as yet, to join the others.

Arms folded, her fingers brushing her upper arms nervously, Mellie's unease deepened as the floor suddenly snapped behind her. With a rush of inexplicable terror, she spun around into the muscular arms of Ephraim Heber. Alarmed and embarrassed by his nearness, she pulled away toward the wall, but Ephraim gripped her wrists. "I need to talk to you, Malvina," he said, his face shadowed with tension.

Mellie's eyes locked on Ephraim's with a cold fearfulness. "You're hurting me, Ephraim," she said. He let her go and Mellie stepped back, rubbing her wrists gingerly. "And what do we have to talk about?" she asked. Only once did she look away from Ephraim's face, and then only to gauge the distance between him and the library door.

Ephraim loomed above her, solid and unsmiling. "We are living for time and eternity, Malvina. Not merely for the moment," he said. "We are born to the world that we might have life. And we live that we might have joy. But we must obey the laws of creation and not destroy the force of life within us."

Mellie weighed these words through rising alarm. "If you mean marriage…" She shook her head and moved to pass him, but he barred her way. In the next instant, Ephraim's hard mouth was on hers, wet and brutal. As she tried to fight him off, he clamped his hands on her elbows and slammed her back against the wall, pinning her arms behind her. With a violent hunger, Ephraim's bruising lips dropped to the hollow of Mellie's neck as he ripped aside her shirt-waist and closed his teeth on the bared flesh of her exposed breast. As the hot, damp wool of his uniform caught in her throat, she pounded a fist on his shoulder with her freed hand, smothered in a mixture of panic, nausea and rage.

"You filthy bastard!" a male voice roared from the far side of the room.

"Lyman! Dear God!" Mellie gasped.

A fist whistled past her left ear and landed with a solid crack on Ephraim's jaw. Blood trickled from the corner of his mouth and darkened one side of his moustache. Fueled with fury, Lyman tossed his jacket and spectacles aside as Ephraim staggered backward. Regaining his footing, the older man plunged into Lyman, and both men crashed to the floor. To Mellie's amazement, Lyman, the smaller of the two men, forced Ephraim onto his back and shoved a knee into the base of his throat. "Now we know you for the son-of-a-bitch you really are," he growled, hovering above

Ephraim for a brief moment and then jumping up to brush himself off. "Are you all right, Mellie?" he asked. Without turning from Ephraim, Lyman reached for his sister, and Mellie let him draw her away from the wall. "You lay one foul hand on my sister again," he warned through smoldering eyes, "and I'll see you in hell."

Ephraim lurched to his feet and put the back of his hand to his swollen lip. "If you think I lend the slightest credence to your threats, Beecham," he rasped, pulling a white cotton handkerchief from his vest pocket to wipe the blood from his hand, "you're sadly mistaken. You've been a disgrace to the Church, to your grandfather...to this whole family for years."

"And you're not?" Lyman sneered.

With a scowl that turned Mellie to stone, Ephraim reeled around and stalked out of the room, Lyman at his heels. The library door had only just closed behind them when Edna bustled in, taking in Mellie's considerable disarray. "Mellie, poor child, are you hurt?" She rushed to her niece, arms outstretched. "Lyman's just told me. Did Ephraim...?"

Mellie shook her head. "Oh, Aunt Edna." She collapsed in the older woman's arms.

"Ephraim Heber." Edna spit the words out like venom, "Why am I not surprised at that man's despicable behavior? I've always thought of him as something of a chameleon, but a scoundrel like that can't hide his true colors forever. There, there, child," she said, brushing a plump hand through Mellie's hair. "We mustn't let this pass, my dear. But for now, we'll mend your frock and gather our wits." Draping an arm around Mellie's slumped shoulders, Edna led her niece from the room.

Shame, anger and embarrassment gathered in the pit of Mellie's stomach as they walked, and for a moment she thought she'd be sick. She scrubbed a hand across her bruised lips and shuddered at the thought of Ephraim's intentions. Only when she'd washed away the taste of him and poured out her heart to Aunt Edna did the turmoil of her emotions begin to subside.

*   *   *

Seated impassively at the head table on Mellie's return, Ephraim introduced his father, Solomon, who called the reunion to order with an opening song, *Oh Ye Mountains High*, followed by a lengthy invocation. At seventy-nine, Elder Heber was smaller in stature and more frail than Father Beecham, but he turned an eye on his audience that was even more penetrating. Mellie had heard rumors about Father Heber's involvement in Danite extremism and blood atonement during his youth, and she feared the old man.

There were whispers that Solomon's unhinged zealousness was cemented in Utah, shrouded in the "reform movement" of the 1850s. Was it true, Mellie wondered, that the mistreatment and even murder of Mormon dissidents was meted out by Church-sanctioned Danite Priests, known as the "Destroying Angels" and that Solomon was among them? Father Heber's grinding moralizing certainly gave such rumors credence.

Among the nonbelievers in the Valley, stories ran rampant, too, that Solomon Heber, at nineteen, had been a member of John Lee's party – a group of Mormons found guilty of the 1857 murder of over a hundred Missouri travelers camped at Mountain Meadows on the west fork of Utah's Virgin River. A handful of children among them had been kidnapped, too. The Church, of course, denied involvement in the entire affair, blaming the tragedy on neighboring native tribes.

Standing at the head of the table, Father Heber beat a fist on the open Bible he always carried with him and demanded health and long life for the family. Fingering his squared white beard, the aging patriarch called mightily upon the power of the priesthood for guidance and protection, a plea reminiscent of many such implorings throughout Mellie's childhood.

At the table across from Mellie, Nephi sat frozen with awe, enraptured in Father Heber's oration. The seats to the right of him were occupied by three of Solomon's sons, Ephraim's older half-brothers. Their mother, Samantha, sat at Mellie's table with her daughter, Abigail, Sarah, the other women of the Beecham and Heber clans and an assortment of Heber grandchildren.

Ephraim, Father Heber's youngest son by his deceased third wife, Alma Saylor, sat at his father's right hand, a place of authority that had come naturally to him over the years. Though his brothers were each five to ten years his senior – Ephraim had turned thirty just last March – they were timid and self-effacing men, easily overshadowed by his impervious nature. Coupled with the fresh allure of his infantry uniform, Ephraim seemed to synthesize pretension with splendor as he commanded the head table. "Look at him," Mellie thought with chagrin. "He's fooled nearly everyone."

Still seething, Lyman had advised Mellie to be forthright about Ephraim's behavior. Having divulged the whole story to Edna, Mellie knew that her aunt agreed with Lyman and would support filing formal assault charges. As she watched Ephraim glance smugly around the room, Mellie's heart tightened. Putting the back of her hand to her still tender lips, she turned away from his pointed stare and again felt his hot breath on her face, the searing pain on her bared flesh. Tears sprang into her eyes. She dropped her hand to her throat and pulled in a ragged breath. Noah would have none of it, she well knew, should she level an accusation against Ephraim. And despite her sickened outrage, she was desperately afraid of the effect such charges would have on Nephi. After Thanksgiving, she reasoned through her fear, Ephraim would be on his way overseas. She might never have to face him again. Was she wrong in the faint hope that her pain might die with him on the battlefield?

As Solomon concluded, Mellie collected herself and announced that Lela would favor them with a solo, *When Springtime Comes, Gentle Annie*. Ill health had taken everything from Lela but her music, and even that had suffered. Until last year, she had sung first soprano with the Church choir but was often too weak now to attend rehearsals. Still, she loved to perform as her health would permit. Sweet and light, her voice now filled the air.

Not the least appreciative of her listeners was Lela's father, Orin Harland, who sat at the end of Nephi's table, his grizzled head held high. Like a halo, a wild shock of iron-gray hair sprang up from the back of Orin's head. An unlit tobacco-stained corncob pipe made its way back and forth between his thin lips and toothless gums. Cotton farming and sharecropping had left Orin's face sun-baked, lined and leathery. Decades ago, the Confederate cause had put the squint of a war wound in one of his eyes, and a sleeve hung empty where his left arm should have been.

By law, Arizona had been dry of alcohol since 1914. In addition to Prohibition, the war effort made it "unpatriotic" to convert food-stuffs into liquor. Nevertheless, Orin brewed a little "white lightning" on the side and, together with an ancient half-blind mongrel named General Lee, he practiced subsistence living, to put it kindly, on the remains of a Cactus Flats farm south of the Valley, most of which had been lost to the drought of 1910. Whenever he made an appearance among the Faithful – which, thankfully for them, was not often – complaints rained on the family like locusts. As for Mellie, she rather liked Orin and admired his resilience.

Lela finished singing to unrestrained applause, and Lyman, seated beside Ephraim at the head table, rose with Duett to escort his mother back to her room. His absence continued through a lengthy recitation from *The Pearl of Great Price* by little Angelina, the youngest of the Beecham children. Perhaps, Mellie thought, Duett needed last-minute help in the kitchen. She knew Lyman would be happy to oblige.

As the program continued, a medley of harmonized hymns was presented by Solomon Heber's four sons, followed by a rousing rendition of *America* by the entire assemblage. Then, at long last, Ira Beecham rose to introduce his father. An uncertain man of forty-nine, Ira had spent much of his adult life avoiding confrontation with Father Beecham. Among the faithful, success in business meant reward for good character, and Mellie knew her father to be both successful and good. Yet, in opposition to Noah, he'd dared to mix with the gentiles of Safford. He bought goods from them and in turn found markets for their grain, their hay, their wood and their garden produce. In Father Beecham's eyes, Safford missed the mark of decency altogether, so there was no forgiving what his son had done.

A solid man of ample but not excessive girth, Ira gave his peppered beard a series of quick tugs. Two short vertical lines creased his forehead above the bridge of his nose and etched a scowl on his face that only rarely reflected his disposition. "The term Elder is a general one," he began. "It applies to all grown men who hold the higher Priesthood." Ira's steel blue eyes locked on the scribbled note card he gripped in his big hands, and Mellie's heart ached for her father's discomfort. "Every officer of the Faith has been placed in his position to magnify the Church. My father, Noah Beecham, has done this with a full and sober heart. He is a pillar of Zion, a defender of the Faith, a man of righteousness, truth and virtue, a good citizen of the state and a staunch and loyal citizen of this great country that we are proud to call our home. We will be pleased to hear from him now." With profound relief, Ira sank back into his seat, and Mellie led a round of applause, while at the same time noting Lyman's well-timed return to the head table.

Father Beecham rose then and delivered a speech that was as lengthy and overblown as it was stirring, touching on "maintaining the dignity of the priesthood," "proclaiming the gospel of the eternal truth" and "welcoming the call to the priesthood as all men should." At this last intonation, Father Beecham's dark eyes fell on Lyman. Like all males of the Church, Lyman had been ordained at the age of twelve with membership in the Priesthood and had risen steadily as a youth through the ranks. In young adulthood, however, he had wavered from the Faith and abandoned many of its principles. In Father Beecham's estimation, Lyman's bachelorhood was of particular insult to the Church. According to his grandfather, Lyman had shunned his duty to "multiply and replenish the earth" and had thereby stifled his progress in eternity.

"This then is our story," Noah went on and lifted his piercing gaze. "In November of 1846, we wintered on the banks of the Missouri. My mother was taken giving me life, my father and brothers by cholera. But Solomon Heber's family took me in and brought me up, and he and I later married sisters, Adriana and Josephine Spratt. Solomon had two other wives sealed to him in the Faith, the last of these bearing us Brother Ephraim in the Mexican settlement of Colonia Juarez, where we'd journeyed to introduce the Gospel."

And not incidentally, Mellie thought, to escape prosecution for polygamy, which was not formally abandoned by the Church until 1890.

"Our families reached this broad and bountiful land in 1883. The soil here was rich and fertile, renewed by the river's flood and abundant sunshine. With a spirit of cooperation, we built in this Valley a garden, a place of refuge where newly-converted immigrants and the persecuted of our Faith were welcomed with open arms." Father Beecham went on to relate in painful detail the history of the Hebers and the Beechams, along with their achievements and an accounting of the many blessings bestowed upon them.

Orin's grizzled head had settled onto his chest early into Father Beecham's long-winded discourse. Now and again, his mouth made soundless chewing motions, while beside him, in stark contrast, Nephi sat mesmerized, starched and stiff in black pinstripes. The older Heber brothers sat hunkered over their folded arms like blocks of granite, while Samantha and her widowed daughter, Abigail, dabbed at tears of nostalgia. The Mexican Revolution, which had threatened the Arizona border since 1911, had driven the Hebers out of Mexico just two years earlier. Many of the men among these "Exodus Refugees," as they were known, worked as tenant farmers in the Valley or on threshing or bailing crews. Along with her children and grandchildren, Samantha had settled out of necessity in the less prosperous Duncan Valley to the east.

"Reckless but eloquent, as usual," Edna whispered to Mellie. She'd frequently used those very words to describe her own life. Edna had participated in a wide array of social programs, the later years of Jane Addam's Hull House in the slums of Chicago among them. She still spoke with a grand enthusiasm of Hull House's social reform movement, proud of her small part in helping to lift a people overpowered by misery to a higher plain. Fueling her worldly reputation, Edna's January march in the suffrage picket in Washington had further set the Valley on its ear. President Wilson had endorsed female suffrage, and the Saints had supported the concept from well before their days in Utah. What offended them about Edna was not the idea, which brought with it greater electoral power for the Church, but rather Edna's freewheeling independence and "progressive" tendencies.

"Every day of the week, except Sunday," she'd written to Mellie in the heat of those times, "and in all kinds of weather – in rain, sleet, hail and snow – we mean to be there, at the White House gates or in front of the Capitol, with our banners unfurled. On the first day, we marched along Pennsylvania Avenue from the east gate to the west gate and stood by the hour with our ribbons of purple and white and gold swaying in the breeze like blossoms against the gray of the pavement." Something infectious and compelling laced Edna's manner, and her influence among the women in the Valley was tangible. This was quite likely what the Elders feared, and last week's arrest of forty-one picketers in Washington certainly hadn't helped her reputation, at least among the men folk.

Feeling a nudge beside her, Mellie's attention turned from Edna's activism to little Angelina, a free spirit in her own right, as her youngest sister began to fidget. Having long ago tuned out Father Beecham, Solomon's grandchildren were pointing and giggling at Shotgun, Angelina's constant companion, a buxom White Leghorn hen. Shotgun, who had worn out her welcome in town, was to be retired to the farm, much to Angelina's dismay. As far as Mellie could discern, Shotgun had apparently bolted from her crate in the backseat of Ira's Model T and had just fluttered onto Lela's empty chair.

At the head table, Ephraim and Solomon drilled the children with contemptible stares until all of them sobered but Angelina, who met their stony gaze with sublime and impenitent innocence. Lyman leaned back with a broad smile as Angelina stroked Shotgun's bobbing head, the errant bird settling comfortably into her new roost.

"Safe in the arms of the True Church in the valleys of the mountains," Father Beecham intoned, oblivious to the disruption. "Praise the Lord for the harmony in our family. But I'm old now and will not be with you much longer."

Each and every birthday Father Beecham made this same prediction with solemnity, and Mellie stole a surreptitious glance at Lyman, who was sure to be rolling his eyes. "Therefore, I implore the young people present. I beseech you. In the midst of many blessings, awaken to your duty and beware the evil within."

As Noah finished, Duett rounded the corner of the house bearing the first dishes of the occasion's meal. Flustered by the sea of eyes washing over her, she stopped midstride and faltered. Sensing Duett's distress, Mellie quickly offered up grace and rose to offer a steadying hand. Soon, well-laden plates of roasted chicken, salad, pickles, olives, baked sweet potatoes, whole-wheat bread and stewed apples were being passed around the tables. Chilled pitchers of lemonade circulated in tandem, slivers of ice clinking in outstretched glasses. A comfortable cacophony settled over the yard as utensils clanked and platters thumped and thudded. Over the din of adult conversation, Mellie smiled at the happy squeals of children.

"An exemplary feast, Mellie, to Duett's credit," Edna complimented warmly as she reached for another slice of bread. Edna's sharp blue eyes flashed in a face round and open. "And a fine and suitable program, though Elder Beecham does go on. My dear departed husband, Lord Sutherland, would have said 'loquacious.' Mind you, he'd have made it clear in no uncertain terms that the trait was common to the family." Edna laughed, patted the curves of her pompadour hairdo and fussed over the contents of her plate, suddenly sobering. "Now you're sure you're all right, my dear? Do give some thought to that man's appalling behavior."

"Actually, I'm trying not to," Mellie answered with a wry smile. "But I'm fine, thank you. Really." There was not much truth to this, but it was all she could manage for the moment without giving rise to fresh tears.

Reassured, Edna leaned in toward Mellie. "Lyman seems quite taken with Duett, don't you think?" She couched the question in low conspiratorial tones and turned her gaze to the beaming pair now working seamlessly to serve dessert to the eager crowd. "He dined with me at Jimmie's the evening after the circus, you know." She removed the jacket of her navy tailored suit and slipped it over the back of her chair. From the cream-colored blouse beneath, pinned at the throat with a pearl-studded cameo, came the faint smell of lavender. "You know, the restaurant there in Safford? I told him you'd closed the school in Thatcher on Wednesday and that we'd taken the children to the circus. Oh…the clowns and concert bands…and those three lovely steam pianos. Well, I said we'd met the most charming young woman from over there by Fort Thomas, and I was certain you meant to hire her for Lela." With great relish, Edna finished another ample helping of stewed apples. "And your mother, my dear, how is she doing under Noah's scrutiny?'

"No worse than without." Mellie sighed, barely pecking at the food on her plate. "His latest remedy is hedge mustard tea, but I'm not convinced it's effective at all."

"Mint tea!" Edna interjected as she stabbed the air between them with her fork. Mellie jumped back instinctively. "Try mint tea instead! Settles the mind…settles the stomach. I've some with me in the Hudson. Mint tea's just the thing. We'll brew some up after supper and see if it helps." She patted Mellie's hands and turned toward Lyman, who filled her plate with a generous sampling of Satsuma plums. "Thank you, dear. I trust that you've got a photo sitting or two in store?"

*   *   *

Lyman's wagon of canvas and wood had a skylight and was divided with small partitions for a posing room, a dark room and a built-in kitchen. Backdrops, developing tanks, printers and glass plate negatives took up the rest of the limited space in his makeshift traveling studio. Most of his photography business was conducted in a flat above one of the drugstores in Safford, but he used the wagon to work on location, capturing images of dances, picnics, reunions and other social gatherings. Although his livelihood came from the people of the Valley, the real joy in Lyman's work came from his own artistic appreciation. He'd haul his camera into the Pinalenos or down into the Gila River bottom, into the Beecham orchard or out into the fields, and then he'd hand-tint the resulting photographs for use as gifts or printed advertisements. He wandered now in the orchard, his driving cap shading his eyes. Lost in reverie, he'd stop now and then to frame a scene with his thumb and forefinger, looking for just the right composition or background light.

The rest of the Heber and Beecham men huddled in conversation in the yard. Nephi, his eyes haunted, soaked up every word, while Ephraim, as upright as ever, dominated the group's exchange, the cut on his lower lip concealed by the sweep of his moustache. When Lyman finally returned to the farmhouse, Mellie set him to gathering the assembly together for group and family photographs. The men shuffled over dutifully, while Edna and Duett fussed over Lela. Orin, who'd skulked off for a pipe, meandered back to join his daughter, oblivious to Samantha's reproachful stares. Edna was tasked with rounding up the smallest Heber children, who, racing after Angelina and Shotgun, kept scattering like a flock of chickens. In due time, Lyman finished each of the requested poses and prepared for a final group picture.

Mellie closed her eyes and had just begun to relax when Nephi dropped down beside her on the porch steps. "You have to promise me that you won't say anything to anyone about what I have to tell you, Malvina," he whispered, as Lyman motioned the gathering in for the last take. Mellie stood up and reached for Nephi's arm, but he remained seated, his face tight and distorted.

With growing impatience Lyman gestured again.

"Promise me, Malvina?" Nephi pleaded.

"Ready when you are, Mellie," Lyman interjected.

"Yes…yes…I'm coming, Lyman," Mellie answered, turning back briefly to her younger brother. "All right, Nephi. I promise."

"Good," Nephi said. To Mellie's amazement, he jumped up and walked off to join the others.

With everyone accounted for, Lyman arranged the families into three tiers. On the ground in front, he centered Lela in her loop-backed chair, surrounded by Angelina and the Heber children; behind them stood Nephi, Mellie, Edna, Samantha, Abigail, Sarah and the other Heber women. In the last row, Lyman posed Ira, Father Beecham, Father Heber, Ephraim, the three Heber men and Orin. Thankfully, the group settled down easily as Lyman set the camera. Still engaged in preparation, he ordered his charges, young and old, to "hold completely still." With her promise to Nephi still fresh on her mind, the resulting silence grew thick for Mellie, and an eerie discomfort filled the air around her.

"Quiet now," Lyman said, lighting the flash-powder.

"I'm going to join up, Mellie," Nephi whispered to her just as the photograph snapped. "I'm going off to the war."

# CHAPTER FOUR

# Tuesday, November 27, 1917

More than a week had passed since the reunion marking Father Beecham's seventy-first birthday and Father Heber's seventy-ninth, and Mellie had yet to return to the farm. Her classroom in Thatcher, ward choir practice and an LDS conference over the weekend kept her busy in town, but her thoughts were often drawn to her mother's continued well-being at the old homestead.

Relief Society, the philanthropic and educational arm of the Church for women over eighteen, had also kept Mellie in Pima. The organization's attention was riveted on the war effort, and Mellie met faithfully with the group on Wednesdays to make dressings and quilts for the war.

Local tensions were mounting with concern for loved ones overseas. Already, the first American warship had been lost in the Atlantic, and still more soldiers of the American Expeditionary Forces had died in the European conflict. Would Ephraim be next? Or even Nephi? Her brother had not mentioned the war again and Mellie dared hope that his cryptic announcement to her had been nothing more than a passing notion brought on by Father Beecham's re-union rhetoric.

The afternoon had passed pleasantly after her teaching duties in Thatcher, and Mellie had driven Ira's Model T back to Pima, parking alongside her father's store and hurrying inside. At the Thatcher Amusement Hall this evening, the Gila Academy planned to present the play *All of a Sudden Peggy*, and Mellie had promised to help Sarah review her lines. The play was being produced in conjunction with the Church's Mutual Improvement Association, a social club of sorts for twelve- to eighteen-year-olds. Sarah had been re-hearsing with the group for weeks.

Stepping into the living quarters in the rear of the store, Mellie waited for her sister to swoop down from the upstairs bedrooms. At fifteen, Sarah was something of a pet with the MIA Social Committee. She accommodated herself ea-gerly to the dances, parties and celebrations of the Church with a warm and open heart. But Father Beecham had once chanced upon Sarah in the kitchen of the old farmhouse on a lazy summer afternoon. Uninvited and unannounced, she was making molasses candy with friends, laughing bois-terously, and in mixed company, no less. The concoction had boiled over onto Noah's newly scoured stove, and as it cooled, they'd tangled the sticky mixture in each other's hair. "Unseemly and immodest" were the kindest words he could now muster for Sarah. In Mellie's eyes, her sister was merely young. A little impetuous, maybe, but certainly without guile.

Pale-gold winter sunlight still filled the large single room at the back of the store where Mellie sat. She'd settled at the base of the stairs on a threadbare couch on which her mother had draped a thick woolen blanket, closely matched in color to a set of thatch-bottomed chairs all facing the fireplace. There was a large dark-oak dining table close to the back window looking out on the dying day, and on the far right side of the room, an ample kitchen.

Laid out in 1874 in harmony with the Plat of Zion, a settlement grid-plan designed around LDS principles of agrarianism and community, most of Pima's town plots were large enough to accommodate fruit trees, modest sheds and a garden. More sizeable barns and stables were erected on the outskirts of town. Located at the town's far northwestern boundary, the Beecham farm was something of an anomaly. Built in 1885, all of its outbuildings stood close at hand, within at least a hundred yards of the house. Ira's Pima store and residence, however, conformed more strictly to the town plan, squarely erected on Center Street within a tidy city block.

The existing mercantile, however, wasn't the original structure built on the lot. The first building, purchased and converted into a commercial enterprise in 1900, had been a scant and airy log cabin of sorts, with merchandise littering the front rooms and the family's cramped living quarters tucked in back. When the store fell victim to summer lightning the following year, the entire Mormon community helped Ira raise another, a more accommodating two-story affair complete with a covered boardwalk. In contrast to the suspended gloom of the old farmhouse, the rooms in Ira's Pima shop crackled with Sarah's vitality and Angelina's beaming innocence. Sunny recesses reflected the melodic strains of Lela's Victrola, which Mellie planned to take out to her mother at the farm on Wednesday afternoon.

Ira's inventory was comprised primarily of dry goods, clothing, groceries and hardware. Many of the canned goods and bakery items he stocked came from non-Mormon merchants in Safford, an indiscretion in Noah's eyes for which Ira dearly paid, though he prospered materially in spite of it. Merchandise lined the walls on bulky shelves, built floor to ceiling and extending lengthwise along both sides. From the right wall at the entrance ran a glass-encased counter that ended near the dividing door to the family's living quarters, where there was a kitchen, a pantry/storage room and a combination sitting and dining area. Cream-colored pillars braced the high, carved hardwood ceiling.

Outside the store, Ira maintained a vegetable garden, a few fruit trees, and a small shed for chickens and a milk cow. (Angelina sold eggs, milk and cheese, a tenth of her scant profits given to the Church as the Law of Tithing required.) A wide, deep irrigation ditch lined with poplars and sluice gates surrounded the one-acre parcel of land. When they'd first moved to the Pima store, Mellie and Sarah had carried in drinking water from this canal. In the summertime, they'd use their bonnets to protect their bare feet from the scorching hot ground. Racing a yard or two, they'd stop to stand on their hats for reprieve, only to start running again, their antics always bringing a smile to their mother's face. There'd be little laughter now, Mellie thought, as Sarah uncharacteristically slumped down the stairs and sank like a rag doll into the sofa.

"You don't look well at all, Sarah," Mellie said and set aside her classroom work. "What's wrong?"

Sarah's hair, in a brown-blonde billow from having brushed out her braids, glistened as usual. But the flash in her pale blue eyes had dimmed and her face was gaunt and chalky. "I haven't been sleeping very well," she answered with a nervous giggle. "I guess I'm not quite ready for *Peggy*."

"You've been out too late too," Mellie reminded her. "Even on Mutual nights. You missed choir again last week, and you know how Papa feels about that cowboy dance in Fort Thomas…and you sneaking out late the very night of the reunion." Mellie's eyes widened.

"I know." Sarah grimaced. "'Fighting and fiddles,' Father Beecham always says. But you've never been there, Mellie. They're not afraid of the devil, those Texans. I mean, there's light and music just pouring out through the cracks and the knotholes. Most of the girls in gathers and tucks and ruffles and frills. It's a sight to behold!" Sarah straightened on the sofa and her eyes flashed.

"They had five gallon cans of coffee. Five!" She threw up one slim hand. "They had them up on two old cook-stoves they used for heaters. And harmonicas and sandwiches and dancing 'til the sun came up. Sometimes down on the Blue, I hear they dance for two or three nights straight…a hundred people. Lyman's been there, and he says it's a hoot and a holler." She collapsed back into the sofa. "I'd rather be Lyman than Papa anyway. You didn't tell on me, did you, Mellie? I mean Papa's one thing. But Father Beecham? He thinks all any Texan wants is to get him a Mormon."

"No…I didn't have any reason to," Mellie answered.

"Most of those cowboys think it's Mormons that cause all the trouble, but I couldn't say."

"Well, it didn't help any when that group of rowdies hurrahed the town after the fall roundup and put Papa's sign up over that sporting women's place outside of Fort Thomas." Mellie stifled a smile.

Sarah laughed and slashed a hand through the air. "'*We*

*will not be undersold. I. Beecham, Proprietor'.* Can you imagine?"

"Well I know Papa didn't see the humor in it. And Father Beecham made a terrible fuss. You know how he feels about brothels and that kind of 'sinful behavior.'" Mellie whispered with embarrassment and put a finger to her lips as Ira's voice rose up in the front room.

"I don't want you coming around here again," she heard her father say, the scowl on his face reaching deep into his words. "Sarah's just a child. She does things sometimes... without thinking."

Mellie glanced at Sarah, who chewed her lower lip and stared at the floor.

"Ain't no reason to put any shame on her, Mr. Beecham," a deep male voice thoroughly unfamiliar to Mellie answered. If Sarah recognized it, she gave no indication. "If you'd just take this new sign here, sir, which ain't to say it was me that stole or shot up the other, maybe we can make things right. Ain't a man could do better'n me with a piece of wood."

"I don't want anything to do with this," Ira said. "And my Sarah will have nothing to do with you. I think you should leave."

Footsteps augmented with the clank of spurs receded then, and the bell over the front door jangled twice. "I'd certainly appreciate some explanation for that," Mellie said to Sarah, breaking an uncomfortable silence. But as Ira stalked through to the kitchen, Sarah went back up to her room without a word. With a startled smile to Mellie, Ira shuffled through the wood-box and then went back out to the shop. Left behind was a polished pine signboard that read, '*We will not be undersold. I. Beecham, Proprietor.'*

✳   ✳   ✳

Nephi walked into Pima from the farmhouse and then he, Angelina, Mellie, Ira and Sarah drove into Thatcher in Ira's Model T. Earlier in the afternoon, Lela had nearly begged to come into town. The prospect of seeing her children perform would do her heart ever so much good, she insisted. But even as she spoke, she'd been overcome by an especially severe coughing spell, and Duett had dissuaded her, promising an evening filled with lemonade and laughter. Moreover, Lyman would be calling on Duett, opening up the evening to the prospect of a piquet round or two – Lela's favorite card game. With that and the assurance of some inventive storytelling, Lela had been somewhat appeased.

From the rear seat of the auto, Angelina, with the innocent enthusiasm of her seven years, kept up a constant prattle, but the overall mood in the car was pensive. Aside from Ira's grumbling as he swerved to the occasional pothole alert, there was no other conversation.

Much to his surprise, Nephi had been invited to debate *The Advantages of Increased Civic Instruction in the Public Schools* during the play's intermission and had prepared diligently for the upcoming exchange. On occasion, he examined his copious notes but otherwise struck a rigid pose in the front seat beside his father. Sarah stared out into the darkness, nervously lacing and unlacing her slim fingers. With such palatable tension in the air, the scant five-mile journey into Thatcher seemed endless to Mellie. But at the door of the Amusement Hall, a rush of activity and confusion met the Beechams, and Mellie breathed a sigh of relief.

Eager for the performance, Sarah and Nephi vanished into the assembling crowd to make last-minute preparations and find their places. Angelina, Ira and Mellie had made arrangements to meet Edna and quickly located her wide-brimmed red hat among the seated throng. As they joined her, Edna dropped a warm smile on each of them, cuddling Angelina and settling herself comfortably between the girls.

"Loosen up now, Ira dear," Edna said, reaching across Mellie's lap to tap her brother's knee. "You look as though this were a funeral instead of a showcase for the children. They'll be fine, both of them. Mark my words. Oh…before I forget, Malvina…" She withdrew her plump hand from Ira's knee and reached into her lap bag, pulling out an awkwardly-carved wooden horse. Barely four inches square, it sat on two narrow black rockers. "I brought this for Duett's little girl, Shadi Lace. She has so little in the way of amusements, you see…but what an exquisite child."

"She is a lovely little girl, yes," Mellie agreed, examining the rough, age-worn toy.

Its mane, tail and eyes were also painted black, and two thin lines – which Mellie took to be reins – had been drawn along either side of the horse's neck. A rust-colored saddle dotted with color – yellow, blue and green – completed the faded embellishments, the pale wood lackluster with wear. Notches had been chiseled on the underside, and just as Mellie asked to examine them, the house lights dimmed and the curtain went up. "Please take it with you and deliver it for me," Edna whispered, tucking the pony into Mellie's purse.

Having browsed through Sarah's script, Mellie knew that *All of a Sudden Peggy* was a lighthearted play designed to invite laughter. But Sarah delivered her lines with a hesitant tension wholly inappropriate to the blithe character she played. The other cast members were confused and flustered, and as the play plodded on, the audience, too, began to sense that something had gone terribly wrong.

With intermission came a promise of relief that was all too short-lived. Nephi captivated the audience with a stellar performance, stunning his family with unaccustomed charisma. Throughout the debate, the usually quiet boy attacked both his subject and his opponent – a squat young scholar several years his senior – with a vigor and volume that drove numerous sympathizers to pity his unfortunate rival. When he finished, the Academy Band played two hit and miss numbers, and, though the sound was not all it might have been, Mellie welcomed the moment for her sister's sake, dreading the approach of Act II. Yet at the appointed time, the curtain swung up again.

Sarah's manner tightened further as the play progressed. Mellie and Edna exchanged nervous glances, and Ira began to tug at his beard more anxiously with each passing scene. Cold as stone, Sarah's lines became bland recitation, and *All of a Sudden Peggy* was reduced to theatrical tragedy. When the merciful end came, the ensemble linked arms for a final bow with Sarah bringing up the end of the line.

A member of the Relief Society presidency then stepped forward to offer a closing prayer, pleading with the Lord for "a world united for peace, even as it is now divided by war." Through half-closed eyes, Mellie watched her sister lean heavily on the cast member beside her. Breathing heavily and ghostly pale, Sarah raised her free hand to her cheek and swayed forward slightly. In alarm, Mellie rose from her seat.

"Let there arise from the ashes of ruined cities," the speaker petitioned, oblivious to Sarah's distress, "towns greater yet, peopled with peace-loving folk…"

Mellie edged her way to the side aisle as the woman droned on. "…Let the world be renewed and reborn, preserving coming generations from the horrors of war. We offer this holy prayer..."

Before the woman's amen, Sarah clutched her abdomen and collapsed.

# CHAPTER FIVE

# Wednesday, November 28, 1917

"I'm just a bit tired," Sarah insisted. "And if you don't get Mama's Victrola out to the farm soon, she'll have Sheriff McBride after you." Mellie opened the lacy lined drapes at Sarah's bedroom window above the Pima store. The late morning's white light flooded across the floor and gleamed on the brass curves of Sarah's bed, planting squares of pale gold on the woven white coverlet. Across the red and gray panels of the papered walls, flowers and ribbons, vines and berries and small birds took shape, their delicacy reflected in the soft lines of the room's sparse white-wicker furnishings – a loveseat under the window and a low bedside table.

As Sarah sank back into the covers, Ira lumbered in, matching the habitual tugs on his iron-gray beard to his slow and even footsteps. "Good morning, Mellie." He acknowledged her with a nod.

"And you, daughter." He turned to Sarah with a tenuous smile. "You'd best put aside these worldly temptations of yours, that dance in Fort Thomas for one. Poor habits reflect poorly on us all, and a child of the True Church should have higher aspirations."

"Oh, Papa," Sarah groaned. "You sound just like Father Beecham. He makes you out to be a wicked man just for shipping in dry goods from Safford – that 'rotted heart of gentile abomination.'" She grinned and ducked her head under the covers.

Mellie stifled a smile. "Papa knows the ways of the world better than we do, Sarah," she said. "What you need is rest and a few more wholesome meals."

"And some of that Composition Tea your mother always gets from Father Beecham for Christmas," Ira added.

"I'll see to it, Papa." Mellie brushed a curl from her sister's pale cheek and disappeared downstairs to the kitchen. The herb and spice drink known as Composition Tea – favored by the early Mormon Prophet Brigham Young – combined ground bayberry and poplar bark with cloves, cinnamon, ginger and cayenne pepper. A satisfying, very popular blend among the Saints, Father Beecham had perpetuated its use in the family for any number of ailments. As Ira carried Lela's mahogany Victrola out to the auto, Mellie asked Angelina to take a cup of the hot tea she had prepared up to Sarah. She followed her father outside with a collection of twelve double-faced records.

"Thanks, Papa. I'll be on my way."

"I'm coming with you!" Angelina called, sliding down the porch banister. "Wait for me!"

Mellie maneuvered Ira's Model T through the wide Pima

streets, into the valley road and out to the Beecham farm on the edge of town. Pulling it from Mellie's handbag, Angelina examined Edna's wooden toy horse with childhood envy. "Why can't I keep it?" she asked, already knowing the answer. "We must give to the less fortunate," she sighed, repeating a Sunday School proverb. "Blessing the lives of others is a blessing unto ourselves." They bounced up the farmhouse lane past a string of barren cottonwoods. When the auto came to a halt, Angelina abandoned the horse on the seat and dashed off to meet Shotgun.

Thankfully, Ephraim had gone to visit the Hebers in the Duncan Valley for several days before he set off overseas, and Mellie was relieved that there'd be no chance meeting. She pocketed the toy and looked for Nephi, who was tinkering with a broken latch on the front door. Nephi helped her lug the Victrola inside and mount it on the washstand in Lela's room, the glassy ruby-red trumpet directed towards their mother's bed. Nephi wound up the machine to play *The Whistler and His Dog*, but Lela had him replace it with one of her favorites – *The Merry Widow* – and waltz strains swept through the room.

Duett's presence had already brought a brilliant splash of color to the otherwise dreary old house, and her company raised a delicate but genuine joy in Mellie's mother. Now that Lela's music flowed again, even more of the gloom was dispelled. She dozed peacefully now, and Mellie left her bedside to visit with Duett, who had just finished tidying the kitchen.

The cherry-wood rocker in Noah's library creaked steadily with a rapid whine. Father Beecham and Nephi had begun some sort of priesthood tutorial that would likely keep them occupied all afternoon. Pulling out a chair for Duett, Mellie sat down at the kitchen table and pulled out the toy horse. "This is a gift for your daughter from my Aunt Edna," she said.

"Well, isn't that the sweetest thing," Duett crooned, running a slim finger down the neck of the carving. "Shadi Lace will be right tickled to have such a fine piece. We surely do thank you for your kindness."

"My aunt said it belonged to my grandmother," Mellie said by way of explanation.

"I reckon she'd be that big-eyed woman pictured in your granddaddy's Bible room?" With a flurry of her hand, Duett gestured toward the library. "And a sweet one she was, too, by the look of her." Duett fingered the toy and brushed away a strand of chestnut colored hair that fell across her eyes. "Meanin' no disrespect now," she added. "But your granddaddy's a whole other crop of hay, so to speak. He makes as though the whole world's down on him, but it's always his word that sticks. He's a hard man, and that's a fact."

Sudden tension caught in Mellie's throat. "But you'll stay anyway, won't you, Duett?" she pleaded. "I know Father Beecham is difficult. He wears on us all. But Mama so enjoys your company. You've given her a new spark of life!"

Duett flashed a disarming smile. "Why, there's no leavin' to be done, Mellie. I only mean to say that the man's…well… peculiar like. He doesn't quite fit with your granny there, or anyone else. That's the size of it."

"I guess a lot of people end up mismatched in this world." Mellie envisioned herself married to Ephraim Heber and shuddered. "I was only twelve when my grandmother died. She hadn't been right in her mind for some time before that, so I don't remember her much. But what about your people?"

"You mean are they right in the head?" Duett laughed. "Why my old Granny Bee Brennick out there at our place, she's an odd duck for sure. Tougher than an old boot when she's riled up, but a real good woman all the same. And, of course, there's my baby girl, Shadi Lace. You're acquainted with her already. Barely three years old. Me and her papa, God rest his soul, named her out of one of them stories on Southern gentility. You know, with some big old mansion off in Georgia or Louisiana, all live oaks and Spanish moss. Sweet as sugar, that child, just like them tales." She paused and lowered her voice. "You know, it's right likely Granny Bee's got the works for what ails your Sarah. She does a lot of nursin' round about, tending to sickness, birthin' babies and what not. A smart old coot, and right handsome for my money, considerin' her age and all."

Mellie tapped the tabletop with her fingertips. "Her fit at the play is the talk of the town, but Sarah claims she's not ailing at all. Just unnerved by the stage, she says. But there's something else going on," Mellie said, speaking more to herself than to Duett. "I don't know what it is yet, but I mean to find out."

"Young folks these days have a powerful bent to changin' their minds," Duett said, though her own twenty-four years hardly put her beyond youth herself. "Why I'd bet a dollar to a road biscuit that the girl's all acted out, but she's scared of quittin' for fear your granddaddy'd go crazy as a peach-orchard boar. A hard mind puts a lock on a man."

"Father Beecham has a lock on his mind if any man does," Mellie agreed. Only the grating of Noah's rocker in the library disturbed the ensuing silence. "We must *all* seem a little peculiar to you, we Valley people," Mellie said after a time.

"Well, folks each got their own way about 'em as I see it, and that's a fact," Duett answered with a smile. "Now it's no never mind to me who goes and does what. But there's some of our Texas kin that don't have the stayin' power you people do, livin' all bunched up together in such a tight clan." Duett smiled. "You all kind of lean into each other like old cottonwoods in a windstorm, while we're off in all sorts of lone places like big old tree stumps, some livin' alone so long they almost forget how to talk.

"When these hard times come and the tanks dry up and the feed gets short, when the land gets so poor you can't hardly raise your voice on it, it ain't easy. We're just out on our luck. None of that Relief Society business lookin' in on us." Duett folded her sun-colored hands on the tabletop, and her eyes deepened with a distant sadness.

"They're bringin' in them starvin' cows from Texas and New Mexico now," she went on. "Two years of drought they've had over there. Well, that's all well and good, except they're snatchin' up all our feed down south. Granny Bee says that the drought from the summer of '92 left dead cows in sharp crusty snow all that winter. They trailed them animals by the bloody tracks they left when the snow broke and cut the critters' legs, clear down to the bone.

"Some of us are still hangin' around Fort Thomas and down there under the Cactus Flats, and there's a few of us left over in the Aravaipa country. But most of us will be bought out before long. There'll be a few big places left, with lots of leased mountain land, but that big money's hell on our kin. And Mormons got the most money I know." Duett shook her head, gave Mellie an embarrassed glance and laughed. "Well, just listen to me carryin' on."

"I *am* sorry," Mellie said, knowing that everything Duett had said was probably true.

"There ain't no fault in it for you, Mellie," Duett said, brushing her fingers across Mellie's arm. "You and me, why we're barely shufflin' the deck. It's just the luck of the draw."

At the sound of an approaching automobile, she jumped up from the table. "Now I thought we'd got shut of that Ephraim Heber for a day or two. Touchy as a teased snake, that man." Both women stepped over to the kitchen window, and Mellie was relieved to see Lyman's auto instead. She relaxed even further when her brother stepped into full view, hauling along the bulk of his field camera equipment.

"Hello, ladies!" With the heel of his boot, Lyman closed the kitchen door Duett had opened for him. He propped a three-legged tripod on the floor and dropped a huge leather carrying case – loaded with camera, plates and sheet film – in a corner of the room. Sweeping off his driving cap, he plunked it on the table, adjusted his wire-rimmed spectacles and pulled out a set of sepia-tinted photographs from under his arm. Shuffling through them, he withdrew one of the largest, cleared his throat and held the picture out at arm's length. "Won't the world puzzle, Malvina Beecham, over such unseemly…" He peered at her over his spectacles with mischief in his eyes. "…and, shall we add, unSaintly, behavior?"

Like wooden statues, the faces in the reunion photo peered out at them from long, sober rows. Mellie's own image had been reduced to a blur of pursed lips, her head turned toward Nephi. Though very much aware of what the expression signified, she had to laugh.

"Like a slick-ear kickin' up, you are, Mellie." Duett had just leaned back against Lyman when the clatter of horses outside drew her attention from the unflattering picture and Mellie's perplexed stare. She glanced out the window, threw open the door and flew down the stairs. Her dark hair shone with a rust-red glint in the cool November sunlight as she scooped up a small child wearing dusty green coveralls. Sun-blonde curls framed sparkling emerald eyes, and

Duett buried her face in the child's soft hair. "Mama's missed her baby, she has. You've been a good girl too, gatherin' kindling for Granny Bee. I can smell bits of it in your hair."

Two men had ridden in with Shadi Lace, the slighter of the two a rough but kind-looking man about Mellie's age, with a swarthy complexion and an easy flash of white teeth. He sported a red cotton bandanna and a black felt hat that offset his lean face. The second man, dark-haired and a bit older, returned Mellie's attentive gaze with unruffled, smoke-blue eyes. A dove-gray Stetson shaded his dark bronzed face. Wearing denim trousers, a pale cotton shirt and a large moleskin vest, the man sat poised and reserved. When Duett released Shadi Lace, he turned his eyes away from Mellie. "Not meanin' to intrude on you folks…." The taller man's voice rolled like velvet in the still air, and when he looked at Mellie again, she held her breath until he'd turned away. "But the little one here had an awful cravin' to get hold of her mama."

With rising interest, Mellie realized that this man was probably the brother Duett had spoken so fondly of during their first meeting in Safford. He was as attractive a man as Mellie had ever seen, and she sensed the closeness he shared with his sister. Lyman passed Mellie on the outer stairs and invited both men to step down. They dismounted and looped their horses' reins on a nearby lilac bush.

Lyman extended his hand. "I'm Lyman Beecham," he said. "You must be Mr. Brennick. We couldn't be more pleased with your sister's work."

The man gripped Lyman's hand, cleared his throat and gave Mellie an embarrassed smile. "Press Brennick, Mr. Beecham. Pleased to meet you."

Mellie slipped down the stairs to join them. With a touch of his hand to her elbow, Lyman drew her forward in introduction. "This is my sister, Malvina Beecham…Mellie," he said.

Press tapped a finger to the brim of his hat. "My pleasure, ma'am."

His smoke-blue eyes scanned Mellie's features, and she was annoyed to feel her face flush. "I'm very pleased to meet you, Mr. Brennick," she said, once again losing herself in the depth of his eyes.

"This here's my main man, Billy Ben." Press motioned to his dark-haired companion, seemingly reluctant to take his eyes from Mellie's. "His pa's cattle ranch was mostly sheeped out up on the Rim a few years back, and Billy Ben dropped down-country lookin' for work. Cowboyed up and down the Sulphur Springs till we took him on as foreman."

"Mighty pleased to make your acquaintance, ma'am." Billy Ben looked somewhat shy and pushed back his muddied hat. Recognizing his voice as the Texas drawl of the same man who had argued with her father in the Pima store, Mellie struggled to remain composed as she acknowledged his greeting.

"Yours too, of course, Mr. Beecham. Mighty pleased," Billy Ben added hastily.

"Uncle Press!" Shadi Lace ducked to the center of the group. "Mama says this lady's gonna give me a new pony. See?" The little girl hitched up her loose-fitting coveralls with one hand and waved Edna's rocking horse as high over her head as she could reach with the other.

"Well now, that's no broomie, for sure." Press swept the child into his arms, and a warm flush crept across Mellie's cheeks as she envisioned herself in the child's place. Shadi Lace thrust the toy into her uncle's face as Mellie regained her bearings. "She's a beauty all right," Press said and drew back to focus on the horse. "Steppin' high as a blind dog in a wheat field, she is."

Just then, Angelina loped in from the front yard with Shotgun bobbing at her heels. "Is this your baby girl, Miss Brennick? Can me and Shotgun play with her?" Angelina looked up at her sister. "Hopscotch or Cat 'n Jacks? Please, Mellie. Please."

Mellie brushed a hand along Angelina's shoulders, smoothing down the ruffles of the young girl's speckled pinafore. "Angelina's very responsible," she said, turning to Duett. "I'm happy to let them play if it's alright with you. There's really nothing around that could hurt them."

Shadi Lace squirmed. "Down! Down!" she demanded. But before Press could set her back on her feet, the toy horse popped out of the little girl's grip and dropped to the ground. Shotgun darted over, took a stab or two at the unfamiliar object and bounced straight up into the air, the chunk of wood fastened to her beak. In an attempt to intercept the old hen, everyone scattered, Shotgun fluttering wildly toward the orchard on spindly yellow legs.

Shadi Lace dropped down into the dirt with a howl. Her small fists scrubbed her face and left bruise-like smudges on her wet cheeks. "My horsey, Mama! That bad old chicken stoled my horsey."

Lyman hunched down beside the little girl and pulled her up onto one knee. "Shotgun won't hurt your horse, I promise." A few strands of hair were matted to her skin with tears and grime, but Shadi Lace quieted, pulled her small round face back from Lyman's and studied him with great intensity. "I've never seen a chicken eat a horse, have you?" Lyman asked. Shadi Lace tucked her chin into the bib of her coveralls and shook her head. "Don't worry, sweetie. We'll catch 'er."

"Angelina," Mellie said. "Would you take Shadi Lace inside and help her get washed up? Miss Brennick's just baked some wonderful corn bread, and you can fetch yourselves some milk from the ice box. You visit with Mama for awhile, and we'll track Shotgun down."

Press' blue gaze met Mellie's again. "You ride on in to your doings in Pima," he said to Billy Ben with a brief glance. "I'll head on back to the outfit after I help Miss Mellie. Seems two could rustle up a chicken better'n one." He touched a hand to the rim of his hat again. "That is if you don't mind the company, Miss Beecham."

"Not at all, Mr. Brennick," Mellie managed. Never before had she been so disarmed in a man's company, but the sensation was not altogether unwelcome.

Angelina led Shadi Lace dutifully up the stairs and back into the house. As Mellie and Press set out for the orchard, they heard Duett say to Lyman, "No one I know tracks a critter better than Duett Brennick, if I do say so myself. If you're of a mind to join me, Mr. Beecham, we'll set to it."

"Delighted, Miss Brennick. Never go anywhere without the works, though. Hang on a second. Camera's just inside."

*　　*　　*

"You've got yourself a fine spread here, Miss Beecham. Seven...eight-month growing season by my reckoning." Press kicked absentmindedly at a clump of brittle winter grass.

"Yes, we do." Mellie stepped lightly beside him. "We grow White Winter Permian apples and Bartlett pears here in the orchard, along with Alberta peaches and Satsuma plums. All but the peach trees were shipped in from Utah years ago. In the spring, the whole orchard just runs wild with bees and blossoms. It's all quite beautiful."

Bordered by a long line of cottonwoods, the Beecham orchard sprawled across five acres behind the farmhouse. The trees produced two to four hundred dollars of fruit per acre each summer, with sweet potatoes, sold at four cents a pound, planted between the rows.

"The rest of the place must go for cash crops then?"

"Yes, except for a five-acre parcel where the house stands," Mellie said. "There's a stable, a granary and a storage barn there. And my grandfather has an herb and vegetable garden, of course." Mellie stooped and tossed aside a lump or two of sandy loam, stood again and brushed off her fingertips. "We have thirty acres in alfalfa with four to six cuttings a year. About ten tons an acre on average. Then there's about ten acres in wheat at thirty-five to forty bushels an acre. Father Beecham sells that to the Army. He gets around three twenty-five for every hundred pounds now, I think. And then we have about ten acres of corn, about seventy to eighty bushels an acre. That sells mostly for feed." Mellie paused and blushed. "Forgive me, Mr. Brennick," she said, catching Press' eye. "I used to keep the books, you see, and the facts and figures just pop up in my mind. Ephraim Heber does all of that now."

"No trouble," Press said. The blue of his eyes swept her so far away that it was only when he finally averted his gaze that Mellie could catch her breath. "Good fertile land too, I'd say, so long as you got plenty of water," Press added.

"Yes, we *are* lucky there. When things get parched in the Valley, the irrigation ditches from the Gila River stay pretty much grass-grown, which keeps evaporation down. It wasn't always that way, as you probably know." Mellie glanced across to Press who lifted a sagging tree limb from her path and returned her smile as she passed under. "The soil was coated with mine tailings just seven or eight years ago," she went on, skirting the edge of a brush pile. "From the mills in Clifton and Morenci upriver on the San Francisco. We thought all of these farms would have to be abandoned. The pulverized rock brought in by the irrigation water spread all over and hardened like thick sheets of glass. The mining companies ignored the problem and, unfortunately, we had to go to court. I think they use those tailings now for reservoirs up in the hills, closer to the plants."

"I believe you're right there." Press stopped and squinted out over the rich soil toward the distant Santa Teresa. "We're back in the hills ourselves pretty much," he said and started walking again. "Round about our place, why you'd think you'd plum quit the country. Dry as any bone. Feed's so scarce some folks have been shippin' cows down south into Pima County."

"So Duett was telling me."

"Might be they'll open up those Indian lands to the north, too, for grazing." Press stooped to finger a fluff of dirty white feathers, stood up again and walked on.

"Your sister called me a 'slick-ear,' Mr. Brennick." Mellie gripped the front folds of her box-pleated skirt and edged her way over a space of lumpy ground where the sweet potatoes had been ploughed under some weeks earlier. A faint breeze puffed the sleeves of her shirtwaist and filled her nostrils with the musky fragrance of dried leaves. She studied Press from under the fall of her hair. "Should I be offended?" Her high-topped shoes gave her some trouble and Press reached for her free hand. With his help, she negotiated the passage and found better footing on the level ground alongside another row of trees. But though Press dropped her hand, he did not step back, and Mellie found herself almost flush against him.

"Slick ear." The blue eyes scanned Mellie's face and she felt an arousing tingle slip across her chest and into her throat. Did Press feel the electricity between them, too, she wondered? "Why that's a calf, Miss Beecham."

"Mmmm…" Mellie's eyes crept along Press' weathered cheek and fastened on the corner of his mouth. She shifted her weight and stumbled over a crevice. Press clutched her upper arms and steadied her, reaching out with a gentleness she had not expected. "Thank you, Mr. Brennick," she said. "Surely even a calf has more grace than I do."

"No, ma'am. I don't think so," Press said. "Not a sign of that chicken. We'd best keep at it."

As he released his grasp, Mellie felt an almost desperate need for some distraction, however small. She stepped away and poked a pointed toe in another tuft of grass. "Your friend Billy Ben came to my father's store yesterday," she said, glancing back at Press. His face was inscrutable. "They were arguing." She leaned down to pluck a tawny shoot from underfoot and began to shred it with the tips of her fingers. "Does he know my sister, Sarah?"

Press' eyes darkened, that much Mellie could make out. Otherwise his face remained unreadable. "Since Saturday before last, I think," he said. "The dance over there by Fort Thomas." He seemed to relax somewhat and smiled. "Your Sarah does like a good time."

Mellie looked up in alarm. "She does?"

"Now make no mistake," Press said, turning to face her again. "I don't mean her any wrong by that. She's just a high stepper. Like Billy Ben. Now you, you've got this sweetness about you…like burnt sugar."

Mellie's lips parted on shallow breath. She wanted to

speak, but an intoxicating disquiet had filled her body and she could think of nothing remotely intelligent to say. Both she and Press lapsed into silence as they skirted an accumulation of firewood, branches and logs stacked against a hay derrick near the open fields. Press walked to one side and Mellie to the other. The warmth of his voice still hummed in her ear as she stopped to catch her breath under a spray of foliage. A twig snapped, and Press reappeared from around the far corner of the woodpile. "I seem to be cursed with a troublesome directness, Miss Beecham," he said. "I apologize." He propped one hand on a piece of wood that jutted out just above Mellie's right shoulder.

"No need to apologize, Mr. Brennick." Mellie dared herself to look at him. "And I take your remark as a compliment."

"As was my meaning," Press answered.

Mellie was still lost in his smoky eyes when he bent forward and kissed her, his warm breath touching her lips before his mouth closed on hers. She raised a hand to brush his chest, but it hung limp in the charged air between them.

"Mellie! Mr. Brennick!" Lyman's shouts spun out from the depths of the orchard. "We've found the little bugger!"

# CHAPTER SIX

# Friday, November 30, 1917

Under the watchful eye of Bishop Tyler, the ecclesiastical leader of the Thatcher Ward, a dance sponsored by the MIA was being held in the Thatcher Amusement Hall as part of the Church's Thanksgiving festivities. Earlier in the day, Duett had prepared a traditional roasted chicken dinner out at the farm for the entire Beecham clan, and the family had enjoyed a peaceful afternoon before heading into town. Lela, in good spirits but not up to much exertion, opted to stay at the farmhouse with Duett, and Lyman and Edna had returned to Safford. The rest of the family set off in Ira's Model T for an evening of community celebration.

The Church deemed it a privilege and a duty to supply "wholesome activity and spiritual instruction for the young people." After fall harvest, the ensuing "amusement season" brought with it regular Friday night dances and Tuesday MIA meetings, focusing on promotion of the Faith, mission reports and recreational games. Such activities structured the social lives of young people between the ages of twelve and eighteen and were intended to give them a solid moral foundation on which to build their adult lives.

Mellie was asked on occasion to chaperone MIA dances, and she enjoyed mingling with the boys and girls who participated. Several of them were her students, and some of the more forthright young men had been known to ask their schoolteacher for a dance.

Once a year, the MIA hosted a hoe-down for both the young people and for married couples and their families. Tonight's event was that occasion and served as a fundraiser for upcoming programs and activities. No one entered the hall without purchasing a ten-cent ticket, and each woman had been assigned to bring a plate of refreshments to be served with homemade sarsaparilla later in the evening. Benches for non-dancers covered half the floor, while at the front of the hall on a portable stage sat the orchestra – a fiddle, a guitar, a piano, and an occasional clarinet.

Behind the stage, women with infants had placed them in the care of some of the younger girls. Angelina was there in a stiff turquoise outing frock, passing the time in endless chatter, reciting scriptures and playing jacks. The makepiece band faltered a time or two, and the instructions being belted out to the *Mormon Quadrille* – a square dance in which each man had two partners – became quite inaudible over the din of the dance hall. But hands clapped nonetheless, feet stomped and couples whirled about the floor to the polka, the schottische, the *Varsouvianna*, the two-step and the Virginia Reel.

Back from the Duncan Valley, Ephraim loomed

throughout the hall with poised reserve. As the dance's official "mixer," he carried messages, parted couples too thickly
entwined, shuffled the old with the young and thwarted at-
tempts by the worldly and rebellious among them to escape
outside – in violation of the prescribed Word of Wisdom –
for a smoke or a drink. Ira, as floor manager, attended to
the musicians' needs and scattered cornmeal at timely in-
tervals across the rough pine floor. He would also oversee
the upcoming refreshments. His blue serge suit gave him
an air of uncomfortable refinement as he fulfilled the evening's duties.

Sarah was radiant, her face aglow with renewed energy.
Any dance at all pleased Sarah, but her favorites – slow
and close – proved a constant affront to Ephraim's watchful eye.

At eleven o'clock, the orchestra wound up a rousing rendition of *Old Dan Tucker*, and Ira settled the crowd first on
the benches and then standing three deep along the back
wall. Rather more sluggish than usual, Father Beecham
inched his way to the stage, while Mellie and some of the
older women replenished snacks of popcorn and molasses
candy and refilled the punch bowls. When Noah reached
the front of the hall, he beat his staff against the floorboards.
The room quieted but for one wailing infant, and his scowl
dropped on the child's mother until she stood in humilia-
tion and rushed off.

A lonesome wind moaned along the outside walls and
the room took on the hush of death in somber contrast to
the evening's earlier high spirits. Only then did Father Beecham speak. "Physical welfare is essential to spiritual welfare," he began. As he bent over his gold-topped cane, one
gnarled hand fussed with the yellow silk rose on his lapel.
"Play is a means of diversion from the routine of life. But it

must also be a means of acquiring wisdom. As a principle, the dance is not objectionable, but when it leads the people into bad company, when it causes them to keep untimely hours, then dancing corrupts the morals of our youth." Father Beecham's accusing glare beat down on the guilt-ridden faces before him.

"But under proper supervision, when the people are not engulfed in a questionable environment, dance can fire the spirit and set it free." He almost smiled then, and a sigh rippled through the room. "'Strip yourselves of all uncleanness,'" he admonished, his upturned expression vanishing. "Ask that you not yield to temptation, but serve the true and living God." Spontaneous applause erupted from the audience, and Noah gestured to Ephraim. "Here is one who will serve…Ephraim Heber." The hall exploded anew.

"There are wars in the world today beyond what men have known," Noah went on as the ovation subsided. "Nation against nation; strife and contention. All because they do not abide in God's Truth. In the True Gospel dwells the light of freedom. Ephraim Heber goes to defend his country's honor with a true and patriotic spirit that only adds to his greatness." Noah raised his hands to quiet the erupting applause.

"His loyalty is unquestioned. He was called to the Colors in the draft last September. And he answered that call with honor, for the citizens of the state must unite and stand together. Tomorrow he departs for the Great Adventure, not to shed blood, but to save the blood of the innocent and unoffending. He is ready to receive his crown of glory and his everlasting reward." Father Beecham turned to the young man and placed a hand on his shoulder in blessing. "Go forth, Ephraim Heber, a fit companion of the Spirit, free from sin. Receive the protection and the care of the Lord."

Ephraim had been through such pomp and circumstance before – the prayers, the praise and the hymns – with others from the Church who had been called to the Colors. When the draft numbers were drawn in September, there had been a program and a parade in Safford, organized for Valley recruits by a host of civilian authorities. He stepped up now to more raucous cheers, giving thanks for the dance and repeating his lengthy farewell speech. Even in Mellie's eyes, Ephraim wore the uniform with profound dignity. His chestnut hair was stylishly groomed, and a rare smile flashed beneath his manicured moustache. But when his cold gray eyes met her gaze, Mellie's memory replayed the iron clasp of his fingers on her arms, the hot, wet mouth on her lips, and she shivered.

The air in the hall had grown thick and tepid, and when Ira announced an interlude, Mellie retrieved her woolen shawl and slipped outside. A double line of Lombardy poplars swayed near the rear of the building, their autumn-tinged foliage shimmering in the moonlight. This secluded lane was harboring more than one enamored couple, Mellie suspected, and would soon be the subject of Ephraim's indignant attention. She settled instead on the side steps of the hall, while the crisp air filled with gentle laughter, whispered voices, and the muffled baying of town dogs. Within moments Nephi slumped down beside her.

"Did you hear him, Mellie?" Nephi pressed his thin hands between his knees and stared into the darkness, an odd glow lighting his pale face. "He said 'citizens of the state must unite and stand together' and 'a patriotic spirit adds to greatness.'"

Mellie cringed. It was evident to her now that Nephi's obsession with the war had remained as firm as his faith. After a moment's reflection, she touched the boy's arm. "We *can* stand together, Nephi," she said. "But do we all have to stand in the trenches?" Pain clouded Nephi's eyes and Mellie regretted her rebuke at once. Nephi jumped up and shoved his hands into his pockets. "I'm sorry, Nephi," Mellie said. "Please don't go." She reached for his arm, and he turned to face her.

A swath of hair whitened to frost in the moonlight splashed across Nephi's forehead. "You made a promise to me, Mellie," he said. "Remember? 'A firmness unshaken.'"

"Nephi…please…" Mellie stood up with a sigh, drawing in her shawl against the cold.

"A firmness unshaken," Nephi threw back at her with a scowl. When he'd vanished around a corner of the building, a part of Mellie wanted to follow him. Instead, she sighed again and sank back onto the stairs, the wind knifing through her shawl and cutting into the thin cotton of her skirt and shirtwaist. As she bent over her knees against the chill, a warm sheepskin vest dropped over her shoulders. She looked up to see Press Brennick, and her mind's eye flashed at once to the pleasurable memory of his kiss. Inordinately pleased but puzzled by his presence, she pulled the vest closer and studied the man's shadowed face, unable to speak.

"Will you walk with me, Miss Beecham?" Press reached for her hand, and Mellie let him pull her to her feet. He dropped her hand with some hesitation, and they drifted to the far side of the Amusement Hall, where the faint glow of the Ward house lights would make them less conspicuous. "You're looking mighty fine this evening," Press said.

"Thank you, Mr. Brennick." Something thrilling caught in Mellie's throat and she smiled in the darkness. In silence, they walked on toward the rear of the building, their spilled-ink shadows dipping and running over the ground ahead. Shredded cloud fragments slipped past the full moon, and

Mellie felt she could have walked by his side forever. "Maybe we'll have rain," she ventured, glancing behind her for some sign of Ephraim. Clearly a Texan cowman at a Mormon dance constituted Father Beecham's "questionable environment." Why was Press here? What did he want?

"Might be," Press answered. "With the wind up." He scanned the horizon above the dark and distant Pinalenos. "Not likely though. Not tonight anyway...Have you seen Billy Ben, Miss Beecham?" he added, seemingly as an afterthought.

"Why no, I haven't." At Nephi's spectral appearance, Mellie felt an instant unease. Nephi eyed his sister with clear contempt and rushed off into the shadows ahead. "Should I have?" Mellie asked, staring after her brother. "Is that why you're here?"

"No, ma'am...Well, not exactly." Fear gripped Mellie's chest. "Billy Ben's a game man," Press went on. "But he gets a little wild now and again. A hard dog to keep under the porch, if you catch my meaning." Something foreboding marred his easy drawl.

"I think I do," Mellie answered, fear rising in her throat.

"Took off this mornin' darker than a wolf's mouth," Press added. "Says your pa read him the law?"

As he said this, a flurry of voices rose up ahead of them. "You get your damn Mormon paws off of me!" Billy Ben shouted from behind the building.

"'Whoredoms are an abomination before me," Mellie heard Ephraim answer. She drew in her breath sharply and threw a wide-eyed glance toward Press.

"You ain't no sky pilot," Billy Ben answered. "You got no right preachin' your fool doctrine to me."

Mellie and Press hurried to the rear of the hall, joining the gathering crowd just as Billy Ben broke the lock Ephraim had on his throat. In a hay wagon up against the trees, Sarah cowered under a heap of quilts and lap robes, her hair and clothes disheveled. In the moonlight, her face appeared wilted and chalky. Lurching from the side of the wagon where Ephraim had pinned him, Billy Ben slammed a fist into Ephraim's chest. Sarah screamed and stumbled to get down, but Nephi reached up and pushed her back.

"What the hell's goin' on here?" Press demanded. Neither man paid heed. His anger mounting, Press grasped Billy Ben's free arm, jerking him away from the other man.

Ephraim doubled over and slumped to his knees. "Our women are pure of heart until they meet the likes of you," he spat. "You've defiled the girl."

Billy Ben tore himself from Press' grip. "You foul Mormon son-of-a-bitch," he snarled. "That ain't so, and you and her both know it." Billy Ben reeled back and punched Ephraim in the face. As Ephraim fell, the cowboy followed up with a boot to the man's shoulder and shoved him to the ground.

"That's enough!" Press shouted again. Ephraim labored to stand while Press slammed Billy Ben back against the wagon slats. Fire shot from the cowboy's eyes. His fists clenched and unclenched, but he withdrew, dark and sullen, to the side of the wagon.

Press reached down to help Ephraim to his feet, but the other man waved him aside. Upright but unsteady, he glared at Billy Ben, one fist clamped against his bloodied cheek. "I shake the dust off my feet as testimony against this man," he said, staring eye to eye through the crowd.

For just an instant, Billy Ben flinched and then he swiped his hat from the ground where it had fallen by Mellie's feet. "I gotta get shut of this place," he sneered. "It's got knots in it for me."

Press gave a soft whistle, and a saddled grey quarterhorse cantered in from the darkness to join Billy Ben's roan. He turned and tipped his hat to Mellie. "Miss Beecham," he said softly. Without a word, she passed him his sheepskin vest. "I'm much obliged to you for your time." The two cowboys mounted and rode off into the darkness.

# CHAPTER SEVEN

# Friday, December 14, 1917

"'The circumstances surrounding the sudden death of Miss Ola May Powers, aged twenty-two years, at the home of her father in the Rattlesnake Mountains, led to a trip for Sheriff McBride and Dr. Platt early Friday morning, when word was received here by the sheriff of the girl's death.'" Father Beecham shook out the newspaper – Safford's *Graham County Guardian* – and laid it back on the table.

"'They arrived at Klondyke at daylight Saturday morning and went to the Haby's ranch, where the body of the girl had been brought,'" he continued reading. "'A coroner's inquest was held by Justice of the Peace Bleak. The girl's father testified that his wife died when Ola was a young child and that she had lived with him all her life at their home in the Rattlesnake Mountains, where he had worked on his mining claim.'" The old man glared at Mellie over the top of his silver-rimmed spectacles and folded the paper, slipping seamlessly into a verse from the *Book of Mormon*. "'And now I, Jacob, spake many things unto the people of Nephi, warning them against fornication and lasciviousness and every kind of sin.'"

As he finished, Lela, wearing pink satin slippers and a fur-lined robe, made her frail way into the kitchen from her bedroom, drawing the curtain closed behind her. "You shame the child's memory, Father Beecham," she said, bracing a hand on the kitchen table as she drew out a chair. "And without cause, I should think." Mellie settled her mother next to Noah and took a crocheted lap robe down from the top of the ice-box to drape across her knees.

"'If we walk in the light as He is in the light, we have fellowship with one another,'" Father Beecham countered. "To live off by themselves as those people do, a young woman in the company of only crude, uneducated men. The Lord finds such living unnatural. We are a people bound to each other, but not in the sinful manner of the uncivilized."

"May not the Lord also find fault with those who judge without merit?" Lela took a deep breath and fanned the infusion of mint tea Mellie set before her, pausing to run a finger absentmindedly across the teacup's raised daffodil pattern.

Father Beecham frowned and took up the paper again. "'About two months ago,'" he read, "'he took her to Safford to be treated by a doctor for throat trouble and again went with her to Safford two weeks ago to get treatment for her throat. Late in the afternoon of last Thursday, the girl came to the house where he and a man named Tom Sisson lived and asked him to bring her a bucket of water, which he did, and later both men went to her house for supper. When he arrived at the house, he said he went into her room and found her lying across the bed and suffering from a convulsion. He called for Sisson and sent him to get assistance and when Sisson left, he held the girl and tried to help her, but that she died a short time after Sisson left.'" Father Beecham cleared his throat. "Can anyone doubt that the girl was used for the most vile wickedness? We've all heard the stories. Brawling and profane, like her brothers, as if that gives them leave."

"Yes, we *have* all heard the stories." Lela glanced at Mellie over her tea. "But where is your compassion, Father Beecham?" she said. "It was only last month that Ola and her grandmother came from dinner in the mountains and their buggy overturned on a woodpile. That poor old woman was killed, have you forgotten? And Ola injured. Perhaps her neck..."

"Well, it goes on to say...," Father Beecham broke in. "'Word of the girl's sudden death was brought to Sheriff Mc-Bride, who left here with Dr. Platt to attend the coroner's inquest. After hearing all the evidence in the case, the coroner's jury brought in a verdict that the girl had died from some unknown cause.'" Father Beecham lowered the paper and glowered. "Some unknown cause." He passed a cold eye from Mellie to Lela and back again. "Who knows what blackness lurks in the dens of such lives. That breed has no restraint, no sense of shame, no decency."

From the kitchen window, Mellie could see that Duett had gathered in the laundry from a tangle of rope lines midway between the farmhouse and the storage barn. She folded the next to last of several cotton sheets and placed it in the wicker basket at her feet.

"Two weeks now since the devil in that Brennick upstart

touched our Sarah," Noah said. "Praise be to God that she preserved her purity."

"No one really knows what happened there," Mellie said. She threw a rapid glance toward her grandfather and then turned back to the window. Outside, Duett unpinned the last of the bed sheets, and Mellie bit her lower lip. "Sarah's made no such claim," she said. "We've no reason to assume otherwise."

But Sarah *had* confided to Mellie that her monthly flow had not yet come. Overdue by only three days, Sarah professed her innocence with such energetic insistence that Mellie attributed the delay to stress from the play, improper meals and too little sleep. The alternative was unthinkable… yet Mellie had approached Duett with their shared concerns, seeking reassurance and advice.

"The wicked cannot hide from the Lord," Noah bellowed, drawing Mellie from her distraction. "The truth will make itself known."

"Yes, Father Beecham." With an air of finality, she passed Father Beecham his cane.

The old man blinked and rummaged a hand over his frazzled beard. He stood up and shuffled towards the library. "Yes, yes…Nephi's lesson," he said. "'Blessed are the undefiled who walk in the law of the Lord,'" he muttered as he left the room.

Duett heaved the wash-basket onto her right hip and started for the side stairs. Just as Father Beecham's weight creaked across the front hallway, she stepped into the kitchen, her dark eyes sparkling. "Always a pleasure to see you takin' to your feet again, Mrs. Beecham." Duett plopped the hamper on the linoleum floor. When she adjusted Lela's lap robe the older woman gave her hand a light squeeze. "Been a day or two now, Mellie, since your ma's been up and around. But we've had a fine time of it telling tales and such, haven't we?"

"Indeed we have." Lela returned Duett's brilliant smile with obvious affection. Moving to the stove, Duett hooked a handle into one of the wood stove's lids, lifted it to poke at the fire and tossed in some fresh fuel. After rattling the lid back into place, she took up one of Lela's cotton nightgowns from the basket. "Boiled these goods past six this morning," she said. "Sudsed them up right good on that old Irish piano yonder." She motioned to the scrub-board leaning against the kitchen wall. "Now that's a white that purely pains the eyes, don't it?" Several irons, each cast in one piece, lined the back of the range. With a wooden handle clamped to each of these in turn, Duett shifted them over the hottest lid of the stove. "Sharp as a thistle out there today." She jerked a padded ironing board down from a wall niche beside the stove and propped the open end on the back of a chair. "Much more of this waitin' for rain and we'll have us a die-up in them hog-back hills 'round Fort Thomas for sure."

"The weather must be such a troublesome burden to your family," Lela said. "I know Mellie's father would gladly furnish you with feed if he could. But he's sold his lot already, I'm afraid. Edna's, too."

"Oh, now never you mind, Mrs. Beecham." Duett balanced a pan of water on the ironing board and began to sprinkle the sleeve of one of Father Beecham's shirts. "We've got us some cottonseed cake set aside yet. We'll do all right. You'll see."

"When Lyman calls on you again tomorrow, he'll see his way to help out in some way, I'm sure. Now I'll leave you to each other's company." Lela draped the lap blanket over one arm and made to rise. "No, no, girls. Never you mind." She waved Duett and Mellie aside. "I'll make my way."

When Lela had gone, Duett drew a tattered leather pouch from the pocket of her apron. "Hedge nettle," she whispered to Mellie, laying the packet on the tabletop. "For Sarah. It's as good a tonic as any I know. Granny Bee swears by it for poor circulation, low blood. It'll do the trick for Sarah."

✳   ✳   ✳

Inside of an hour, Mellie returned to the Pima store, making her way through the wide streets in the gloaming of twilight. She would return to the farm the next morning to allow Duett to spend the weekend with her family at the Fort Thomas ranch. At the store, Ira and Angelina bustled over a shipment of dry goods newly arrived from Safford.

"Letter for you, Mellie," Ira said as Mellie entered the store. "On the back room table?" he asked Angelina.

"Yes, Papa." The little girl popped up from behind the counter, her blue eyes twinkling with mischief. "It's from Ephraim Heber, Mellie. I can tell by his s's. Snakes with little eyes."

"Snakes indeed." Mellie chucked Angelina under the chin. Taking the letter up to her room, she dropped it on the bed. At the dressing table, she unpinned her hair and began to brush it with brisk, measured strokes, her eyes fastened on the envelope. When she finished, she snatched the letter up again and turned it over in her hands. Only then did she notice the postmark – November 10th – well before Ephraim's leave. With marginal relief, she opened the letter and read:

> *Kansas, November 6, 1917*
> *My dearest Malvina,*
>     *We arrived in Camp Cody in New Mexico from Holbrook and lived there in tents, our time given over*

*to drills and training with guns. Our camp here in Kansas is alive with enthusiastic recruits. It is magnificent to see such a large number of men working together for one purpose. I am perfectly content here. We drill and learn under gallant and gifted men who instruct us in the peculiarities of trench warfare. We live in large, well-ventilated wooden barracks, clean, dry and sanitary. Nonetheless, there are those less able to resist the temptations of the flesh. But we who love the Lord above life honor the daughters of all men and keep ourselves pure and unspotted. If then we lay down our lives in service to humanity, we will ascend into the presence of God, pure and clean as the spirit of a newborn child. Though many may perish in valor and splendor, I await this war with anticipation, excitement and eagerness.*

*With regards,*

*E.H.*

"Pure and clean," Mellie muttered. She tossed the letter back onto the bed. So much for "temptations of the flesh." Hearing Sarah slip into the room next door, Mellie sat tapping the hairbrush in the palm of her hand for a moment. With a long sigh, she took up Duett's packet of hedge nettle tea.

When she entered Sarah's room, several items concealed in old newspaper lay on the wicker side table. Sarah quickly gathered them into a small wooden crate. She shoved the carton under the table with the toe of her shoe and sat down on the edge of the bed. "You scared me, Mellie," she said, leaning back. "I didn't think you were back from school yet."

"Late MIA rehearsal?" Mellie asked.

"Yes." Sarah clenched her hands in the lap of her flowered frock. "That's just a Christmas box," she said, following Mellie's gaze.

"Well...I have something here that might help you with your female trouble." Mellie untied Duett's packet and pulled out a pinch of dried nettle leaves. "Miss Brennick's grand-mother says hedge nettle tea should bring on your flow." She replaced the fingerful and passed the pouch to Sarah.

"Will you thank Miss Brennick for me?"

"Yes, of course I will." Mellie sat down on the bed be-side Sarah. "Now you're sure you're all right?" She brushed a hand across Sarah's slim shoulders and swept a few errant strands of hair from her sister's face.

"Don't be silly, Mellie. Why wouldn't I be?"

Mellie sighed. She tried to catch her sister's eye, but Sarah turned away. "All right then, I'll put the kettle on." As she stood to leave, Mellie's eye fell on a scrap of paper Sarah had left lying on the tabletop. "Ephraim Heber," the note read. "American Expeditionary Forces."

"That package is for *Ephraim*?" Mellie turned and stared hard at her sister.

"It's nothing," Sarah answered with a vague smile. "It's just that it's Christmas, you know, and he's alone and so far away."

# BOOK TWO
# Duett Brennick

# CHAPTER EIGHT

# Saturday, December 15, 1917

Duett's eyes skittered across the landscape as Lyman's auto rattled down the three miles of ruts and dust that led up from the Fort Thomas–Geronimo Road to the Santa Teresa Ranch. "The Brennick Place," they called it in town, or sometimes just "Granny Bee's."

In years past, the Santa Teresa had taken in a considerable scope of country. Some valley flats, but mostly dry, rolling malapai hills. Five hundred cows they'd fed in those best of times, with free-range land and plenty of rain. But like so many other non-Mormon ranchers in the area, the Brennicks had not fared well in the drought of 1910. When the Fence Law came down six years later, they were "powerful low at the equator," as Granny Bee put it – short on cash. All that land they'd worked for so many years, they couldn't buy it up now. At thirty-five cents a head, even leasing was out of the question.

Hills beyond hills rose up from the road in tangles of soap-weed and mesquite, creosote and cat-claw acacia. Palo verde, agave, yucca and sotol overlaid distant blue mountains. Ocotillo, cholla and prickly pear dusted the hillsides, and streambeds, filled up with cottonwood, sycamore and hack-berry, were shadowed in the early afternoon sunlight. December was half dead now, along with most of the bunch-grass and the hair-fine grama Press liked to call "dog's grass." Even a heavy dew on the west end of the Valley would have set folks dancing, but there was not a cloud in the sky from one sun-up to the next.

"So has Father Beecham got the best of you yet?" Ly-man asked, grinning. He eased the high black body of the Packard across a gaping rift. The wide slash ran squarely between the tires, and scrappy twigs snapped along the running boards.

Duett tucked back a few strands of wispy dark hair and reached down to steady Lyman's field camera as it bounced on the seat beside her. "Well, now," she said. "Folks each got their own way about 'em, I know, but that man's ornerier than a stuck pig." The Packard crawled across a rocky chan-nel and jounced into a dust-filled depression on the other side. "But he'll not get the best of me, Lyman Beecham." She leaned over and rapped Lyman's knee with the palm of her free hand.

"He's an odd duck, I'll give you that." Lyman picked his way across another boulder-studded creek bed and twisted through a thicket of mesquite followed by a long line of stunted oaks.

"And that little brother of yours, that poor child Nephi." Duett clutched the open window frame to keep her hips from jostling against the door. "Well now, pardon my directness, but Nephi's no more'n a broken bell mare to that fool hoe-man Ephraim Heber. That man's on the prod, mark my words. We're all a sight better off with him a Sammie now and gone to the Colors."

"Arizona's loss is the Kaiser's gain." Lyman laughed again and maneuvered the Packard across the sand and gravel of another dry wash.

"But now your other kin – little Angelina, Sarah, your ma. And Mellie too, of course. Why they cheer up the place. They're like blooming filaree after a winter rain to that gloomy old house. So when do I get a go at this old devil wagon, anyway?"

"The lady wants to drive, the lady drives," Lyman answered with good-natured surprise. He pulled the Packard to a stop, and Duett hopped out to open the last of three Missouri gates marking the Santa Teresa road. When Lyman had driven through, she closed the gate again, fastening its heavy wire clasp on a freestanding post. Lyman idled the Packard at the head of a half-straight stretch of road ruts, and Duett returned to the cumbersome old car, taking the driver's seat. Lyman gave her some brief instructions, and the auto buzzed and shuttered as Duett coaxed it into a forward crawl.

"Granny Bee talks up the Hupmobile 'cause it's built high and clears uneven ground. Like an airship, she says. But this machine of yours does fine by me." With jolts and jars, Duett prodded the buggy on while Lyman glued his eyes to the roadway ahead, holding his camera in a white-knuckled grip. High and low, right and left, they bounced along, spinning around the shoulder of a greasewood-covered hill. "My, but she does sashay," Duett said. "Just needs a little unroostering is all." With the wind on her cheeks, she swung up into the hills again.

Up and down and up again the Packard jostled along. Duett slipped under the Santa Teresa's signpost and whirled into the ravine on the other side. The old gas buggy rattled on past the milk-cow pasture, past the bell mares and past the Santa Teresa's first corral. And then…there were chickens! A whole bustling flock of chickens, scratching in the dust, smack in the middle of the road. Now there was no telling what those chickens would do, or just how they would do it. But God's truth, they would *not* stand still.

In lopsided circles, the birds spun around, doing mad little dances in the dirt. With a blur of color and a scatter of white feathers, one hen shot straight up into the air. Duett shrank back and ducked her head as its fat gray body – wings flapping madly – hurled over the hood of the auto with a crow of despair. The old black Packard jumped the roadway and came to a screeching halt against the interwoven mesquite limbs of the second corral.

Through a swirl of dust, Duett slumped in her seat and glanced across at Lyman. The man's face drooped a little, and a shock of his sand-brown hair poked straight up from his forehead. He stared across the space between them with narrowed blue eyes. "Lord, woman! Who's been teaching *you* the finer points of motoring?"

"Why, this fine Mormon gentleman from Safford," Duett purred and clutched the wheel again.

"Uh…no," Lyman laughed and grabbed the wheel. "I think we should walk from here, don't you?" He nodded so vigorously that his spectacles quivered on the bridge of his nose. Reluctantly, Duett agreed and scrambled out of the automobile. To her relief, only a snatch of down and feathers was strewn across the roadway. Lyman slapped his pin-striped trousers with his driving cap, snapped his suspenders a time or two to raise the dust and adjusted the black garters on his upper shirtsleeves. When Duett had dusted off likewise, she re-fastened her wind-whipped hair in a loose knot at the back of her head with a couple of pins from the pocket of her skirt.

The Santa Teresa's main house – a low, dust-colored adobe – sprawled on the crest of a hill directly ahead, though still some distance away. Pinon pine and juniper ringed the building with a sprinkle of earthen green. In late spring, Virginia creepers and lizards would vie for a warm spot on the front wall. But for now, there was only a string of rust-red chili peppers and the angle iron Granny Bee used to call the family in for chuck. Canales – roof drains – tilted out high in the exterior walls. The mud roof they once emptied had long since been covered over with sheets of galvanized iron. Duett tentatively took Lyman's outstretched hand and they started up the slope.

"Did a little blacksmithing myself in the old days," Lyman said, motioning toward the open-ended shack opposite the first corral. Ferrier equipment hung on the sagging walls and cluttered the dirt floor.

"Billy Ben's been workin' the shop since he joined up. A real sally dog with horses, he is. He's real good with 'em. Riding...roping...racing." Duett warmed to the feel of her hand in Lyman's and smiled.

Beside the blacksmith shop stood a horse barn – part stalls, part tack-room and part feed storage. West of the barn was a weathered-pine bunkhouse, from a time when the Santa Teresa could afford a crew. It was shaded on the north side by elderberry bushes. Billy Ben bunked there now.

Last in the line of buildings on the left was an adobe hay-barn littered with old wagon parts, other rusted scraps and machinery, and two large freight wagons for hauling in supplies. To the right stood three large corrals of mesquite fencing, behind them a small brown alfalfa field – a "trap" – used as pasture for milk cows and a few favored horses. The upper-end gates usually stayed open so the stock could wander in for water and then leave again to graze on the open range. The gates were closed now, the water nearly gone.

In the early days, the Brennicks had ranched wild, snaky cows that bolted if a jackrabbit crossed their path. Years of hard work had gentled the cattle and bred up young ones that could be handled more easily. Now, the remaining herd stood around, big-eyed and half-starved on the rocky hillsides.

"See that black walnut yonder, next to those boulders?" Duett indicated the large bare tree in the center of the middle corral. "Right there, a band of Chiricahua Apaches surrendered to some soldiers from Fort Thomas after a bloody shootout back in the 1880s." She raised an eyebrow and winked at Lyman. "Or so Granny Bee says." Hand in hand they continued towards the old homestead, Lyman taking in Duett's every word.

He eyed the remains of a sun-dried brick jacal – a small survival shelter tossed together when the Brennicks had first come in from Texas by covered wagon in 1892. "It had three small windows," Duett said, nodding toward the rickety ruins. "And Pa faced the fool thing south so's the sun would shine in the door near noon and Ma would know the time. They all lived there with Press like lambs at a sheep dip until Pa built the new place the next year."

Duett squinted from the blacksmith shack across to the weathered façade of the main building. Under a cottonwood tree nearby stood the "summer house." Four posts and three cross pieces, the middle one higher than the others, gave a slant to the heavy canvas roof, and the sides were screened. On hot summer nights, Granny Bee threw buckets of water over the ground to cool the air for sleeping.

Lyman had stepped closer, and Duett had just begun to hope that he meant to kiss her when Shadi Lace bounded into view from behind the smokehouse. A hefty black Shorthorn bull with a ruffle of white hair across the shoulders lumbered at her heels. Lyman took a hesitant step backward as they approached.

"And how's my best girl?" Duett swept Shadi Lace up into her arms. The black bull froze, a wild spark in his small brown eyes, and Duett dropped back and touched Lyman's arm. "This is Torito," she said. The bull's ears swiveled toward her voice. "Come, Baby." The bull cocked his head, stamped the ground with one stunted foreleg and shifted his great bulk. "He's just a little shy around strangers," Duett added as Torito started forward.

"I had some trouble with a bull once," Lyman ventured, fixing his gaze on Torito's wide, flat face and motioning down the road toward the abandoned Packard. "Front tire punctured," he said. "I'd just put in a spare tube and was inflating it when this bull lowered his head, got a good grip on the road and launched himself. Oh, I stepped aside sure enough…" He nodded to Duett and turned back to the bull. "But he hit the tire head-on and broke his neck."

Duett laughed, and Torito came to a sluggish halt. "This fellow here's nothing but a two-year-old bootblack kitten." She teased the bull softly. "Shadi Lace helped nurse him through some sickness about a year ago when she was barely two years old herself. He follows her around the place now like a moon-eyed calf looking for handouts. He's a timid thing. Rolls his tail when he's fussed up, like she-stock in a stampede. But he wouldn't hurt a soul, man or beast."

"Come, Baby," Shadi Lace called to the bull from her mother's arms. The big animal stepped forward again.

Lyman stood his ground and Duett reached out as Torito sauntered up, the hot breath from his nostrils fanning her hand. His thick tongue snaked out across her palm. Just as Billy Ben stepped through the front door of the ranch house, Lyman reached out to scratch the animal's wide muzzle.

"You leave the boy alone out there, you spoiler!" Granny Bee's words flew after the cowboy. "Don't you make no trouble!" Startled, Torito lurched sideways and rammed into Lyman who was left sprawled in the dirt as the beast trotted off across the yard. Shadi Lace squirmed out of her mother's arms, flanked the animal and tapped his rump. Torito's gait slowed, and he ambled away.

Billy Ben reached Lyman just as he'd pulled himself to his feet. "As the fella says, he's a wild one, that Torito." Billy Ben grinned and winked at Duett. "Yes sir, wild is what he is. You played it right smart to stand back of him, Mr. Beecham." He laughed again and beat his hat up and down the other man's dusty outfit. "You gotta come prepared for a scuffle with an animal the likes of that one." He gave a sharp snap to Lyman's suspenders with soiled buckskin gloves. "Why all you Mormon hay-men harness up like that confounds the hell out of me."

"Ease up there, boy." Granny Bee reached the group and pushed the cowboy aside with a flourish of her hand. "And, by God, I'll crack your jaw if you ain't talkin' proper 'round the place," she added. "Quit your swaggerin'. Hell's for them that sins, and you're up to some devilment by the mile." She glared at the young man. "Yessir, there's plenty of hell left in you, boy." She turned to Lyman.

"Claireanne Brennick here, Mr. Beecham," she said. A

slight, wrinkled woman awash in oversized denim coveralls and a battered straw hat, Granny Bee jabbed a thin arm at Lyman and then pumped his hand. "Pay the boy no mind, Mr. Beecham. No use pickin' on 'em when they're so young and tender."

Billy Ben laughed. "These Mormon folks shook the dust off their feet against me, Granny," he said. "We just give a little of it back, is all. Which is more'n they'd do for us. We're a damn sight better for the lay of the land than some fool hoe-man suckin-up all the water."

"That'll about do it, boy." Granny Bee drilled the cowboy with small dark eyes.

"Billy Ben can think whatever he likes, Mrs. Brennick." Lyman squinted through his spectacles as he hooked them back over his ears. "Maybe some day he'll just have to prove it."

Billy Ben beamed and rocked back on his boot heels. "I'm a game man, Mr. Beecham. You just name me the place. God never made a hole you could stick your head in that I wouldn't. I shoot like the devil, fight like hell – no offense, Granny." He dipped his head to the old woman. "And I ain't no rail-bird when it comes to ridin' neither. Just you name me the place."

"The horse race, then," Lyman said. "That horse race you cowboys always run on New Year's Day over there in Fort Thomas." For a hair's breadth of time, Billy Ben looked stunned.

"You're no horseman, Lyman," Duett said under her breath. "And Billy Ben here picked up a fifty at the fair in Tucson last month. First place. Three hundred yards on that sweet-tempered, collected horse of his, that Russian River Bill."

Lyman stood firm, impassive to Duett's half-whispered

warning. "You're on," Billy Ben said and lifted his hat. "To the best man. I'll be up in the hills workin' on the check dam with Press if you need me," he said to Granny Bee and set off for the horse-barn.

*　*　*

Duett always felt at peace in the main house. She'd been born there, in the front room, and the old place had hung on so well through all the years of flood and drought and hardship that she'd made herself believe it always would. The pine-plank floor in the front room had been laid down so green that it had shrunk over the past twenty-plus years, and the dirt brushed into the cracks over time had packed in nearly even with the wood. The walls were thick and dust-colored. The high ceiling of mud and cottonwood beams was shirted with an unbleached cotton-muslin, as were the three bedrooms. These rooms, along with a storehouse and a meat house in back, formed a rectangle of the building, leaving a central courtyard. Each bedroom had whitewashed stone walls and a concrete floor, poured when Duett's pa added on those rooms in the year 1900.

The front room was Duett's favorite. The walls there, pale as a wild rose, caught sundown from behind the house and the hills, and the twilight play of color gave the room a warm and blushing feel. Small recessed windows split the outer walls with grillwork, two in front on either side of the door and two in back, with an adobe-and-tile fireplace between them. Next to the back porch door, Duett had placed a plain unpainted pine chest, a gift Shadi Lace's father had given her on their anniversary a year or so before he died.

Kerosene lamps and tin candle boxes hung high on the walls. A long table made of cured ash and ten slat-backed chairs with woven rawhide seats took up the remaining space, accented by a scattering of colorful braided rugs. Outside Press' bedroom hung a collection of long-guns and ammunition – Pancho Villa still raided north now and again for cattle.

The pungent aroma of vinegar and bacon grease filled Duett's nostrils as she entered the house. "Now that'd be Granny Bee's bean pie," she told Lyman as she sniffed the air appreciatively. Granny Bee mixed mashed pinto beans with vinegar and sugar, when it could be had, and then baked them with thin strips of bacon that turned brown and curled on top. Granny Bee hustled Duett off to the kitchen to lay out some refreshments.

"Oh, my, my yes," Duett heard the old woman mutter over the scraping of chairs in the outer room. "Why I give up a prayin' for rain in January way back. I want mine *now*." She slapped the table and turned to Lyman. "We folks know dry. Why our fish pack canteens and our frogs don't swim a lick. But a hundred sorry critters ain't about to pack into that old cow pasture out yonder. We was hopin' awhile back that one of your people, say that Heber fella, might plow us up a few more acres to seed with alfalfa, helpin' out with his works like he does down there in the Valley. Takes two teams to break the land here, the sod's so thick with rocks and roots. Too heavy for our teams. But Lordy, we grubbed out old stumps and hauled off stones by the barrel. Too little, too late, though. And besides, your granddaddy put the hoof to any help from Heber."

"Ephraim put up the last of his alfalfa last month, I think," Lyman said. "I didn't know you'd asked him for help. I'm sorry he turned you down."

"Asked him right decent, too. Ain't you to blame though. We seen this warm dry spell comin'."

Duett stepped to the back porch, hoping the old woman

wouldn't get herself in a dither again over this alfalfa business. She pulled a slab of butter from the icebox. Even at the height of summer, this porch – its roof made of peeled saplings spread with earth, grass, flat brick and lime – kept the icebox fixings fresh.

"West Texas has been dryin' up two years now," Duett heard Granny Bee say as she reentered the kitchen. "The low country in New Mexico, too. Creepin' into the Valley like a snake losin' skin. Folks that's short of feed hereabouts been shippin' south since a couple weeks back – down into Pima County. Some of that beef hangs around there in Fort Thomas like flies at a picnic, waitin' for rail cars. We cut back to winter pasture mid-November. But that's the end of it for us. Let me tell you what rain means to a cowman in these parts, young fella.

"Two cowmen was on the ark with Noah, don't you know. And on the day they landed on that mountain, why they went out to look at the range on behalf of the two head of cattle on board. So one of them cowmen looks at the flood waters backin' down and he says, 'Had a pretty good shower here.' And the other says, he says, 'Be all right if we get another one just like it in a day or two.'" Granny Bee howled.

"Get another one like it in a day or so," Lyman laughed along with the old woman. "That's a great story, Mrs. Brennick."

"That ain't no story, sonny. That's God's plain truth."

"Duett tells me you've been here quite a while. I bet you've seen a lot of dry weather, Mrs. Brennick."

"Indeed, boy, I have." Granny Bee took great pleasure in her life stories and commenced another yarn. Back in the kitchen, Duett took down a set of blue-rimmed tin plates and a dish of cornbread from the high open cupboard opposite the stove.

Whatever else they might have to worry on, the Brennicks still had plenty to eat. There was always fresh milk and cream for homemade butter, and once a month, they stocked up on enough groceries from the Valley towns that shelves of food lined the storeroom – sacks of beans and potatoes, bins of cornmeal, rolled oats and rice, cases of coffee, baking powder, tomatoes, molasses syrup and lard. A screened cupboard in the meat house held slabs of salt pork and bacon, and stone crocks of dried apples, prunes and apricots filled the cellar.

In cold weather, the butchered beef that hung out at night to cool was wrapped at dawn in heavy canvas and put in the storehouse, too. Summer meat was jerked into strips and dried in the sun, and sacks of it hung from the storeroom rafters.

Midway through slicing the cornbread, Duett paused to tend the stove, shoving a piece of wormy oak deep into the glowing front hull of "Old Ironsides." A bitter winter in the eastern States had brought on a nationwide coal shortage. But the Brennicks' stove had always burned wood gathered from the mountains. Duett placed a blackened coffee pot on the stovetop, finished slicing the bread and went back to the porcelain sink to dust off three tin plates. Press had installed the faucet two years ago before the drought, tapping into the second of three springs on the ranch.

Spilling from the Santa Teresa Mountains, the first water source backed up behind the diversion dam where Press and Billy Ben were working and channeled down to a stock tank high on the summer range. The second spring fed the house, about a gallon a minute on a good, wet-weather day. The overflow slipped downstream to meet a third spring, which spilled over a concrete tank at the north end of the alfalfa pasture and trailed down to the Gila River. Once bubbling and clear, the first two springs produced well below their normal levels now. The third had gone completely dry.

"Oh, been here some years, I reckon," Granny Bee was saying. "My man just disappeared one day, years and years back. Left us high and dry, so to speak. We ranched a place in West Texas, me and a whole batch of young'uns. Sure knew how to grind out the work, we did. Never did make a go of it though. Bad times drove us out. Me and my youngest – Duett's pa – why, we came here with his woman, and little Press, of course. Been here since '92. Lordy, when I first saw Mount Graham over there in the Pinalanos, it weren't no bigger'n a molehill."

Lyman smiled and then grew sober. "The drought and the depression brought a lot of people out here from Texas in those days, so I've heard."

"I bet you have, Mr.Beecham."

The Mormons had never warmed to the steady stream of "gentile" southerners that had cramped the Valley from the turn of the century. Most of the Texas cowmen around Fort Thomas would likely be bought out in the next few years. The high demand for beef to feed the men in the trenches and training camps, and all those folks living under the hostilities in Europe, that demand would dry up with the end of the war. And there was always the threat of another sheep trail, this one right through the Valley, from the high country above the Mogollon Rim.

"Arizona's first predators," the cattle ranchers called those woollies. They'd been brought in from California in the drought of '76. Then in the dry years of '91 and '92, they'd crossed the Salt River below Florence to winter in the low country. Twice a year now, they came along to winter on the desert and summer in the White Mountains, ninety thousand sheep at the Salt River Crossing. In her sixty-five years, Granny Bee had lost a mother, a father, two brothers and a cotton farm in East Texas to the War Between the States. And then more hard times in the Texas hill country had taken an Angora goat herd, a cattle ranch and a husband. Rough living, no doubt about it, but Granny Bee's staying power had yet to be bested.

Duett grabbed a handful of coffee mugs from the top of the flagstone shelves, lifted the coffee pot from the stove with the skirt of her apron and sailed back into the front room before Granny Bee could start in on Lyman. "It slipped my mind entirely," she said, passing the cups to Lyman. "But you folks don't abide by no java." She balanced the pot on an old horseshoe to keep the direct heat from marring the tabletop.

"Ah, yes…Father Beecham would say we should, how does he put it? 'Set our faces like flint against strong drink or it will fasten its fangs upon us.' Something like that, anyway. But I prefer Saint Paul. 'Use a little wine for thy stomach's sake,' he said. Or a little coffee, I might add. Passion for the heart, revival for the spirits."

"Too much liquor is the bane of any man," Granny Bee said, but she laughed with the others. Duett poured a cupful of coffee for each of them and then went back to the kitchen for the cornbread and molasses. Sugar had gone to the war effort, along with wheat flour and coal.

"Now just what would you be doin' riding against Billy Ben?" Duett asked Lyman as she stepped back in from the kitchen. "That race in Fort Thomas brings out a lot of good cowboys and a lot of good horses."

"Nephi has a real good horse out at the farm," Lyman said, sipping his coffee. "Kitty Clover, he calls her. A bay mare speckled all over with white. I've run her myself, a mile in just under two minutes."

"Oh, the boy should have his ears knocked back, I suppose," Granny Bee piped in. "Too proud to cut hay and not wild enough to eat it, as I see it." She slurped her coffee and gulped. "Stuff's strong enough to strip the hoof off a boar hog, girl." She scowled but slurped again. "But he don't mean no harm, that Billy Ben. Just wild with the times is all. Should have been drafted to burn off some of them wild oats, but them flat feet of his got the best of him. I expect your eye trouble kept you from the Colors, Mr. Beecham?"

"Yes, it did." Lyman adjusted his spectacles. "I guess the Army thought I might just shoot *before* I saw the whites of any Prussian eyes."

"Your ma's heart-set against this war, Lyman." Duett sat down for the first time since they'd left the old Packard down by the corral. "Doesn't hold with no killin'. She says the Bible teaches 'All them that take the sword die by the sword,' and she says…" Duett squinted to the ceiling, searching for the very words Lela had used. "She says 'the Republic ought to have a cause for war so plain, so just, and so necessary that the people rise up as one.'" Pleased with her memory, she nodded to Granny Bee and Lyman in turn. "Told me just before you came by the place yesterday, Lyman. She said some high-ups in the government, a Mrs. Rankin and some others, stood by their country, but they couldn't vote for the war. And she said, your ma now, she said, 'God bless 'em. There's something so much greater to do than fight.' Your ma says President Wilson himself feels that way. Now, of course, your ma don't speak out much with your granddaddy's ears around. I swear that man can hear corn growin'."

Granny Bee made a harsh throaty sound and guzzled her coffee again. "We got us a cause for war that's as plain as the nose on your face, child. Feed every one of them pacifists raw meat, I say. Hang them traitors from a lamp-post. Them foreign devils make war like murderous savages. 'Slaughterin' the innocents,' the Reverend Billy Sunday says. Ain't that so, Mr. Beecham?" A revival preacher much to Granny Bee's liking, the Reverend Billy Sunday had never struck Duett's fancy, and she cringed.

"The Reverend Sunday does say so," Lyman agreed. "But war is also good for business, Mrs. Brennick. You come to terms with someone, or he takes his business someplace else. This country's more prosperous because of all the trouble with the Prussians. Government loans, business loans, food and equipment sales to the Allies."

Granny Bee pursed her thin lips as Lyman went on. "Then there's this blockade business. England mines the North Sea, and not a word about it. But Germany's war zone is ignored, and we expect the Kaiser to let our people tramp around there unharmed, just because they're Americans. Makes no sense to me. No, this war is more about the preservation of power than about the defense of innocent people."

"Humph!" Granny Bee's eyes spit fire. "That wolf of Berlin or whatever the hell they call that fella, he's a get-down, cold-steel man. Why if he has his way with the world, the lamb'll lie down with the lion all right. But he'll lie down just where the damn lion tells him to. The Reverend Sunday's doin' his patriotic duty."

"The Reverend Sunday can't afford to make war into the butcher's business that it is," Lyman countered. "Or he's lost the crowd. Maybe he should get down on his knees and ask forgiveness for wasting young lives on the altar of greed."

"Well now, it's a shame about that young Powers girl over there in the Aravaipa country." Duett's interruption broke off the heated debate. The light in Granny Bee's eyes softened, and the war evaporated. "Your ma showed me Friday's newspaper story," Duett said to Lyman. "How they brought poor Ola Power down last Saturday from Power's Garden. Such a pretty girl she was. And so sweet."

"My…my, yes." Granny Bee shook her head. "I caught me all the range gossip on the poor thing's demise. Always had a smile on her face and a kind word for everybody. Fine people them Powers. Their womenfolk went to church regular even after they moved up there to Rattlesnake." The old woman gave Lyman a pointed stare. "Good God-fearing folks *they* were, just like the Reverend Sunday."

"Touché, Mrs. Brennick," Lyman said, leaning back in his chair.

"How's that?"

"I've not darkened a church door in some time. You've got me there."

Granny Bee looked pleased with herself and was about to reply when Shadi Lace flung open the front door and raced over to her mother.

"Mama, Mama," the little girl spluttered on the edge of tears.

"What is it, child?" Duett reached for the toy horse Shadi Lace held up to her. "Why the poor thing's broken." The bottom of Edna's toy had fallen clear away, leaving a crudely carved hollow in its place.

"My horse's belly falled out." Shadi Lace sniffled and handed her mother a square of faded white cloth. "Is this his belly, Mama? Can you fix it up again?"

Duett spread the snip of cotton, no larger than four inches square, on the tabletop. Ringed about with a running line of butter-bright yellow embroidery were the words: "For Hal from Josie, 1856."

"What does it mean, Lyman?" Duett asked.
"Honest to God, I have no idea."

# CHAPTER NINE

# Saturday, December 22, 1917

When Ira led the family in a prayer meeting at the old house after Angelina's baptism, Duett took in the affair with some interest. The ritual itself had taken place at ten that morning in town. Duett had stayed at the farm to prepare the evening meal, but as she understood it, the child had been dunked under water with not so much as a toe popping out.

Eight was a crucial year for children "born under the Covenant," Mellie had explained. At that age, a child came to "a true consciousness of right and wrong." Now, Duett knew many a man – and many a woman too – not so blessed, and eight seemed a snip of an age to lay such a burden on a body. Mellie's people believed, too, that in every Stake of Zion – which Duett took to be a parish of sorts – formal baptismal services should be held monthly, as each new crop of children turned eight. Stand-in baptisms for folks already passed on too, though Duett never craved the finer points of that one. Tomorrow was the birthday of the founding Mormon prophet, Joseph Smith, who had been martyred in 1844. It would be a "fast day" for the people. No food or drink beyond water could be taken from sundown Saturday to sundown Sunday.

On an ordinary Sunday morning, Mellie had told Duett, the men went off to priesthood classes at eight o'clock, the women to their Relief Society meetings. At nine, everyone went on to Sunday School for doctrinal instruction and scriptural lessons, which broke at eleven. Then folks went home to eat before trooping back for an afternoon sacrament meeting, where assigned speakers railed against the congregation's darker nature and sent the people home again to sing and pray, read the Good Book and hash over Church doctrine. On a fast day, though – typically the first Sunday of every month – an hour and a half long testimony meeting took the place of the afternoon speakers. Members of the congregation bore witness to their beliefs as the "Spirit" moved them or gave short speeches, with a moral, of course, on travel or personal hobbies. Lyman said that to escape the boredom, some of the smaller children crawled under the benches and stole out the side door to play.

The money saved by foregoing meals on fast days was given to the Ward Bishop for the Mormon needy. And maybe they even prayed for rain, Duett thought. Mormon customs surely did puzzle her. They were an odd bunch, no getting past it, but being Lyman's people, they'd roused her curiosity.

A big bear of a man with an open heart, Ira closed the meeting in the parlor with a blessing. "Dear God, the Father of our Lord and Savior Jesus Christ," he beseeched, "Maker of heaven and earth. Let Thy spirit be with us. I bless you, dearest daughter, Angelina, in the cause of Zion, with all my soul and by the authority of the priesthood that I hold. From the depths of my soul, I bless you, my brethren and my sisters, that you may be stronger in good works, that your hopes may be realized and your faith increased. In Jesus' name, amen."

Hymn singing commenced around the parlor piano, and a gaggle of off-key voices drifted through the house. Even in her weakened condition, Lela's rose sweetly above the others, and she beamed with pride and pleasure at Angelina, who reveled in her mother's attention.

"Lordy," Duett muttered from the doorway of Lela's empty room, as Lyman hummed his way backwards from the parlor through the kitchen shadows. "May the good Lord bless y'all would have been a sight less windy."

"A couple of more hymns, a few more prayers, and they'll all be hungry again." Lyman gave Duett a playful wink. "But we'll have you back out at the ranch well before that. They've got no weekend claims on you."

"Now suppose Mr. Smith's ma had birthed him at the first of the month and that day fell on Saturday," Duett said as Lyman straddled the spindle-backed chair in Lela's room. She took a seat next to him on Lela's blanket chest. "Would that be two days runnin' without any chow-up for you folks?"

"Not this folk," Lyman said with a broad grin. "Fasting's for the pious, for hermits and fanatics. Lord knows I'm none of those. Scandalized the whole Valley with my own baptism," he added. The gleam in his eye told Duett that he meant to make a tale of it. "My other grandfather, Orin Harland – you know, the frowzy fellow from the reunion, smelled of tobacco and whiskey?" Duett nodded.

"Fine man," Lyman said. "Well, old Orin had me smoking before I was eight years old. And no good Mormon is ever allowed a smoke, you know. He used bits of Manila paper to roll the weed and showed me how to work it tight. Out behind the barn, I broke the Word of Wisdom a hundred times if once." Lyman laughed. "Well, I was terrified when I first saw the baptistry. In the old days, well before my time, they used to baptize everyone in a field canal north of town. A head-gate there backed up the water deep enough for a solid soaking.

"As it was, the room where I was baptized was damp and noisy. The font was square and white and level with the floor. A man dressed all in white stood there in water up to his waist, his hands on his daughter's shoulders. He held her hands together and after the prescribed prayer, he plunged the little blonde girl backwards, deep enough to drown the float of her hair. She came up wide-eyed and sputtering."

Lyman rolled up his sleeves. "And then it was my turn. I took off my shoes and started down into the water with my father. Some fellow read my name and then the names of my parents. And then Ira baptized me. Well, I'd forgotten that I had my pockets full of Grandpa Harland's weed, and the water floated it all right up to the surface. All I could do was stare at it as I went down."

"Well, I never." Duett laughed and rapped her knuckles on Lyman's knee. "Ain't you the one. And I reckon old Noah was all aggrieved?"

"Well, I made my escape and ran outside, but I'm sure I owe everything that happened after that to Mama. She found me skulking alongside the building, dried me off and talked me into going back in. Father Beecham pronounced me a full-fledged member of the Church and gave me what they call a confirmation blessing…something he no doubt regrets."

The music had stopped in the outer room and Duett and Lyman dropped their voices. "Mr. Harland doesn't come 'round much now, even to see your ma," Duett said. "That would be your granddaddy's doin', I expect. Looks to me like your ma doesn't quite belong. Least not to Mr. Beecham. A hard man gets like that, if you know what I mean."

"Noah Beecham's the hardest man I know," Lyman agreed, as he moved to the doorway with Duett. With the curtain still closed, there was only a small slit on the right of the doorway through which they could peer across the empty kitchen into the parlor. Lyman stood directly behind Duett, one hand resting lightly on her shoulder as the family drew around the table. Duett warmed to his nearness, leaning back into his chest, his soft breath falling on her hair.

Hunched over his walking stick, Noah shuffled into the kitchen first. Forgoing the kerosene lamp, he reached for the pull-chain to light up the bare bulb in the ceiling. His hairline, considerably receded, seemed to dip further in the shadows, and a spray of iron-gray hair shot up from the back of his head. In Duett's eyes, the speck of yellow in his lapel was all that kept old Noah alive.

Before Father Beecham's crimped fingers could clasp the light switch, Nephi, always at Noah's side, reached up and pulled it down. Behind his boxy silver spectacles, the ice in the old man's eyes thawed a degree or two as he smoothed his frazzled beard.

"Something's been eatin' at those two…I mean Mellie and the boy," Duett said, more to herself than to Lyman. "Ephraim Heber might be overseas but he's really still there in that poor boy's face. Mellie doesn't say a word about it, not a word." Duett glanced up at Lyman and then back out into the parlor. Nephi, thinner and more fragile than the old man whose arm he took, swept a tuft of pale hair from his eyes and steered Noah to the end of the oak table. Nephi's birth had come at a time when his father, Ira, had been back east on a mission for the Church, Duett remembered hearing. For all the big-eyed wonder Nephi had for Noah Beecham and Ephraim Heber, Ira Beecham needn't have come home at all.

"She eyes him all the time, Mellie does…like she's afraid he'll disappear. See there?" Duett stabbed a finger toward the parlor door. As Mellie helped Lela to her chair, her skittish eyes cast about for her little brother.

Little Angelina bounced into the kitchen next, her long blonde hair wild with curls. Angel had a face as innocent and bright as a patch of sunflowers, and the sight of her seemed to give Mellie some comfort. Sarah had been like that once, Mellie had told Duett. All grins and giggles. But not since Duett was hired on, if not longer. The time or two she'd come by the old house to visit with Lela, Sarah seemed a pile of raw nerves, pale and thin and scared. No more meat on her than a jackrabbit, Duett thought. Young Sarah came in with ghostly silence and took a seat beside her mother.

Duett had a hunch that Sarah was with child. Though some of the others surely must think so too, no one else quite had the courage to name it. There'd be hell to pay when the old man found out, that was as true as the Bible. Duett considered sharing her suspicions with Lyman but decided against it. The man had enough on his plate just belonging to these Beecham folks.

As Lyman and Duett returned to their seats, everyone but Noah made a great fuss over the evening meal Duett had laid out on the sideboard – cold sliced beef, cheeses from the ice-box, a basket of oven-warmed sourdough biscuits and a pitcher of milk. As the meal progressed, Edna joined Lyman and Duett in Lela's room. Two women could hardly be more unlike, Duett thought as Edna opened the curtained doorway and looped the panels over hooks on either side. Lela, soft and frail, had an unbreakable spirit of faith that bent more heavily with every gust of wind. Edna, feisty and full of courage, her round face creased with smiles, seemed as healthy as a gray mare in a spring pasture. Edna greeted Lyman and Duett in turn with a kiss on the cheek. "I thought you two might be hiding out in here, away from the bustle."

From the corner of the room, Lyman pulled up a chair for his aunt and once again straddled his own.

Edna wore a gray tailored suit that stood up well against the salt and pepper of her hair. "I do hope you'll get home Tuesday for Christmas, Duett dear," she said as she sat down. Duett reclaimed her place on the blanket chest, and the three of them settled affably in a loose semi-circle. Beyond the now opened doorway, the rest of the family had gathered around the kitchen table in low conversation.

"The young'uns are finished with their schooling for a spell, so there's plenty of other hands for Christmas dinner here," Duett answered. "Mellie says you'll eat 'round about two o'clock, so as to get all the preaching out of the way. That means I can be out at the place all day." She beamed. "Granny Bee's puttin' on a big feed. Roasted chicken with Mormon dip…" Edna raised her eyebrows.

"That's a hot browned flour and milk gravy built up so's you can handle it," Duett explained. "Don't know why it's tagged with such a name. But there'll be celery and cranberry sauce and, mmm-mmm, minced pies and fudge." She glanced at Lyman and blushed. "And then Lyman and me, well we're goin' on into Safford at suppertime for our very own Christmas dinner at Jimmie's." Duett's brow crinkled. "Now what's that the paper said? Oyster cocktail, roasted turkey, creamed cauliflower, fruitcake and...oh, I forget now what-all," she added with a flourish of her hand. "But my mouth's been waterin' with just the thought of it."

"What a lovely idea, Lyman." Edna squeezed Lyman's arm and looked extraordinarily pleased. She had a soft spot for Lyman, and with her growing affection for Duett, she was always tickled to see them together. "Just see that Noah Beecham doesn't get wind of it. Not that we should care," she added. "I know he's my father, and a fine man in his own way. But I hear he's been positively frothy over this business in town with Mellie and your brother Press yesterday. I've been told all the poor boy did was bid on a basket supper at a Mormon function, but a Texan/Mormon social mix is sin itself to Noah.

"That being said, Lyman, don't you let him scare you away from this charming young woman." Edna pressed Duett's hand.

"Not a chance," Lyman answered, smiling at Duett so warmly that she felt her face redden. "Father Beecham's been threatening Church discipline ever since I was baptized, but I'm still holding my own." He winked at Duett and turned back to Edna. "Do you remember that spring when we had to clean up the main canal for the new season?"

"Oh, my yes," Edna nodded.

"All the male students and teachers were supposed to work on it one Saturday morning," Lyman explained to Duett. "As you no doubt know, what with the springs out on the Santa Teresa, waterways can get pretty clogged up over time – weeds, Russian thistle, whatnot. When two of the teachers didn't show up to help, we tossed them into the ditch the next day...me and a couple of friends. We were expelled from school, of course. But old Noah spoke up for us – God knows why – and they let us back in. I think that's the last time he's looked me straight in the eye."

"Lyman, you didn't!"

"Oh, yes he did." Edna looked thoroughly pleased again. "So what exactly went on at this basket social yesterday? Now, do tell me the whole story."

"Well, you know Mellie's been workin' on that basket of hers for nigh on a week now," Duett answered. "All lace and roses and scraps from all the sewing she does. Well, I let the cat out of the bag when me and Lyman were out at the place last week. So Press knew exactly where they'd be and when. And most of all, he knew the makings of Mellie's basket.

"I'd been watchin' after Mrs. Beecham when all the fuss started up. The bids for Mellie's basket had already gone up some. Eight, nine dollars and then..." Duett's eyes widened. "From out of the blue and the bushes came my big brother and says, 'twelve dollars,' all soft and firm like. Why all those respectable folks nearly dropped their teeth. It was a sight all right." Duett wagged her head and settled back on the blanket chest. "Press took Mellie off, and they picnicked with the others. But big black holes burned through the pair of them from that cavvy of folks. It was a sight all right. And Mellie, bless her, she never paid them any more mind than a hare in a snow storm."

"My, my." Edna smiled and shook her head. "Father Beecham must have been livid when he heard the news."

"How's that?"

"Angry, child...in a rage...fit to be tied."

"Oh, yes, ma'am. He was all of that and more. Mad all over, he was, readin' us all his hellfire. And then he caught sight of this snip of needlework I was fixin' to show your ma." From her apron pocket, Duett drew out the square of embroidered cotton Shadi Lace had discovered inside Edna's toy horse. "Went plumb crazy, he did. Roared like the devil to have hold of it. But it bein' from that toy horse you gave to Shadi Lace, why it weren't his to have."

Edna took the needlework and spread it on her lap. "From inside the horse, you say?"

"Why yes, the belly of that horse fell clean away. Mind you, Shadi Lace did give the critter a firm goin' over."

Edna laid the cloth in the palm of her hand. "'For Hal from Josie, 1856,'" she read.

"Now isn't that just a treasure," Lela exclaimed as she stepped gingerly through the doorway. She stooped to examine the frayed cloth. "Look at those ragged lines." She ran a thin finger along the rough stitching. "Wherever did you find such a pretty little piece?"

"I've only just discovered it myself…this very moment," Edna answered. "It's from a trinket my mother passed on to me when I was eighteen years old or so, about the time I first left home. Duett's little girl found it tucked inside."

Lela turned the square side to side in her hand. "Remarkable work. A child's hand, I'm sure. You know…" She straightened and glanced from Mellie to Lyman with clear surprise. "It's a very curious thing, but my father, your Grandpa Harland, was called Hal as a child. What a remarkable coincidence."

# CHAPTER TEN

# Monday, December 24, 1917

"Most folks never come to God so long as there's someplace else for them to go." The Reverend J.J. Carlisle thundered out his words, his black eyes burning like bull's-eye lanterns. A snicker floated over the crowd.

"Amen!" Granny Bee called out, and the word was taken up and echoed by a score of other voices. Granny Bee prized almost any revival meeting, but she was loathe to give an ear to the whole of those weeklong works that featured some saddlebag preacher hollering day and night between testimonials. Some folks stayed on night after night – women sleeping in wagons, men out in the open, children in the straw by the foot of the altar. But Granny Bee never held much to the neglect of one's chores, so she was inclined to pick and choose among the sermons. "The Lord don't just want us to have milk and honey in heaven," she always said. "He aims for us to have some ham and eggs on earth, too."

Lord knows she'd heard enough grief to pack hell a mile, but words from any man of the cloth never seared her soul quite the way they did Noah Beecham's. Still, the roar of a preacher declaring city life "a sewer of vice and immorality and corruption" – a notion Granny Bee was drawn to – just shook her to the bone.

The first night of the Reverend J.J.'s weeklong run was on Christmas Eve. Preaching from a tent in the winter fields around Fort Thomas, he thumbed his plump pink hands through the pages of a white leather Bible and slapped the book on the back of his makeshift pulpit. He flung his arms around like he was fighting off a swarm of bees and whirled his words like death and destruction down on the plain folk before him. The men sat to one side; the women to the other. Now and again, one of the harnessed horses from the circle of wagons, buggies and automobiles that surrounded the assembly would snort and stamp as the Reverend's rantings shot through the air.

"Who cares about old hell, friends," he shouted, shrouded in a long black overcoat. "We all know about hell. I want to know about heaven. And I want to know how to get there. Lift up your hearts, dear friends." He bobbed his pink bespectacled face to the rhythm of his words. "I say, lift up your hearts and come to God. When God is in the home; when God is in the schools; when God is in the workplace; when God is in the government…" His fists stabbed the air with each fresh phrase. "Then, and only then, my friends, will this world cease to crumble." And then he was silent. Tilted back on his high-heeled boots, he clutched the Good Book to his brocade-vested bosom, his florid face squatted on heavy-set shoulders. "Getting what the other fella's got and not getting caught." Beside Duett, Shadi Lace jumped as the preacher roared again. He pierced the front row with an unwavering black stare. Right or wrong, Duett knew she could get anything she wanted from Lyman Beecham.

The Reverend J.J. snatched at the guilt he'd sown in the audience. "Is that what it's all about, friends?" His black eyes drilled Duett's face, and she pulled Shadi Lace in close. "Is that what the Lord is all about?" A staggered chorus of no's flittered up from the congregation. "Praise the Lord," he hollered again. "Hard work makes the soul shine. America has a mission to lead the world to perfection, to be the guardian of liberty and justice, 'a city on a hill that draws the world's admiring glance.'" He paused. "This Great War is as sacred as the crusades of old. A battle for the Lord; a fight for what we believe in and wish to be the rights of mankind; for the future peace and security of the world."

So loud and long was the Reverend J.J.'s tirade that the skin began to prickle along the back of Duett's neck. His voice dropped again to a hush but soon swelled anew. "To make money honestly is to preach the gospel," he bellowed. "But let us use ourselves, and all that we have, all that we are, and all that we do, to the glory of God and to the holy crusade on which we…as a nation…under God…have justly embarked. Amen!"

An "Amen" murmur rose to shouts over prolonged applause, at the end of which the Reverend called his flock forward for his blessing – and his ministry's financial need. Duett kept her place, while others, some who she knew had never before picked grapes in the Lord's vineyard, trooped dutifully down the aisle happy as heifers, as Granny Bee would say. They got down on their "prayer bones" and stacked their burdens of sin and their hard-earned dollars on the Reverend J.J.'s altar.

"A genuine ring-tailed snorter, that one." Granny Bee scrambled to her feet and fixed a lean hand on Duett's elbow as they hauled Shadi Lace through the flow of the crowd. Men, women and children, decked out in their finest, milled about under the trees and between the wagons. "That Beecham man of yours would have had a heap of trouble with that honest-money talk."

"He ain't my man." Duett wedged the old woman between the last row of wooden chairs and a lofty, round rancher in musty pinstripes. "Besides, Lyman Beecham's worked hard for what he's got." She guided Granny Bee along the back row and out toward the Brennick buckboard.

"Well, if it weren't so, we'd never know it, now would we? Them Mormon folks take care of their own. They've been bailin' hay and plowin' up for winter wheat like there's no day of reckonin'. And the rest of us without feed enough to spring a chicken." With Duett's help, Granny Bee hoisted herself into the wagon. "He won't be wantin' for nothin', not while his folks got their hooks all over this damn Valley. That ain't honest, child."

"Now I thought you'd taken a shine to Lyman Beecham," Duett said as she swung Shadi Lace over to Granny Bee's side of the wagon and climbed up to the driver's seat.

"Oh, he's a good enough boy, all right, and I reckon you're sweet on him." Granny Bee raised a knowing eyebrow. "Well off to boot. But just don't you go fallin' for the moon, girl." She cleared her throat and spit over the side of the wagon. "Most of them Mormons is crazy like a fox. Can't trust 'em." She scowled and spit again. "Lordy be. It's dark as a panther's mouth out here."

Duett pulled a lantern out from under the front seat and struck a match to it, handing the burning lamp to Granny Bee. With a whistle to the horses, she gathered in the reins and released the brake. "You've been beatin' 'round Ly-man Beecham for a good while now. What's on your mind, Granny?" she asked. "We shouldn't take what's the other fella's, ain't that what the Reverend said?"

"That gate's wide open, girl." Granny Bee cranked the lantern's smoky glass down over the open flame. "You can go on through or not, just as you please. But you'd best watch your back, whatever you do."

# CHAPTER ELEVEN

# Tuesday, December 25, 1917

"In early winter, why the filaree just hugs the ground and waits." Duett dropped down on bent knees and plucked up one of the red-stemmed forage plants, the deeply-lobed leaves brown and curled. "The summer rains are for bringing up the grass, you know," she told Lyman. "But the winter rains, why they belong to us. They send the rivers down in flood and store up water in the mountains to fill the springs." She crushed the dead plant in her hand, and fragments swirled to the ground like scraps of paper. "But without winter rain, when a cold wind blows high and dry for more than three days, well, the filaree just goes red, dries up and blows away. In a good rain year, I've seen it come up nearly belly-high to a horse." She squinted out over the low hills of the Santa Teresa, dusty brown and flat under the midday sun. "Makes over the whole land in green and purple, like patches on a great big quilt." She smiled with the memory of better days.

Christmas had dawned as clear and raw and windy as any Duett could remember. The sharp cold still bit through the wool of Lyman's overcoat heavy on her shoulders, but only an errant breeze was left to rummage about in her hair. Directly after the Reverend J.J.'s salvation show last night, snow had capped the mountains, but none of that was left now. And still not a drop of rain for the Valley.

Lyman crouched down beside Duett and fingered bits of the shriveled plants. "I've seen it at the best of times too," he said. "After the winter rains. You're right. It's like a delicate blanket draped all over these hills. There's nothing can hold a candle to a properly watered desert spring." He flicked away the filaree scraps. "This drought's got to break before much longer. Filaree's the least of its victims."

"Sheep from California brought the stuff in," Duett said. "Seeds in their wool. Freight wagons, too, I reckon. Haulin' in hay and such. And from the old country before that. Came over with the Spanish, they say. In Granny Bee's day, stockmen hit the trail when the filaree went, so as not to lose their animals. But that's a poor man's dream these days, what with rail lines and cattle cars."

"Father Beecham says the drought's been overdone. That things aren't really as bad as some people make them out to be."

"People like us, he means." Duett tossed the last crisp specks of filaree into the wind and stood up. "If we were one of yours out here on a thread and a prayer, why he'd be all over us with hay-feed and seed cakes and what not." She half-smiled. "We've been down before, us Brennicks. But we're not out yet, no matter how much that old man might wish it."

"I've seen the way you and Press and your grandmother – maybe especially your grandmother…" Lyman laughed. "I've seen how you look at your land, the stock, the hills, the washes, the cactus…the filaree." He motioned toward another dormant plant. "And you're right. No insufferable old man like Noah Beecham can ever take that away, not a love of the land like yours." A snatch of Lyman's sand-brown hair fell across his spectacles, and he swept it aside as he stood up.

"I knew you had a feelin' for the place, Lyman." A twinge of excitement coursed through Duett's chest. "At least I always fancied you did."

When Lyman took her in his arms, his woolen overcoat dropped from her shoulders and his hands, warm and strong, pressed against the back of her cotton shirtwaist. "Marry me, Duett," he said, tilting her face up to his. "You know I could love you better than any man that lives." He kissed her then, and her body warmed like sunlight on a bed of snow.

When she'd regained her bearings, Duett ran a finger across the front of Lyman's shirt. "Well now, Lyman Beecham," she said. "You plainly took my breath away. And I believe you, I do. You're a fine man, and we'd have us a time, we would." She smiled and laid a palm gently on his cheek. "I'm much obliged for all of your caring. But there's a lot more on the line here than just you and me. Now I'd understand if you cut and run, seein' as how I can't rightly say 'yes'…But then I ain't rightly sayin' 'no' neither."

"That suits me just fine," Lyman answered.

\* \* \*

From the Santa Teresa, Lyman took Duett into Safford for Christmas dinner at Jimmie's. Though by the new laws of the Great War, the holiday was a Meatless Tuesday, Arizona and other western states with big business in meat production had been excused. After all, it *was* Christmas Day. At Jimmie's, they relished all that Duett had anticipated and more, taking to heart a plaque on the west wall: "Food will win the war, don't waste it." For a brief and savored evening, neither of them belonged to either a place or a people, and Duett allowed herself to fancy building a future with Lyman.

As they jostled along the road back to the Beecham farm, Duett leaned over to knead Lyman's aching shoulder. He always set the spark on the Packard's steering wheel and lifted the hood to regulate the choke before he started cranking. But the old Packard had a tendency to ease forward against him once the engine started, and Lyman had leaned his shoulder hard against it to try to hold it back. This time, the car had kicked, too.

"Seventy-five cents…for oysters, turkey, dressing, cranberries, mashed potatoes, cauliflower…"

"Pumpkin pie and coffee," Lyman finished with a laugh. "Worth every penny, and a sore shoulder, too."

"Granny Bee's always braggin' on how her grandkids are strong as mules. Well I could move the barn with my bare hands after that feed."

"I expect you could do anything you set your mind to, Duett."

Savoring his words, Duett followed the play of the headlights along the road ruts a few feet ahead. As they twisted among tree trunks and boulders, lamplight bounced up into the black night air. What a fine day they'd made of it. Christmas morning at the Santa Teresa was all Shadi Lace, big-eyed with a child's pleasure. And Granny Bee's popcorn and berry garlands draped on a pinyon pine in the front room. That blissful stroll by the river – and Lyman's proposal – followed by a fine meal at Jimmie's. They'd even managed a hurried visit with Edna Beecham in her Safford boarding house before stopping to fetch out Lyman's Christmas gifts from the studio.

"I can loan you enough for cottonseed cake until the drought breaks," Lyman said, breaking the silence. He tapped nervously on the steering wheel. "Press is still exempt from conscription – keeping the troops in red meat and all that. You could go back to Shadi Lace and your grandmother then and be done with Father Beecham once and for all. Just say the word."

As the emptiness slid by outside her window, Duett turned to Lyman with a tenuous smile. "You know, we had this big black mongrel on the place once," she said. "We called him Troubles, because that's what he was. And that's what we got a lot of the time, us Brennicks." The night air turned icy, and she tightened Lyman's woolen overcoat around her. "But we always come through on our own. Ma and Pa, Granny Bee and Press – they came by train to Fort Bowie from the deep-well country of west Texas when the water dried up. Freighted up to Fort Thomas to settle on the place. Pa had a contract to feed mesquite to the railroad for a year or two. They lived there in two big tents, one to cook and eat in and the other one for sleeping.

"The drought in the 1890s nearly killed Pa and his stock with him. The mines over there by Silver King finished him off when I was just a baby, and Ma died along with my baby sister the same year Pa was killed. It was just Granny Bee and Press after that, rebuilding the herd. They sent me to school in Willcox, doing laundry and housework for folks that'd feed me and give me a place to sleep." She paused and brushed a swag of hair from her eyes. "I stayed in town until I was seventeen. Then I ran off with a cowboy from down on the Blue. We flagged down the train outside Pima and went over to Morenci to get married. But he got himself killed in them damn mines, too, scramblin' to make us some money just before Shadi Lace was born. After that, I went back to the ranch to have our baby. Granny Bee pulled me through."

Lyman's hand covered Duett's, its smoothness taking her by surprise. "Ranchers live by the seasons," she went on. "Calving and branding, haying and roundup. They're always uncertain. But it's a life worth living. Press branded over some calves for me and Shadi Lace way back, so now we got us our own cows. I thank you, Lyman, truly I do, but I can't take your money. We might know troubles like the neighbor's dog," Duett finished with a laugh. "But we gotta do for ourselves. Besides," she added as an afterthought. "I like your sisters and your ma too much to leave them to the black-eyed mean spirits of your granddaddy."

The old Packard slipped down the Pima road cast in thick patches of shadow. In the distance, the lights of the town began to flicker and blink. "So now, about this horserace in Fort Thomas," Duett ventured, pulling herself upright in her seat. "Billy Ben's been lower than a bow-legged centipede since mention of the fool thing. No…longer than that. Black as a boot heel since way back to Thanksgiving, when Ephraim Heber put a curse on him."

Lyman's face shifted between amusement and confusion. "Put a curse on him?" he asked. "Oh…you mean his foot-dusting routine. He does that for all the girls."

"Oh, go on." Duett slapped Lyman's arm. "Billy Ben says he knew a fella once who had the dusting done to him for spurning a couple of Mormon Bible men. And do you know what?" Duett's eyes widened and she leaned further toward Lyman. "Not a summer passed, and every last one of his cows got the black leg. Went belly up right before his eyes. His horses too...blinded. Cursed he was."

His eyes still fixed on the road, Lyman kissed the tips of his fingers and brushed them across Duett's lips. "You're a treasure, Duett," he said. "A pure treasure."

"Are you makin' fun of me?"

"Not a bit. And it's *your* horse race, remember? It's a Fort Thomas affair. And not one Noah would condone either."

"You're bound to race then?"

"Looks like it." Lyman hauled the black Packard into the space left of the lamp-lit farmhouse next to Ira's Model T. "Ready for a roust?"

"A what?"

"The wrath of God is about to descend upon us, my child. I've deserted the flock on Christmas Day for a woman of 'questionable virtue,' as the old man would say. An innocent Mormon boy like me." Lyman grinned and chucked Duett tenderly under the chin as he reached across to open her door. He stepped out to the running board and pulled up a flour sack from the rear seat. "Sure you're up to this?"

Duett nodded and Lyman closed the collar of the overcoat snug against her neck. "Ready as rain," she said. "I'm back on the job tonight anyway, remember?"

Night air stood black as pitch over the old house. The spun gold of lamplight spilled to the ground from the parlor and kitchen windows. Bare-branched fruit trees clattered in a rising wind that rustled along the wall of the house and settled on Duett with the same disquieting stillness she'd known sometimes out on the range.

With a thunderstorm coming on, she recalled, cows old and young feared the lightning. They'd mill about, skittish and wide-eyed. But strike a match and they'd be halfway up the mountain and still going, feet clacking on the rocks like a butcher's knife. When Lyman cracked open the farmhouse door, Duett knew he'd just lit that match.

Aglow with festivity, the kitchen smelled of roasted turkey, popcorn and pine greens. From the spindle-work of the pantry opening, a garland of red berries and pine boughs dipped in grand loops. Thick white candles encircled with sprigs of juniper and a sprinkle of tiny silver stars had been arranged in the center of the kitchen table, and Christmas carols filtered in from the parlor, the piano keys clinking above a rousing swirl of voices. "That old man can't carry a tune in a corked jug," Duett whispered.

"Well, he does have something of a reputation for sour notes," Lyman snickered.

"Lyman!" Angelina skipped into the room from the front of the house and spun around on the heel of her black-laced boot. Beaming, she spread out the white cotton pinafore that covered her sky-blue frock and curtsied.

"Merry Christmas, Angel." Lyman gave his youngest sister a hug and took out a yellowing box from the flour sack he'd brought in from the auto. The singing voices in the parlor dimmed to mumbles, and the piano fell silent. Unaware of any simmering tension, Angelina pried the ribbon off her package, opened the lid and dug out a lace-trimmed handkerchief embroidered with the letters "A" and "B."

Duett wedged the handkerchief into Angelina's pinafore pocket, its gold-threaded letters standing out bright as poppies in a hay field. "You look mighty fine, Angel," she said.

Braced between Sarah and Mellie, Lela entered the room next. "And a joyous Christmas to both of you," she said with a warm smile.

Lyman kissed his mother and sisters in turn and settled

Lela in the chair nearest the wood-burning stove. Ira lingered in the dining room doorway as Lyman opened the sack and passed out more beribboned parcels. Noah and Nephi were yet to be seen. They'd be the ones to lead the run when it came, Duett thought, toying with a button on her collar.

Unruffled, Lyman went on emptying his gift bag. For Sarah he had a sleeveless slip-on sweater with a tasseled gray belt. "I'm no fashion expert," he said. "But I heard these were all the rage." Sarah put the sweater on and whirled around like a firefly, hammering the newcomers for a rundown on Jimmie's Christmas dinner. But behind her spunky spirit, the poor child seemed worn as a mud-baked brick in a wash of rain.

Lyman had a stylish new breakfast cap for his mother – a band of taffeta edged with lace and trimmed with a zigzag of little pink blossoms. Under a bow of satin ribbon, the cap fastened at the sides of her head with dainty snaps. Lyman had a photo-print for his mother too, tea-colored and mounted on dark cardboard.

"Your father and I at the reunion," Lela gushed. "A lovely remembrance of a lovely day. My thanks to you, Lyman."

"You're welcome, Mama," Lyman said. Smiling broadly, he turned from Lela to Mellie. "And this, my dear sister, is for you." Lyman gave Mellie a Liberty Bond and a smartly ruffled collar and cuff set.

As Duett unwrapped her own gift, Father Beecham lumbered through to the kitchen, glaring at Lyman as though he were the devil himself. Lyman had given Duett a small framed portrait of Shadi Lace with Torito – as promised – along with a gorgeous silver and turquoise hair pin and a collar and cuff set in pale sandstone brown, similar to Mellie's.

Noah stopped short and leaned over his walking stick. "The depravity of my people," he muttered. "The Lord is pleased to see us acquire riches, for He intends to give us the whole earth as an eternal inheritance. But it is the *love* of riches that kills. 'My soul delighteth in plainness,'" he said, picking up Mellie's cuffs from the tabletop where she'd placed them. In an instant, he let them drop again, as if they'd burned his fingers.

"A small thing, Father Beecham." Lela made to stand but sank back into her chair. "A token of celebration."

"The boy meant only to please," Ira added, stroking his chin.

"To please whom?" Noah scowled. Duett's cuff set slipped silently from her hands. "Not the blessed Lord, I'll wager." He thumped the cane a single time on the linoleum floor, and Nephi came and stood beside him. The pale-faced boy looked like a sun-sickened sheepdog Duett had seen once in the Mexican camps up north. Only fifteen years old, Nephi was. But as he hovered at his grandfather's right arm, he seemed ageless and ghostly. "I will afflict thy seed by the hand of the Gentiles, thus saith the Lord," Noah said, a pronouncement clearly meant for Lyman and Duett.

Ira sagged against the icebox, and Mellie and Lyman traded helpless stares. Sarah, looking like she'd be sick, managed a sympathetic glance in Duett's direction. In the silence that followed, Lela cleared her throat. "'Wherefore the Gentiles shall be blessed and be numbered among the house of Israel,'" she reminded Noah in a voice stronger than she'd mustered in some time. "A gift is an expression of the love of the giver."

Ira coughed and continued to stroke the salt and pepper of his beard. "What have you got there yet, son?" He strode past his father, the crease on his forehead deepening. Sarah drifted back to the piano with Lela and began to pick her way meekly through *Silent Night.*

"This is for Nephi. It's just a bow-tie." Lyman slid another box along the tabletop toward his grandfather. "And these are for you and Father Beecham," he said to his father. The two calendars he pulled out from the flour sack were identical. The Beecham orchard, bare and beautiful, stood out against a shadow of distant mountains. In the foreground, perched poetically in the angles of an apple tree, rested Edna's toy horse.

"Why, this is fine work, Lyman," Ira said with genuine enthusiasm.

"Mighty restful," Duett added with an inward sigh. Things would be all right now, she thought.

But things would never be all right. Father Beecham's hands began to shake, and he clutched methodically at the silk rose in his lapel. Ira attempted to steer the old man to a chair, but Noah resisted. Instead, he silently snatched up the two calendars and shuffled through the parlor and on up the staircase to his room, leaving his bewildered family behind.

\* \* \*

Long after the others had gone, Duett discovered the smoldering remains of Lyman's calendars in the library fireplace. In the morning, Nephi swept up the ashes and scattered them in the orchard.

# CHAPTER TWELVE

# Saturday, December 29, 1917

Mellie and Sarah had been at the farm since school broke for the Christmas holiday. Sarah stayed in the upstairs bedroom that Ephraim had occupied on the west side of the house, sharing the room with Angelina on those occasions when her father and little sister stayed overnight. Mellie used the room on the east. Duett's small room lay between them. Both Noah and Nephi had larger rooms at the rear, where there was more space for their religious studies but less heat.

Granny Bee's hedge nettle hadn't done the trick for Sarah. Nor had Ira's composition tea. Mellie had also given her sister a dose of Canutillo, a Mexican remedy for stomach ailments that Noah's former housekeeper often brewed from a plant called Mormon Tea. Despite these home remedies, no monthly flow came to Sarah, which meant the only trick left was to shelter the girl from the wrath of Noah Beecham as the child in her womb grew. How Mellie kept herself together without a Granny Bee to fall back on was beyond Duett's understanding.

In recent days, Lela's coughing fits had taken more out of her than ever. She tired more easily, and Duett was troubled by the black smudges under her eyes. She'd heard the old man say that there'd be a "laying on of hands" for Lela, and she wondered if as much Mormon magic came with that as with the dusting off of Ephraim Heber's feet. Folk treatments had failed as miserably for Lela as they had for Sarah. The hedge mustard plasters, mint tea and brewed-bark remedies Noah gave her "to revive the heart" did nothing to ease her consumption.

Nephi and Noah had gone off earlier in the week to fetch Solomon Heber and his sons in from the Duncan Valley for an upcoming priesthood meeting in Pima. The old man had little use for gasoline machines, so he and the boy had set off in the old black buggy that was otherwise stored beside the thresher in the barn. With neither of them about the place, the farmhouse seemed almost cheerful, its shroud of self-righteous intolerance lifted.

Weak and unsteady, Lela had taken to bed soon after breakfast. With preparations for the noonday meal hours away yet, Duett sat gazing out her bedroom window, looking down the long road that led out to Fort Thomas toward the Santa Teresa. Pale morning sunlight slivered through the bare black branches of the mesquite trees bunched at the front of the house, their long shadows stretched across the dusty roadway.

With the check dam in the back hills already prepared for winter rains – if and when they finally came – Press and

Billy Ben would be out on their own this time of day. Having finished her morning chores, Shadi Lace would be off in the hills, rambling about with Torito and Granny Bee. Duett needed the work, no doubt about it, but Lord, she missed her baby girl.

Lost in thought, Duett was startled to hear a squeal of panic from Sarah's room next door. "It's not true, Mellie! I swear it!"

Drawn by curiosity, Duett inched open her bedroom door, but the sisters' voices dropped and disappeared as she stepped outside into the open hallway. Vents in each of the front upstairs bedrooms brought a scrap of heat to the upper rooms from the fireplaces below, but a small square of emptiness hung between the hall railings that looked down on the entryway. Very little warmth made it this far up the staircase, and cold air from an open window on the stair landing filtered through Duett's thin sleeves. She rubbed her hands together and moved to close the shutters, but the hardwood floor creaked like saddle leather underfoot and she froze.

The voices in the next room rose up again, though not quite as loudly as before. The door to Ephraim's room opened, and Mellie backed through, resting one hand on the doorframe. "I can only help you if you tell me the truth, Sarah." Mellie's voice faltered with emotion. When Sarah was silent, Mellie turned to leave, and her eyes met Duett's with surprise. From inside the room, Sarah whispered through desperate tears. "It was Billy Ben, Mellie," she sobbed. "My child's to be Billy Ben's." Duett gasped and gripped the hallway railing, and Mellie slumped against the open door. The burden of Sarah's plight was more than either of them could bear alone.

"It'll be all right, Mellie," Duett said, instinct prevailing over her own shock and confusion. But even as she spoke, she knew, of course, that she was wrong.

# CHAPTER THIRTEEN

# Tuesday, January 1, 1918

**W**ith the annual Fort Thomas horse race drawing up, the little town overflowed with ranchers and cowboys, horses and buggies, dust and smoke. This race, like many others, had begun as a Mexican tradition that the Texas cowboys had long ago pounced on as their own – any excuse for a wild ride. Dressed in chaps, Stetson hats and the short heavy jackets Granny Bee called "Levi jumpers," these boisterous men packed the main street, testy and fired up with anticipation. "A cowboy could be wet all over and still get by," Granny Bee liked to say. "That is, until his hat leaked." Truth be told, most of these boys treated their headgear better than they did their women.

The ranch owners and their foremen – cowmen, as opposed to cowboys – lolled about in huddles, chewing on their troubles and triumphs; how the railroad had gone over to the government last Friday, predators on the range, and stock-grazing in the forest reserves. They'd all heard rumors of another sheep trail from the Mogollon, and they bemoaned the plague of the ongoing drought. Sheriff Mc-Bride and Deputy Kempton had rounded up twelve cases of homebrewed Cedar Brook just last week, but by the complexion of the crowd there was still plenty of bootlegged whiskey to be had.

The ranch women, especially those off in the wilds for most of the year, visited with far-off friends and kinfolk, trading yarns about women's work and lamenting the weather. The worst blizzard in forty years had pounded the east coast just three days after Christmas, making fuel shortages worse than ever. Being blessed with relative warmth was some compensation for the land going dry, the women claimed, but none of them really believed it.

Some of the Mexicans, the ones Billy Ben said would rather fight than eat, blustered around puffing on cigarettes made of tobacco rolled in cornhusk. Along with the other cowboys, they cursed, drank and flirted with all the girls in town. Their own women and daughters watched them from closed circles. Wrapped in striped serapes of red, yellow and black, their sober dark eyes were full of suspicion. Everyone knew that sooner or later, some Texas cowboy would get drunk and ride into a Mexican dance to rope the dogs. Then, for a long while, the Mexicans would run around saying that all Anglos were crazy – raucous, thieving sorts "worse than poison." And the Anglo cowboys would set about proving this, brawling in the saloons and swooping down on some Sunday night Mexican do to shoot out the lights.

Granny Bee, Duett and Shadi Lace had come to town in the old buckboard hours earlier, hitching the wagon on the outskirts of town and walking in toward Main Street with other far-flung ranch families. Right after their arrival, Duett spoke briefly with Lyman, who'd ridden in on his own. A bit of an odd man out in the Fort Thomas crowd, Lyman planned to keep to himself at the back of Dietrich's saloon down on Fort Thomas Avenue, biding his time until the call-up for the race. With Father Beecham's volatility, he'd thought it best to keep the proceedings from his family. There was no real need for them to know, though the news had quite likely reached them already. Press and Billy Ben had arrived mid-morning, Lyman had said, and were tending to Russian River Bill across the road outside the town stables.

"Billy Ben thinks a heap of that red-eyed devil he rides." Granny Bee plunked herself down on a corner step and clamped her straw hat over ash white hair.

Through the thickness of bodies and dust, Billy Ben's black hat bobbed up on occasion from behind the red-brown rump of his horse. Duett had seen Billy Ben on the prod a hundred times, but never before, so far as she could recall, had she ever seen such alarm on his dark face. A numbing fear from the curse of Ephraim Heber, she surmised, of Mormon Bible men and a die-up on the Santa Teresa.

For now at least, Sarah's fingering of Billy Ben as the father of her unborn baby had not gone beyond the farmhouse. Whether or not he really *was* to blame, Duett was convinced Sarah would keep silent until she and Mellie could work out the best course of action.

"He ain't hisself, child. Somethin' ain't right." Granny Bee cleared her throat and spit into the street. "That Mormon hex has been eatin' at his insides like cows on a lick. I ain't seen Billy Ben so fussed up since Lord knows when."

"I've seen him jumpy before," Duett agreed. "But never quite this fearful."

"Them Beechams ain't got nothin' to do with this evil eye business, do they?" Granny Bee asked.

Duett looped an arm around Shadi Lace's waist and set the child down beside Granny Bee. "Ephraim Heber's got nothin' on the curse Noah Beecham could lay on a man, I reckon. But I don't think so."

"They're against us, those Valley folks." Granny Bee slapped her hands to raise the dust on her coveralls and pulled Shadi Lace up into her lap. "That Beecham man of yours seems a tolerable sort. But you'd best look to your own kin, Duett Brennick. And maybe you'd best start doin' it now, 'fore you end up in the paper like poor Ola Power, God rest her soul." The old woman spit into the roadway again. "Them Mormons is tighter than a tick on a bloodhound. I've heard the stories they tell about Ola May, her brothers and her daddy and the way they lived up there in Power's Garden. They're shamin' the child's memory with all them rumors of evil doings, and they'll treat you the same if they can, by God. You mark my words."

Granny Bee might be right, Duett thought. She could be camped out on some big old fire-ant nest, a swarm of cuttin' jaws at the ready. But, Lyman aside, she valued her friendship with Mellie and felt a deepening kinship with Lela. She'd even taken over a loaf of "war bread" on her weekend off. "Victory bread," Granny Bee called it – cornmeal mixed with any other grain but wheat, all of which had gone to the war. There was no way around the Beechams now.

"I've told you before, Granny, Lyman's not my man," she said, jumping to her feet. Billy Ben and Press, Russian River Bill in tow, wended their way across the crowded street. Now and again, they stopped for a word with an acquaintance or two, and man after man slapped the cowboys' backs and grinned with well wishes.

"So I says I'd buy that Heber bastard a shot of whiskey if he was here to take it, so's the grievance would be done," Billy Ben said to Press as they neared the women. "But I don't beg nothin' from no man." He scrubbed a gloved hand over his horse's muzzle and nodded to Granny Bee. "And that Nephi, that god-damned little bastard, he stared right through me like I was a pane of window glass. How you all put up with them Beechams," he added to Duett. "Well it confounds the hell out of me. Odd a bunch as ever I come acrost. And that Nephi, ask any fella, he's plumb possessed."

"The devil's in a few of 'em and that's a fact," Duett said. "But there's others have a good heart, and it's them I pass my time with. Besides, there's money in my bein' there, and Lord knows we're broker than the Ten Commandments."

"There ain't enough money in hell to set me to workin' for the likes of them folks," Billy Ben shot back.

"I reckon you didn't need no money to mess with Sarah Beecham." Press tugged down on Russian River Bill's saddle blanket and adjusted the cinch. Duett's ears pricked up at the mention of Sarah's name.

"I'd swear on my mama's grave. That is, if I knew who she was and if she's passed on or not." A flash of white teeth offset the tan of Billy Ben's face. "But I swear I never touched that girl at that damn dance or ever. Though I might have had a mind to once or twice, her bein' the looker she is." Billy Ben grinned and winked at Duett, but his smile faded with an icy rage that snuffed out the spark in his eyes. "If you ask me, one of them Mormon bastards got to her himself. They'd dance with the devil if he was one of 'em. Crooked as a jay-bird's hind leg, the lot of 'em."

A call went out for the race to begin, and Billy Ben

shoved a hand into his pocket and sulked off with Russian River Bill toward the edge of the main road. Folks drifted aside to clear a path for the running horses. With a hand from Shadi Lace, Granny Bee rose to her feet and took a seat on the next step up from the roadway, Duett and Press standing behind her. Shadi Lace looped her legs over a rung of the side rail and dipped her body backward, the tangle of her sand-colored hair spilling around the crown of her head like bristles on a hairbrush.

Laid out on a puckered, potholed road, the racecourse followed the river out of town, sloping toward the bank. A mile and a half in length, most of the makeshift course was lined with mesquite trees and cactus. The contest was to finish on a bend – a quarter of a mile beyond the cemetery – where a thirty-foot high hillock of black volcanic rock and thick tangled brush rose up from the roadside. Every year, one or two of the McKittrick hands, ranchers out of Fort Thomas, were stationed in the gulch to oversee the race's outcome. As Duett watched Billy Ben climb aboard Russian River Bill, the intensity of the crowd sent a chill through her body. No…it wasn't the crowd. It wasn't even the crisp winter weather or the sinking sky overhead. It was Billy Ben himself who worried her, raising a cold sweat on her palms. Before she could focus her thoughts, the starting gun snapped, and the crowd jumped to its feet.

The first horse, Russian River Bill, lunged into view. He strained against the wind, and his hooves dug up clumps of dirt from the hard street. Bent over the horse's neck, Billy Ben whistled by, lashing the reins with a crazed wildness. The darkness on his face reminded Duett of Torito – fierce on the outside, but fearful in the heart. If Billy Ben had done what Sarah Beecham said he had, a Mormon curse would surely put the fear of God on his face. Beside Duett, Granny Bee squinted and shook her head. She'd seen it too.

Nephi's bay mare, Kitty Clover, with Lyman atop, edged in against a chorus of hoots and hisses from the cowboy crowd. Just past where the Brennicks stood, the spirited horse was neck and neck with Russian River Bill. A horse-length behind them rushed two past champions of the Fort Thomas race – Salim, a bay from the Monk brothers' ranch, and Jack Green Horn, an appaloosa run by a sheepherder from the Mogollon Rim country up north. At the appaloosa's approach, obscenities ripped from the crowd. These southern folks could cuss a sheepman as loud and long as the Reverend J.J. cussed the devil. Each year, Duett marveled that this unwelcome horseman showed up at all.

A rag-tag mix of sleek quarter horses and shaggy draft-horse nags followed. Four or five lengths back chugged a scrappy Mexican tenant farmer from over near Solomonville. He brought up the rear on a dull, long-eared mule called Conejo – "the rabbit." No one paid much attention to either of them, the whole Valley being inclined to view its Mexican population with a jaundiced eye. When all the horses and cowboys had plunged into the dust, buggies and horses fell in on their heels toward the finish line.

Press had gone on ahead with the earliest riders, leaving Duett in the thick of it with Granny Bee and Shadi Lace. A swarm of people slowed them as they made their way to the Brennick wagon. Duett offered Granny Bee her arm as they maneuvered through the stampede, and once or twice, she had to lift Shadi Lace up out of the crowd and carry her.

Above the general melee, Duett caught a splay of firecrackers. The Mexicans along the racecourse were known to toss a few skyrockets under the horses' legs to jump the riders and spook the animals, and Duett paid little heed to the pops and crackles. Piling into the buckboard, she and Granny Bee started off after the others.

The first half-mile whipped by with ease, twigs snapping along either side of the wagon. But as Duett dipped down toward the river bottom near the cemetery, one of the wagon's wheels snagged on a rut. She worked the horses back and forth until it could be loosened, and on they sped. Just past a thicket of granite headstones, the lofty boulder-strewn outcrop that marked the end of the race loomed ahead.

As the road began to curve, Duett was seized with an unnamed dread. A lump of terror settled at the base of her throat, and she could hardly breathe. Time seemed to slow to a stand-still as she strained to see beyond the bend, which seemed to stretch out twice its length and more.

When at last they'd taken the turn and reached the other side, Duett saw Russian River Bill, foamy and riderless, rearing up in the midst of a paralyzed crowd. When she pulled the wagon to a stop, she was met with a silence you could plug a nail in. The way parted solemnly, and Duett could see Press hunched over the lifeless body of Billy Ben. His curly black head had a sickening crook to it, his twisted neck surely broken.

# BOOK THREE
# Mellie

# CHAPTER FOURTEEN

# Wednesday, January 2, 1918

Father Beecham held Josephine's worn black Bible up in one hand to catch the sun from the west window of the Beecham farmhouse. Backed by the light, the frazzled outline of his bearded face became a confusion of sinister shadows. "'They that were foolish took their lamps, and took no oil with them,'" he read.

Concealed behind the doorway, Mellie peered through an opening in the closed curtains of Lela's room, where her mother had been confined to bed for the better part of a week. On the far side of the bed, Ira stood stiff with discomfort, his large hands clasped in front of him as Noah prepared to pronounce a blessing of healing. Mellie well understood her father's struggle with the Faith, especially now. Father Beecham's reaction to Sarah's condition, whenever he learned of it, would certainly be cruel and unchristian; worse, even, than his callous response to Billy Ben's death.

Watching them together, Mellie herself felt an unsettled curiosity about this priestly rite, this "laying on of hands." But her misgivings were coupled, she had to admit, with the nebulous hope that her mother might recover, or at least somehow improve.

"'But the wise took oil in their vessels,'" Father Beecham read, pulling a length of fine muslin embroidery from the back of the book. On her journey west, Martha Heber, Solomon's first wife, had fashioned yards of this needlework as trim for infants' clothing. All of it had a fine yellow/red line of iron rust from a wire on the bow of the wagon where she'd tied her work. Generations of Hebers and Beechams had been christened in blessing gowns embellished with Noah's adoptive mother's embroidery. In Mellie's estimation, these christenings, with the needlework that accompanied them, were the most cherished of Father Beecham's many rituals.

Noah marked his place in the Bible with a piece of the fine trim and laid the book aside as Lela lifted an arm to each man. "I have faith enough to be healed," she said, a peculiar glow transforming the features of her face. "Bless me."

The old man took up a vial of "consecrated" olive oil from the highboy and passed it to Ira. The fluid in the flask, rich as molten amber, had been blessed by men ordained as Elders in the Melchizedek Priesthood. Invoking the spirit of God, they had asked for divine power to pass through the liquid, to sanctify it and make it holy.

All her life, Mellie had heard miraculous tales of this "balm of Gilead," given to fortify "the mortal tabernacle of the spirit." In his early days, Father Beecham had said, olive oil had been taken by the spoonful for its "vital and life-giving elements." It was used now primarily for anointing purposes, and Mellie watched with wonder as her father carefully poured a precious drop onto the crown of Lela's head and whispered a short prayer.

For those who had faith in such things, consecrated oil worked miracles of great healing. Lela, whose belief was without blemish, seemed already flushed with new health, her formal blessing yet to be offered.

Changing places, the men placed their hands once again on Lela's head. An almost tangible rush of energy spun around the room, and Father Beecham wrenched his eyes from Lela's enraptured face and lifted them, closed tightly, to the ceiling. Ira shifted his weight from one foot to the other and back again, his head bowed. As Noah drew a breath to speak, a pale smile touched Lela's lips, and unwavering devotion sprang up in her eyes. "Lela Beecham, by the power of the Holy Melchizedek Priesthood which I bear, I seal this anointing upon you and command you to rise and be made whole, that you may hereby fulfill your mission on this earth." His hands pressed firmly on Lela's head, Noah was consumed with fervor. "I invoke this blessing upon you, according to your faithfulness, in the name of our Lord and Savior, the Giver of all that is good. To the Almighty be all the glory. Amen."

Mellie shuddered. What comfort in an untroubled faith, she thought. Both fear and anticipation shivered along her bare arms, and she glanced into the darkened pantry behind her. She quickly turned back toward Lela's room, surprised that tongues of flame did not leap out to consume her doubting soul. Could it truly be that Ephraim Heber *was* the man to save her soul and give her children? Was there safety here for both Sarah and Nephi? Billy Ben had mocked the Faith. Had he died for that sin? Father Beecham seemed so certain.

Lost in contemplation, Mellie jumped when Noah and Ira dropped their hands. Only then did she realize how long she'd been holding her breath. She glanced at her father and saw raw bewilderment in his face. Was he, too, questioning his life's path? Too often, she knew, he'd lost his way altogether, unable to determine whether or not he'd chosen the way of the world over the way of the Lord. But Ira was a good man, without question; a faithful husband and loving father. He understood his customers, and he worked tirelessly to meet their needs. Their individual feelings and failings were neatly catalogued in the back of his mind, and he'd developed affable relationships with many of them. Some of his most loyal patrons came from the "gentile hordes" of Safford and sometimes even from Tucson, and they were hardworking, honest folk, wholly undeserving of Noah's condemnation. Ira was left to question his father's ways in solitude, but for fleeting hints visible only to Mellie.

Father Beecham would never understand such spiritual confusion. Never doubting his own interpretation of the Faith, he questioned only the dedication of others, their "lack of wisdom" in inviting the wrath of God through "imprudent pursuits and unseemly behavior." His self-righteous devotion, Mellie thought, his singularity of purpose, might once have engendered praise among the Saints, even nobility. More often now, though, his arrogance and intolerance made it increasingly easy to defy him.

Stooping toward Lela, Father Beecham eyed her intently. "I have blessed you by the power of God, the Father of our Lord and Savior Jesus Christ, the Maker of heaven and earth and the Father of our spirits," he said. "His blessings be upon you, Lela Beecham." He collected Josephine's

Bible and the flask of oil from the highboy, as Ira reached to part the curtain in the doorway. Back in the kitchen, Mellie ducked across the room and pulled the chain of the electric light bulb in the ceiling, as though she had just come in. For her, at least, the wonderworks were done. Nothing left but the strength – or the weakness – of the human spirit.

"Does Mama feel any better?" Mellie asked her father as the two men emerged into the sudden flash of light.

"'If thou believest in the redemption of Christ, thou canst be healed,'" Father Beecham answered, shuffling toward the dining room.

Mellie looked past him. "May I see her, Papa?" she asked.

"Leave her to rest now, Malvina," Noah ordered as he passed them.

Mellie slipped an arm around her father's elbow. "Papa?" she asked.

Ira tapped Mellie's fingers with his free hand. "Let it go, Mellie. Give your mother some time." He cleared his throat. "It would have pleased Nephi to have witnessed his mother's healing," he said to his father.

Upon her arrival at the farm this afternoon Mellie had asked Ira why Nephi hadn't come to class that morning. They'd assumed he'd gone off to meet Noah on his way home from the Duncan Valley, but there'd been no sign of him all day.

Father Beecham froze at the mention of Nephi's name. He churned his hands on his walking stick and blinked his cold eyes repeatedly. A shock of fear rose up in Mellie's heart, and she swallowed hard. After the news of Billy Ben's death had reached the Pima farmhouse the night before, Nephi had come to her on the porch swing of the Pima store, distraught. He'd *seen* the Three Nephites this time, he'd insisted.

"I saw them in Fort Thomas, crouched in the bushes during the New Year's Day race."

"Nephi?" Father Beecham's eyes darkened and he stared at the floor. "He's none of your concern. I expect there's a debate going on at the Academy."

"There's no debate," Mellie snapped. "Did you know Nephi wasn't in class today?"

"There must be some..."

"You know where he's gone, don't you?" Mellie broke in.

"On my return from Brother Heber's this morning," Father Beecham said. "He asked me for a blessing of protection. And so I obliged."

"Did it ever occur to you to ask why?"

"I have no cause to question Nephi's faith." Noah answered with a flippant mixture of annoyance and puzzlement, but Mellie could see the uneasiness rising in his eyes.

"Why would he seek your blessing now?" she persisted. "Weren't you the least bit concerned?"

"Now, Mellie," Ira put in. "It's the right of us all to ask Father Beecham's blessing, and it's his duty to give it..."

"But why?" Mellie asked again. "Why now?" She looked expectantly from one man to the other.

"The boy will be fine, Malvina." Father Beecham spoke with his customary sternness. "He makes more of his duty to God than of his worldly studies. Have you forgotten? 'The righteous are favored of God and need not fear.'"

"Oh, stop it!" Mellie shouted.

"Hush now," Ira implored, glancing in alarm toward Lela's room.

Mellie dropped her voice and turned back to her grandfather. "You of all people must know what being righteous means to Nephi," she said.

Father Beecham swayed over his cane and blinked at the ceiling. Then, as though in pain, he dropped his head, a cold flash in his steel blue eyes. "'To walk upright before God,'" he said, his voice quivering.

"I said stop it!"

"'To harken to the truth.'"

"And what *is* the truth for Nephi?" Mellie demanded, her voice restrained but shaken. "God knows you've defined it for him enough."

"What's come over you, daughter?" Ira asked. His gentle voice belied an obvious confusion.

"It's what's come over Nephi. That's the question, isn't it Father Beecham?" Mellie threw an accusing glare at her grandfather. "You know where he's gone, don't you?"

Ira looked to his father as if expecting an explanation and tried to smile despite Noah's silence. "If I know the boy, he's back at the shop this minute with Angel and Sarah."

Father Beecham drew in a deep breath and shaded his eyes with a gnarled hand. "'All of His ways are judgment,'" he mumbled. By then, Mellie knew it would be futile to pursue the discussion. Noah had nothing more to say.

\*   \*   \*

After supper, Mellie made arrangements to drive Ira's auto back to the Pima store. Sarah would continue to look after Angelina there while Mellie attended a Relief Society meeting. With the Church's approval, the women of the Stake had partnered with the Red Cross in Safford to stitch Army-issue pajamas for American soldiers, sending crates of clothing to Safford to be transported overseas. Hoping for news of Nephi, Mellie would return to the farm later in the evening with Sarah and Angelina and then return with Ira and her youngest sister to the Pima store.

Had Father Beecham lived with him at the shop, Ira would likely have dissuaded Mellie from driving at all. Noah harbored great anxieties about the mobility of young people, and Ira made every effort to keep the collective peace. In his father's estimation, access to moving picture shows and dance halls threatened religious stability, and driving the Model T was a sure and swift path to hell. "Keep away from worldly enticements altogether," Noah insisted. "There may be some good in them, but there is so much more evil entwined. The safest bet is to leave them alone."

For Noah, Satan himself rode around in a four-wheeled motor car, frightening buggy horses with the engine noise at every bend. Automobiles were designed for the devil's minions, the old man said. That is, of course, until Solomon or Ephraim Heber took the wheel, when angels themselves could lead no finer motorcade.

Before Father Beecham's bulk could creak up the staircase to his bedroom, Ira had ushered Mellie outside. In the face of her father's barely concealed alarm, Mellie's heart broke. How could she tell him what she feared most for Nephi? She was certain, now, that he'd followed Ephraim to the war – with Noah's blessing and even encouragement. As Ira plied the engine crank, she slipped behind the wheel of the Model T. The auto sputtered and choked down the drive and on to the main Valley roadway.

With the Pima store keeping shorter holiday hours, the family had arranged for Ira, Sarah and Angelina to stay at the farm on occasion with Lela so Duett could catch up at the ranch. Her teaching duties lightened at the onset of the New Year, Mellie had been able to take a turn caring for her mother as well.

As she drove along toward town, Mellie rummaged in the satchel of needlework on the seat beside her. Her hand closed on a small glass flask of alfalfa tonic Duett had given her when she'd arrived at the farmhouse earlier in the day to meet Lyman. "Granny Bee swears by alfalfa tea for low blood in women with child," Duett had explained. "Poor Sarah will make a wreck of herself, bein' so young and in the family way. Her with no husband. And your granddaddy to stand against to boot." Mellie had been on the edge of confiding her secret fears about Nephi, but Lyman had pulled his Packard into the grassy space next to Ira's auto just as she prepared to speak. With boyish enthusiasm, Lyman had whisked Duett away for a picnic by the river, leaving Mellie alone with her worries.

Mellie's eyes welled up with tears as she pondered the day's events. "'Those who have endured the crosses of the world, their joy shall be full forever,'" she said aloud. The auto thumped and rattled through the falling darkness, headlights pulling twisted shadows from the roadside. The tiny bottle fell back into Mellie's lap bag as teardrops inched their way down her cheeks. "Nephi...Oh, Nephi," she sobbed. "What's to become of you? Could my promise of silence cost you your life? And what about Sarah?" The road ahead began to blur, and she shook the moisture from her eyes, wiping her wet cheeks with the back of her hand. "'It was not the hand of God that put affliction and trouble upon us,'" she said aloud, with a strong but shaky voice. But the tears only sprang up again, fuller and faster this time, spilling down her face to dampen the cool cotton collar of her shirtwaist. "Whose hand was it then?" she begged an answer through her tears. "And why?"

# CHAPTER FIFTEEN

# Thursday, January 3, 1918

Alone in her bedroom, Mellie picked up a postcard from Ephraim Heber, a tea-colored sketch of three soldiers with fixed bayonets. Addressed "To the Heber and Beecham Families," Father Beecham had brought the card to Mellie on his return from the Duncan Valley. A poem, under a stamp marked "Soldier's Mail," read:

> *Strike manfully for liberty*
> *Stretch helping hands across the sea*
> *And keep your own heart clean and free*
> *Americans, Americans.*

On the reverse side was printed:

> *The ship on which I sailed has arrived safely overseas.*
> *Name: Ephraim Heber*
> *Organization: American Expeditionary Forces.*

At Thanksgiving, Ephraim had explained that such post-
cards would be printed and held in New York City. If a troop
ship crossed the Atlantic without incident, a wire sent to
New York would release the cards and notify families that
their soldiers had arrived safely in Europe.

Mellie laid the card aside and took up a letter she'd personally received from Ephraim.

> *December 14, 1917*
> *We are at Sea*
> *My Dearest Malvina:*
>
> *I have viewed myself in my own carnal state, and
> I am less than the dust of the earth. I cry aloud for your
> forgiveness that I may purify my heart. May you remem-
> ber what glory comes with passing over a transgression.
> I tell you now how we came to be here. I took the train
> from Bowie at four-thirty, then on to Camp Dix in New
> Jersey. Five days from start to finish. Mid-afternoon the
> next day, we sailed down the Hudson and out into the
> Atlantic Ocean. I am told that the Kaiser's submarines
> take more time than we give them to raise their peri-
> scopes. So we are safe.*

> *December 18, 1917*
> *La Havre, France*
>
> *The crossing was stormy. Eleven days altogether,
> and we fed fish to pass the time. We came to Liverpool
> and traveled to a tent camp where we are to stay one
> week. Then we move on to an American base and to the
> front lines. I look forward with eagerness and excitement
> to confronting the enemy, locked in glorious battle for
> the Lord. The blessings of Father Beecham and Father
> Heber will see me through the darkness of war. As for
> the evil within your house, "And then shall the wicked
> be cast out and they shall have cause to howl and weep."
> Such is God's punishment for those who defile the inno-
> cent. But forgive and ye shall be forgiven.*
> *Regards,*
> *EH*

Mellie tossed the letter to her dressing table, plucked the metal pins from her hair and let the sandy drape fall down over her shoulders. Mellie's room in the Pima store was one of the front bedrooms, the larger one that overlooked the roadway. The furnishings, though sparse, made a haven of the room – a brass bedstead with an ivory coverlet, an oak wardrobe and a white vanity table with a paneled mirror. Crossing to the front window, she was soothed by a crisp rush of wintry air. She settled on the low window seat and reached for her hairbrush.

As she pulled the bristles through her hair, Mellie looked down on the quiet street below. She'd just come from the schoolhouse, and already the sun had dipped down behind distant Mount Graham. A swath of lucid purple light hung over the Valley – the tree-lined streets, the orchards and gardens, the unpainted hay barns. The whole town spread out before her, detached and peaceful. Over at the Pratt drugstore, three of her best students raced off into the twilight. Shops closed, and automobiles rumbled off through clouds of dust, unaffected by the raging tumult overseas.

Where *was* the war for this town? In the propaganda films at Gilpin's Theater in Safford – the pacifist-leaning *Civilization*, Mary Pickford's *The Little American*? In two wheatless days, two porkless days and a sheaf of Liberty Bonds? Other people and other places had far more at stake than what was visible within Pima's sheltered boundaries. Until Nephi had disappeared, it had been that way for Mellie, too. But what about Nephi? What about Ephraim's zeal? Did all wars generate such ambivalence, she wondered? Or were these the peculiarities of an isolated Valley and men like Ephraim Heber?

If he fell to the war, Ephraim would be accorded all the grandeur of a hero's death. But who would see any glory on the battlefront if Nephi died in the trenches? Other people's sons and brothers went to war. Were they all heroes, too? And what of men like those Texas cowboys up in Power's Garden? Some said they'd refused to register for the draft, and there was talk of riding in after them and bringing them out by force.

Nephi had not come back to the Pima store overnight, and Mellie and her father had agreed to keep the news from Lela until his whereabouts could be established. Though she insisted she was much improved after Noah's laying on of hands, an unnatural flush tinged her cheeks, and her eyes were far too bright for Mellie's liking. "'If we do what is right in the sight of the Lord,'" Lela had often told Mellie, "He will put no affliction upon us." Her mother's illness aside, Mellie ached to know where Lela would put the fate of Nephi, Sarah and Sarah's unborn child. But, of course, she couldn't ask. How she longed for her mother's lost wisdom and strength, those long-gone days when her mother could take pain and sorrow and turn them into hope with just a word or a look, a touch or a smile.

Mellie forced herself back to the task at hand. Tonight was choir night, and she knew there'd be questions. She would explain Nephi's absence as a scheduling conflict, and she'd respond gracefully to inquiries after Ephraim. Sarah, she expected, would prattle on with her friends as usual. But she would no longer look Mellie in the eye, and behind the flirtatious pretense would be a frightened child unwilling to lean on her sister. Out of fear or guilt, shame or anger, Mellie didn't know. And Sarah wouldn't say.

Mellie stood up, gathered a few errant strands of hair from her cotton shirtwaist and dropped them in the wicker basket under the table. She had just wrapped her hair to be re-pinned when the clip of horse's hooves at the front of the store drew her attention back to the window. A wave of excitement washed over her as she watched Press Brennick step out of the saddle and sling the reins of his mount over the mercantile's hitching post.

Mellie had neither seen nor heard word of Press since the basket social two weeks earlier, but her memory of their evening together remained blissfully vivid in her mind. No man of the Church had ever struck Mellie's fancy in such a way, and she'd found herself smiling fondly whenever she thought of him. What boldness he'd shown, singling out her basketwork at a Mormon function. The bids had already climbed to around eight dollars, she recalled. And then Press stepped up. "Twelve dollars, here," he'd said, tapping a hand to the brim of his hat.

His sudden appearance in the grassy picnic lot behind the Amusement Hall created an instant scandal among the Saints, but he was unaffected by their embarrassment and alarm. Some of the younger women held their indignation at bay with curious fascination. Beyond Press' physical attraction, he also represented the forbidden "ways of the world." "The wild enticement of the lost and the fallen," Father Beecham would have said. But what Mellie most recalled about Press were the soft lines around his eyes and just how blue they were as they met her appreciative gaze. With a deep sigh, Mellie adjusted the folds of her skirt, pinched her cheeks at the dressing table mirror and swept her hair into a knot at the base of her neck. Closing the door behind her with care, she left the room and tiptoed to the top of the stairs.

"Mr. Brennick, isn't it?" she heard her father say. Press had been to the store before.

"Yes, sir, Mr. Beecham." Press rapped his knuckles on the countertop. "Looks like you're fixin' to shut down for the day."

"In a minute or two," Ira said. "I've got a shipment to unload. Might as well keep the door open." There followed a painful silence. "Is there something in particular you're after, Mr. Brennick?"

"Well, we're in bit of a winter slump," Press said with a light laugh. "I've read more labels on them tin can airtights than I care to admit. What we do mostly this time of year is just keep our cows located. Passing the time, don't you know." His knuckles tapped again. "The fact is, Mr. Beecham, things haven't been the best of late between your people and mine. I wonder if I might have a word with your Miss Beecham, if she's still of a mind to speak to me. Miss Mellie, that is. I won't take but a minute, and then I'll clear out of your way."

Without seeing her father's face, Mellie sensed his dilemma. Here was a man of the same "breed" – to use Father Beecham's ugly epithet – as the one Ira believed may have troubled his young daughter. But Billy Ben was dead, and the Brennicks' grief naturally kindled Ira's compassion. "I'll get her," he said and strode through the store into the back rooms as Mellie darted back into the bedroom. "Malvina?" he called up the staircase. "You've a gentleman caller here. Mr. Brennick from Fort Thomas."

"I'll be right down, Papa." Mellie answered with faint apprehension. Just what, if anything, she wondered, did Press know about Sarah? She composed herself quickly. "I'm coming."

Press was standing by the counter turning his hat in slow circles in his hands. At Mellie's approach, he nodded. "Miss Beecham," he said.

Mellie smiled back, a delicate flush warming her cheeks. "Hello," she answered softly.

Ira cleared his throat. His brows came together over the

bridge of his nose, and he stared hard at the countertop before looking up again. "Let me just say, Mr. Brennick," he said, "as a family, now, we never willed any harm against your boy, Billy Ben. I came down hard on him for my Sarah's sake. But we're a peaceful people. We're all sorry for his passing." Press fumbled with the brim of his hat. "Understood, Mr. Beecham," he said.

"I'll see to Angel." Ira excused himself and walked back to the kitchen, where Mellie had set her little sister to peeling a small sack of potatoes.

Mellie snatched a shawl from a hook beside the front door and ushered Press outside. The air closed in around her, colder than she had expected. But at least the wind had died down. "We were all sorry to hear about Billy Ben's accident, Mr. Brennick," she said. She settled in the swing Ira had installed on the front porch for Lela, half afraid that Press would join her and half afraid that he would not. He stood aside, leaning over, one hand in the pocket of his sheepskin vest, the other on the upper end of one of the swing's vertical bars. He was so close to her now that she could have reached up and brushed his chest.

"Some sorrier than others, I expect." Press watched her intently.

Mellie drew in a sharp breath and let it seep out silently through her parted lips before she spoke. "I don't know what you mean," she said, her gaze dropping to the floorboards.

"Oh, I think you do, Miss Beecham."

Mellie fixed her eyes on his. "*I* don't know anything." she said. "What are you getting at, Press?"

Press straightened and squinted off across the street. "Somebody tossed firecrackers down on Billy Ben from the brow of that big bluff just past the cemetery."

"My brother Lyman says they do that all the time," Mellie said. "The Mexicans. They try to scare the horses. Make them jump or some such nonsense." Mellie made to get up, but Press stopped her with only a glance.

"And they do," Press agreed. "But they throw them under the horses' feet. Not in a man's face. A fella from the Monk Brothers claims he saw some boy skitter off the bluff afterwards. They had their man on Selim, you know. And Billy Ben had powder burns on his face…Mexicans don't aim to harm a man."

"And Mormons do?" Mellie countered. Before she could get up, Press grazed a hand up along her arm and rested the palm on her shoulder. The warmth filtered through to her chest.

"That's not what I meant," he said. "They're just after scarin' the horses. But your boy, Nephi, was there. Seen him myself."

Mellie swallowed hard and turned away. "Nephi would never do such a thing," she whispered.

Press put his hand under her chin and turned her face to his. "That boy's not right," he said with marked gentleness. "I think you know that." He studied her in silence, letting the blue of his eyes float across her face.

"Besides," Press added. "He's thick with Ephraim Heber, and that man had a hankering to make good on his curse. I mean to get to the bottom of this, Miss Mellie, whatever might turn up. I thought you should know that." He brushed a tear from Mellie's cheek, dropped his gaze momentarily to her lips and left.

# CHAPTER SIXTEEN

# Saturday, January 5, 1918

**W**ith Lela in capable hands, Mellie had driven Ira's Ford the five miles down the Valley into Safford to see Lyman. Duett had agreed to come back to the farmhouse Friday evening after Billy Ben's burial in the old Klondyke cemetery. Mellie marveled at Duett's ability to step back so easily into the bramble bed the old farmhouse had become. Since Billy Ben's death and Nephi's disappearance, which could no longer be kept secret except from Lela, suspicion and dread lurked in every corner. Not even the lively strains from Lela's Victrola could dispel the gloom. But with the feed shortage still acute in the Fort Thomas area, Duett's wages would no doubt keep her family together until the winter rains came back to the Valley.

In contrast to Pima, Safford was something of a

metropolis. At the end of her half-hour drive, Mellie maneuvered through the busy tree-lined streets with a mixture of trepidation and excitement. In the last year alone, a hundred new homes had been built in town, most of them in the bungalow style still popular in California. There were millinery shops and dressmakers, hotels and a café. And the Safford Creamery and Ice Company even had its own milking machine on display.

In the heart of the bustling town, the Graham County Motor Company sold everything from runabouts and touring cars to couplets, town cars, sedans and one-ton trucks. Safford also had a choice of three movie houses – Bryer's Hall, the Safford Theatre and, Mellie's favorite, Gilpin's. These offered everything in entertainment from Mary Pickford's *Ramona* and *Rags* to serial Westerns, which played at Gilpin's on Saturday nights. William Duncan, Carol Halloway and Pauline Fredericks were among the many performers who passed through town.

In November, Mellie and Edna had met Duett when A.G. Barnes had come to town with his four-ring wild-animal circus. There were social dances and road shows and even a Chautaqua lecture series in the spring at the Safford Opera House. Once or twice, Lyman and Edna had taken Mellie to the Amos Cook Best Drugstore. With its twelve-foot-long white marble mirror-backed bar striped in black, three ice cream compartments and twelve syrup pumps lit at night with a dozen electric globes, the choices at the soda fountain summed up the excitement of the whole town for Mellie.

Just past noon, she reached Lyman's studio and parked the auto in the street below. If Nephi was somehow connected to Billy Ben's death, as Press had implied, she needed to find out what Lyman knew about the accident. He had,

after all, ridden alongside the cowboy, at least into the last
half mile. As a precise and detail-oriented man, he may have
noticed something others had missed. Surely he'd heard the
skyrockets. Surprised but pleased to see her, Lyman was taking an engagement portrait of a longtime forester friend and
his future bride. He settled Mellie on the horsehide sofa in
the waiting room and promised his full attention when the
photography session ended.

Lyman had designed the portrait studio himself in 1912.
The room where Mellie sat entered off a landing at the top
of an outside flight of stairs on the north side of one of Safford's several drug stores. It was a neat green room, with
four modest chairs and a potted palm. Behind a heavy curtain, explosions of flash-powder alternated with laughter
and snatches of muffled conversation.

With its adjoining living quarters, the studio fused the
cultivated taste of a well-educated man with sentimental-
ity and a winsome carelessness. In this first room, Lyman
had enshrined the box camera built for him in 1910 by the
Safford photographer who'd first encouraged his picture-
taking. He'd regularly escaped Primary on Saturday after-
noons to walk the five miles to Safford so this man could
teach him the use of the camera. As a result, Noah regularly attacked Lyman's livelihood as a danger to the Church
that "narrowed the vision, darkened the mind, and puffed
up a haughty spirit." Lyman's negatives and prints included
"painted" women and smoke-filled gambling halls, word of
which had filtered back to the farmhouse to give great offense to Father Beecham's sense of propriety. But Mellie
admired both Lyman's collections and his artistry.

There were leather-bound volumes of English poetry
and Russian playwrights on Lyman's bookshelves, too, and
sets of phonograph records that trailed off into a tiny white

kitchen, where the walls, as Mellie remembered, were hung with photographs of creek beds, blossoming fruit trees, desert ravines and lofty mountain ranges. Listening to the voices in the other room, she envied Lyman's affable irreverence, even his "Jack Mormon" reputation among the Saints. Unruffled by their judgment, he nipped Orin Harland's white lightning now and again, played at cards and sometimes even smoked.

The curtains parted, and a stately woman swept through, her cheeks flushed beneath a pompadour sweep of rust-colored hair. An apple-green organdy skirt topped a pair of high-buckled slippers, and on her head she wore an ornate bonnet of shirred silk, taffeta and chiffon. Mellie had never seen such an elegant creature before. Suddenly self-conscious, she tugged at the box pleats of her plain skirt, a light wool shepherd-check in black and white. The woman paused and flashed Mellie an effusive smile.

In the next moment, Lyman emerged, engaged in quiet conversation with the forester. Long in body, with pea-green knee breeches and shirt, the forester pulled a timepiece from his pocket and punched open the face. To Mellie, his hobnailed boots and feathered, peaked hat looked more like a costume than regular daily attire. The man's job, Lyman explained on introducing them, was range management. "Counting prairie dogs and coyotes, measuring trees and pressing worthless weeds," the forester said with a laugh. His fiancée had been a performer in the most recent road show at Brier's Hall, *When Dreams Come True*. It certainly seemed as though hers had.

As Lyman closed the door behind the couple, Mellie's ears pricked up anew at another round of their convulsive laughter as the forester and his bride made their way down the outer steps. "I know what you're thinking." Lyman unbuttoned the cuffs of his shirtsleeves and rolled them up past his elbows. "You've got that look on your face, like someone propped a door open and let you have just the tiniest little peek inside."

"I know," Mellie said. "Like a slick ear."

"A what?"

"Oh, nothing." She smiled and shook her head. "Never mind."

Lyman sat down in the chair next to Mellie's. "You know, you don't have to dress to the nines and wear ostrich feathers," he said gently. "Just be yourself. You always take on everyone else's battles." He paused. "And you don't have to marry Father Beecham's man to save your soul, either."

"Oh, I know that," Mellie scoffed. "I'm not a child, and I've no intention of marrying Ephraim." She paused and chewed on her lower lip. "But that's not it."

"It's Nephi, then," Lyman said. The brothers had so little in common and so little contact with each other that the prospect of Lyman knowing anything about Nephi's whereabouts was beyond remote. But Millie had held on to a slim hope. "Hasn't turned up yet, eh?" Lyman went on. "What the hell's gotten into him now?"

"No one's seen him anywhere," Mellie said.

"Well, I suppose Duett's told you about the calendars." Lyman stood up and began to pace the room. "The plates are missing too."

"Calendars? Plates? I have no idea what you're talking about."

"Ah...so she didn't tell you." Lyman stopped and adjusted his spectacles. "The calendars I gave to Pop and Father Beecham for Christmas. Duett found them burning in the library fireplace."

"What?" Mellie was stunned. "And you think Nephi...? But why?"

"She found them Christmas night, just before she went to bed. By next morning, there wasn't a scrap left. Even the embers were gone, and she saw Nephi scattering ashes out in the orchard. Of course, she can hardly go rooting around the garden to see what's what, but Nephi's been tinkering for the old man for years now. He was certainly up to something. My guess is that Father Beecham's behind it all."

"But why? And you said something about plates?"

"My glass-plate negatives. They're missing too. Now, I leave the door unlocked sometimes when I run out for a bite. But I never even noticed they were gone until Duett told me about the fire. I thought I could at least make up another one for Pop. But Nephi must have skulked in here too. You know, there's nothing unusual about those photographs but Edna's toy. There must be something about that horse that Father Beecham doesn't want us to know. Duett found a piece of embroidery inside. Did she tell you?" Mellie shook her head. "It said 'Hal from Josie,' and a date. Eighteen-sixty, I think. I don't care much what the old man does anymore. But this is different. This is my work. This is my home. They've got no business in here and no business making off with any gift I've given to Pop."

"Mama's always been so sickly," Mellie said after some reflection. "And Papa's never had the stamina or will power or whatever it takes to hold Father Beecham off. But you and me, Lyman, we should have done something for Nephi."

Lyman smirked. "Like what?" His voice was laced with sarcasm. He sat down again, leaned back and locked both hands behind his head. "What more could we have done? Going up against Noah is like going up against the whole Church. Sometimes you have to do for yourself before you can do for anybody else, or we'd all be as crazy as that miserable old man."

"But that's not the whole Church, Lyman," Mellie insisted. "Not for Mama anyway."

"Well that's the Church for Nephi now. And for Ephraim. Their Church tries to make other people's weaknesses permanent so they'll be desperate for whatever they think the Church can give them. I think it's a common failing, hardly restricted to *our* grandfather or to *his* faith." He stopped suddenly. "But you have to decide those things for yourself, Mellie. Frankly, I'm more interested in my missing plates."

A long silence followed Lyman's words as Mellie considered her own. "There's something else we probably should decide," she said. "Do you think Nephi could have killed Billy Ben so Ephraim's threat would come true?" Lyman eased the back of his chair from against the wall, his manner telling Mellie he'd already considered the notion. "Press Brennick seems to think so, Lyman, and he's not going to let it go without some answers."

"I fell behind there at the end," Lyman explained. "But I heard the snap of the rockets from down the road. Billy Ben had already gone into the bend past the cemetery. By the time I got there, his horse was rearing up and screaming like a banshee, and the poor lad was on the ground. The boys from McKittrick's got to him, and when they turned him over, you could see that his neck was broken and his face was badly burned. All I could do was think of Duett. You should have seen her face, Mellie. You should have seen Billy Ben. Now, did Nephi do that?" Lyman's eyes roamed the room in thought and came back to Mellie's. "Honestly, I don't know. But *could* he? Yes…I believe he could."

# CHAPTER SEVENTEEN

# Sunday, January 6, 1918

Willy was a roustabout, a big-eyed kitten that nibbled Mellie's toes just after six o'clock in the morning and kept her awake until seven, when Edna got up. Mellie followed and straightened the bedding as her aunt gave Willy and the other cats the table scraps from the night before, when Mellie and Lyman had joined her for dinner downstairs. The evening in Safford, with Edna's warm hospitality and Lyman's good-natured banter, had lifted Mellie's spirits.

The rooming house in Safford where Edna lived embodied the casual eloquence of the woman herself. Edna had been there since her return from Chicago in 1904, after her husband Lord Lambert Sutherland's death. Her second floor rooms were small but homey – a short entrance hallway papered in burgundy florets on a creamy beige background, with a tall oak coat-stand right of the door. A well-furnished sitting/dining room opened up straight ahead with a single bedroom right of the hallway furnished with an oversized cherry-wood bedstead, a matching mirrored dressing table and a wardrobe. A tiny kitchen with a gleaming porcelain sink and icebox opened up off the far end of the sitting room. Edna's was a corner flat, and the windows, hung with white Spanish lace, flooded the rooms with light. Shared bathing and toilet facilities were in the outside hallway near the stairwell.

At breakfast in the downstairs dining room, the conversation centered on the riddle of Nephi's disappearance and the tragedy of Billy Ben's death. Edna was in firm agreement that both affairs seemed somehow connected to the destruction of Lyman's orchard calendar plates and prints. That brought Mellie to Edna's wooden toy horse, the focal point of Lyman's ruined work. Mellie had just touched on the subject as they re-entered Edna's upstairs rooms. "So the only explanation," she said. "Is that there's something about that toy that Father Beecham finds very upsetting. Do you have any idea what it could be?"

Edna placed the pitcher of hot water she'd brought with her from the dining room below on the kitchen counter. They'd do up the tea service from the night before in a minute or two, she told Mellie. She settled herself in the sitting room's padded rocker, and Mellie took a seat at the nearest window ledge, looking out on Safford's awakening Main Street below. "Well, my dear," Edna answered. "I know so little about the toy. As I say, it belonged to Mother Josephine, and she treasured it above all things. I never knew exactly why, and I don't suppose she remembered anymore either. Her mind had quite gone by the time she gave it to me." Edna patted her lap and Naboth, a sleek gray and black striped tabby, sprang up, circled head to tail and dropped into place. The fur on Naboth's back rippled as Edna's hand rummaged about his neck. At the foot of the chair sat Fogarty, a sloppy red-brown tomcat with lazy green eyes.

"I don't remember much about Mother Josephine myself," Mellie said. "Just that in my child's eye, she was a distant and rather vague woman, though I couldn't have put it that way then. I used to sneak up that creaky farmhouse staircase and hide outside her door watching her swaying back and forth. She'd sit forever in that old chair." She motioned to Edna's heirloom rocker. "I'm ashamed to say there was always something unsettling about her, a sort of creeping vacancy that I found unnerving."

"You're quite right," Edna answered. "Mother Beecham was from the Spratt family in Logan, Utah," she said. "Mind you, those were trying times, my dear. Especially for women like my mother, who married under the principle of polygamy.

"As you know, the Church teaches that if a man wants to attain the pinnacle of glory in the next world, he must enter into a Celestial Marriage, one made for eternity and sealed in a Temple. Back then, this commandment was sometimes interpreted as a directive to take on a second wife or even a third." She rolled her eyes heavenward with clear disgust. "Now it's beyond me how one man could love all these women equally. But he can surely treat them with equal indifference. Some wives were made capable by such forced independence – heading up households on their own. Your grandmother, I'm sorry to say, was not one of them.

"Believe me, she was once a dear, sweet soul, Mellie." Edna smiled faintly and gazed out the window as Naboth rearranged himself.

"I've always been of two minds about her," Mellie admitted. "There was that kindly woman in the mantle portrait in the library, and then there was that shadowy figure at the top of the staircase." She laughed. "How did women handle plural marriage?"

"Well, Mother Josephine thought the principle worthwhile," Edna went on. "It was a character test, she used to say. To build nobility, generosity, sympathy, patience...self-control. She was barely fifteen when she married Father Beecham. And as you know, her sister, Adriana Spratt, was sealed to Solomon Heber that same year, as the first of *his* three wives. By the time she was nineteen, Josephine had borne a son – your father Ira – and lost two daughters in childbirth. And then Esther and I came along." Edna's round face softened with the memory of her twin sister. "Just before I left for Chicago with Lord Sutherland, at age eighteen, Mother gave me that horse." She paused, smiled again and leaned over to pat Mellie's arm. "Now there was a man to charm the moon right out of the sky. Like that Texas beau of *yours*." She winked at Mellie, who blushed and turned away to glance out the window.

"Nothing can possibly come of that," Mellie said with unconcealed bitterness. "There was so little hope from the beginning. And now, whatever might have been...well, it's too foolish to think about." She turned back to her aunt.

"Lyman and Duett seem to have made a go of it." Edna dipped her head and raised an eyebrow. "Now why couldn't you?"

"It's different for Lyman, Aunt Edna. He's...I don't know... he and Duett seem to move about more freely in the world somehow. And then there's Billy Ben. Press Brennick thinks..."

"You'll see, my dear. This, too, shall pass."

"Nothing like that ever passes in the Valley." Mellie laced

her fingers in her lap and stared out the window again. "Press Brennick thinks Nephi killed Billy Ben."

"What?" Edna's jaw dropped, and she put the back of her hand to her mouth. "Is that possible?"

"It's what they all think…I know it."

"But little Nephi?"

"He hasn't been little for some time," Mellie answered grimly. "Press thinks Ephraim put him up to it. I don't know what to think, but Lyman insists Father Beecham's behind the whole thing. You know how controlling he's been of Nephi's life over the years."

"But to cause a man's death?" Edna slumped back and shook her head. "Well, I suppose it's entirely possible, given the way things are in this family. Could that be why Nephi's left us? And what does Mr. Brennick propose to do with his suspicions?"

"Well, he never directly accused Nephi, I should make that clear. But he'll get to the bottom of it, whatever it takes. That's what he said. But tell me more about the horse. It might give us a clue or even some answers. Can you think of anything at all that might help?"

"Why I'm afraid there's nothing more to tell." Edna stroked Naboth's long body in silence. "Do forgive my romantic spirit, my dear," she said after a long pause. "You're quite right. Things have never been simple in this Valley, have they? Sometimes, that's too easy to forget."

Mellie reached over and squeezed Edna's hand. "It's all right, Aunt Edna," she said. "We may be a simple people, but the way we live gets more complicated and confusing all the time. Press Brennick is just one complication I haven't time to worry about." She smiled, leaned back in the window seat and folded her arms. "Didn't your mother tell you *anything* when she gave you that toy horse?" she asked again, intent on an answer, however tenuous.

"Only to remember a mother's gift," Edna answered. "And to someday share it with a child less fortunate. That's why I passed it on to Shadi Lace.

"That horse," Edna mused, "was the one thing in Mother's life that was truly hers, and hers alone. I was to have it for my courage, you see, a piece of home to carry with me on my travels." Edna laughed. "I suppose your grandmother was worried because I'd found another way in the world." She leaned over and took Mellie's hand. "Women who choose a profession *do* have a place, Mellie, a purpose. If and when they marry, they can do it for love and for children, not because their lives are meaningless until they do." Edna sat back, and Naboth, who'd been displaced, reclaimed his position on her lap. "Mind you, I was only eighteen when I left home. But I'd witnessed the life my poor mother had lived, and I knew it wasn't for me."

"I can only imagine," Mellie remarked. Yet that was just the kind of life Father Beecham had most likely conjured up for her and Ephraim. She shuddered. "What was it really like for Mother Josephine, do you remember?"

"Well, she was forty-three the year we moved to Pima from Utah – in the spring of 1883," Edna answered, getting up to gather last evening's china. Naboth dropped to the floor again with pointed disapproval. "They moved south to shelter Solomon Heber from persecution for polygamy as I recall, though no one said as much around us children. And then Noah took a second wife in September – Stella Luft." Edna sighed and stepped into the kitchen, where she poured half the pitcher's now tepid water into the stoppered sink. Mellie followed with saucers and spoons, set them on the countertop and took the linen towel Edna offered her. "I think you're old enough now to know the full circumstances of my sister Esther's disappearance," Edna said softly. "Father Beecham has always demanded silence on the matter, but it speaks to Mama's state of mind, and possibly to that wooden horse as well.

"Esther had gone into Pima to sell eggs, you see," she explained, slipping three gold-rimmed teacups into the dish water. "We all did this on occasion to earn a few pennies for our tithe. We also gleaned the fields, like all the Mormon children in the Valley. But a day or two earlier, Esther had told my mother that she'd been followed home by a strange man, whom she described in some detail. She didn't want to go into town alone again, she said. Couldn't she just stay at home?

"Well, Mama laughed and wrote the story off, telling Esther to focus less on her imagination and more on her chores. She sent us off the next day as usual, Esther into town and me into the fields." Edna paused and handed one of the teacups to Mellie. Her eyes filled with tears and her voice faltered. "Well, we never saw the poor child again." She brushed a tear from her cheek and gazed out the kitchen window onto the brilliantly blue desert sky.

"I had no idea!" Mellie's own eyes welled up. She laid aside her towel and teacup and wrapped an arm around Edna's hunched shoulders. "I've always known that Esther had died young," she said. "But that was all I've ever been told."

Edna drew herself up and patted Mellie's fingertips. "Of course, Mama never forgave herself," she went on. She gave Mellie's hand a tight squeeze before both women went back to their work. "Eleven we were, Esther and I. And Ira was barely fifteen. I tell you this now, Mellie," she added, rinsing a second cup under the tap and handing it to Mellie.

"So you can better understand the dreadful emotional state your grandmother was in. She suffered for a very long time. There Mama was, you see, a soul already possessed by her husband's need for another woman, feeling overlooked and unloved, a failure at every turn. They say that the patriarchs of the Old Testament had more than one wife. And there are souls aplenty clamoring to be born to some man who will lord it over them in the hereafter. But that's not an easy thing for some women to accept. And on top of that, she'd lost a child to an incredulous and inexplicable horror. To know of Esther's certain death would have been so much kinder."

"How dreadful for all of you!" Mellie exclaimed. "And your poor mother, bearing it all alone. I can see how a man of Father Beecham's temperament and controlling character might want to keep such a truth hidden. He probably silenced her out of guilt."

"There have been times when I thought that myself, but I have my doubts." Edna sighed, finishing up the silverware and passing the handful to Mellie. "But guilt calls for some measure of concern for others, and my father has none of that." She pulled out the stopper. When the water had drained, she gave the sink and counter a final swipe. "Two years later, plural marriage became illegal. Stella had to live 'on the underground,' as they say, posing as Josephine's widowed sister. They were to keep two separate households, the first wife's as the primary residence, with supplies dealt out from there to the second. Then, to add to their difficulties, Father Beecham was called on a two-year mission for the Church to Oregon." Edna rolled her eyes and shook her head. "Lord knows he had mission enough in his own family.

"What a time of it Mama had then, even with Ira and me to help out. She worked as a seamstress, and she traded butter, eggs, milk and poultry for baking powder, salt and such at the local mercantile. She also sold baked goods and garden vegetables. A priest quorum of older boys came by every Saturday to work both her lot and Stella's, pruning trees and plowing up the garden, helping with the planting and what not. Whenever someone killed a pig or a cow, Mama got the liver and usually some spareribs. And sometimes we'd find a sack of flour or potatoes on the front step.

"She was already quite unstable by then, and Aunt Stella was such a sickly young thing. She tried, bless her, to pick up some of the load, but just after Father Beecham left, Stella died in childbirth. The child died too." Having shelved the cleaned dishes, Edna led Mellie back to the sitting room, where they regained their former seats. Caesar, a regal beige Persian and the last of Edna's cats, claimed her lap at once. "I was only fourteen then, but I understood what was happening. Poor Mama just had no place left for any more guilt. She was convinced she'd envied and resented a good woman, you see. She retreated altogether after that. She never came to your father's wedding. Never even knew Lela's family, or Lela herself, for that matter. She kept to her room most of the time, as you well know." Mellie nodded.

"It was a full five years before Noah finally succeeded in persuading her to venture outside for Sunday services, and then she was killed by one of his supply wagons. Well, he went straight back to the farm with some hoopla about her death being a sign from God of some sort, a message to withdraw from 'Gentile commercialism,' as he called it. You know, I don't think he's ever accepted a single ounce of responsibility for Mama's failing mental state or for her death," Edna finished with obvious disdain. She brushed Caesar from her lap as she rose. "So you see, my dear, I not only lost my mother, but I buried my father years ago, too."

She ambled off to the kitchen and opened the icebox, the four cats trailing behind her.

Mellie stared out the window – tense and perplexed yet determined to make sense of this new information. But how? Wherever could these pieces fit into the puzzle?

"Now, I never meant to upset you, my dear," Edna said as she re-entered the room and passed Mellie a mug of fresh milk. One by one, the cats, having been given their own treat, drifted back in, stopping to wash whiskers in the doorway. "No one, I'm sure, has ever talked to you so openly before about either Mother Beecham's death or Esther's disappearance. I only tell you now to better explain my mother's failing state of mind as it relates to the toy horse she gave me." Edna set a second glass of milk on the tea table beside her rocker and went back to the kitchen for a plate of shortbread. "These events have all been so hush-hush with Father Beecham over the years," she continued, coming back in and offering the plate to Mellie. "I must confess to a long-suppressed need to share the burden their memories carry." She sat down again. "But I'm afraid that's all I can offer by way of illumination. So far as I know, Father Beecham never even knew of the horse's existence. *I* surely didn't tell him. He and I had a bitter parting of the ways after Ira's marriage, and we've hardly spoken since."

"Because of your mother's sufferings I would imagine," Mellie said.

"Not entirely. When I left the Academy at eighteen to clerk in Safford, I more or less left the Church, too. Of course, given Mama's ordeal, I'd broken away in spirit much earlier. And then I met Lord Sutherland." Edna's eyes sparkled again. "He was a land investor from East Anglia – in the British Isles, you know. And the most handsome, gallant gentleman I've ever known. What brought him to me was a miracle, isolated as I was here in the Valley. He'd been looking at land in the Willcox area and around Aravaipa. He believed, as I did, in the social roots of so much poverty and despair. Certainly my mother's life had demonstrated that. Anyway, Rockford College and my Hull Settlement work kept me from the Valley for many years after he and I were married, and my subsequent visits were always with Mama and you children. I avoided my father altogether…I still do. But I assume he has no knowledge of the toy." Edna paused to catch her breath and glanced at Mellie. "There's always a price to be paid no matter which path we choose, Mellie dear," she said. "When I came back after my husband's death, Mama had only a year left to live. I came to oversee my interest in the farm and to see that your father got his rightful share of the profits along with mine. I suppose I might have done more for her if I had stayed here all along."

"But how would that have made any difference?" Mellie spoke with clear resignation. "There's only so much one person can do for someone else."

"It's Nephi again, isn't it, my dear?" Edna asked quietly. "I might have known."

"Partly, Aunt Edna." Mellie fingered the lacy curtains. "Oh, I hardly know where to begin." She tapped her fingers on the window glass.

"What is it, Malvina?"

"There's just no easy way to say this, I'm afraid." Mellie turned back to her aunt. "Sarah's to have a baby."

"Oh, my word!" Edna gasped, her eyes wide with disbelief. "A child? Are you sure? But of course you are. How could this happen to our Sarah? And who's the child's father?"

"Sarah says it's Billy Ben," Mellie answered quietly.

"And do you believe her?"

"I don't know what to believe about anything anymore." Tears filled Mellie's eyes, and she bowed her head in despair.

Edna rose and laid a gentle hand on Mellie's shoulder. "For Sarah's sake, I'm hoping Father Beecham is none the wiser at the moment. And of course, there's the child to think of. We'll take care of them both, Mellie," she said with fixed determination. "She can stay with me here in Safford, or I'll take her with me to Chicago, if it comes to that. My Hull House work taught me nothing if not compassion."

"But what about Father Beecham?"

"I swear to you on my mother's grave, Mellie, that my father will not drive another soul in this family to destruction."

# CHAPTER EIGHTEEN

# Sunday, January 13, 1918

With Lela becoming ever more fragile, the Beechams had decided to retain Duett's services into the New Year, allowing her one weekend off each month. Having spent the past couple of days with Shadi Lace, Press and Granny Bee, Duett was due to return to the farm in time for supper. Since Lela had enjoyed a restful day at the farm, Mellie decided to drive out to the Santa Teresa with Lyman to pick her up.

As the Packard spun along the dirt road, Mellie passed the time mulling over Nephi's disappearance, considering it in light of the burning of Lyman's Christmas prints and the theft of his photo plates. Did it make sense, somehow, to hope that Nephi had forgotten the war? That, instead, he was hiding because he'd played a part in the destruction of Lyman's gifts? There had to be some relationship!

If Father Beecham would divulge what he knew about Edna's toy horse, Mellie reasoned, perhaps Nephi would come home again. But what about Billy Ben? What about Sarah? There were just too many unanswered questions. Mellie shook her head and turned her attention to the surrounding landscape. "I've never really looked at the land out here before," she admitted to Lyman. "It's hard to see how people can be so comfortable living in such forlorn places."

"Our point of view isn't the same," Lyman answered. "We're all using the same camera, so to speak. But we're each looking through our own lens."

Mellie glanced out at the grizzled hills. In the heart of the Valley, where most of the Mormon farms lay, complaints about the drought centered on nuisance dust and warmer than average days. The Gila River still flowed, and life-giving water still reached the fields and orchards by canal or artesian well. But out here at the far end of the Valley – back in the foothills and far from the riverbed – the lack of water was tangible. From the Beecham farm and from Mellie's room above the Pima store, these hills and the front line of the Pinals to the east bore only a distant freckled appearance. But here, the parched gullies and bony desert hills were dotted with scraggly bushes, the soil chalk-white, cracked and raw. Here and there, the single spear of a yucca plant caught Mellie's eye, bleak survivors that had somehow thrust through the desolation.

Back toward the Pinalenos and up ahead in the hills of the Santa Teresa Mountains, twiggy brush and dying scrub flattened the landscape into gray smudges. Cream-colored boulders sprang up from clumps of juniper and pinyon pine, as the road turned and dipped into a wash of loose sand and drought-stricken, red-brown oaks. The grass among the trees was sparse and brittle, spotted with shriveled clumps of cactus.

"The same as what?" Mellie asked at last.

"Pardon?"

"Our viewpoint isn't the same, you said. The same as what?"

"The same as the people who live here." The auto rumbled up out of a sandy wash and threatened to roll back again, but Lyman coaxed it forward.

A slice of winter air slipped along Mellie's cheekbones, and she shivered. "It's frightening to be so alone in such a wilderness," she said. Ahead, looming gray and stony in the heart of the Santa Teresas, Cottonwood Peak cradled a tiny patch of snow – the remnant of a lackluster cloudburst that had capped the mountaintops and sprayed a misty rain along the Valley floor several days earlier. Nothing was left of it now except the vague hope that a bigger storm would follow.

"Doesn't Father Beecham say there's 'tribulation in the wilderness?'" Lyman asked. "That it's 'infested with wild and ravenous beasts?' It's in the Book of Alma, I think." He laughed.

"That's not what I meant," Mellie said, swiping at his arm.

"I know. But for some people it's frightening *not* to be here. This land gets in their blood. It's *home*."

"Do you suppose that's why those Texas miners are staying up there in Power's Garden? They won't even register for conscription."

Lyman picked his way through a knot of scrawny chickens littering the roadway, and through rising dust, Mellie caught sight of several dilapidated outbuildings. The Packard rattled up a gentle hill, where two or three horses bolted from the fence and raced off across a long, brown field. Up ahead, outside what Mellie took to be the Brennick ranch house, Duett waved from amidst the cactus and brush.

Both Lyman and Mellie returned Duett's greeting. "I don't know enough about those Texans to say," Lyman said. "I think the Powers ranch in there, but I can't say much else. As for conscription, well, I think a person can be right to refuse to go to war. Fighting's not always the answer. Look at Ephraim. I know he was drafted, but we've said it's all about duty to home and family and country; about the honor of dying for some great cause. So now we've got this army of medieval warriors, and we expect them to fight in a modern world. There will always be old men who talk up a good fight as long as somebody else takes all the chances. Like I said before, it's a matter of your point of view. Now what would happen if Nephi marched off to war and got himself killed?" Lyman pulled the Packard to a halt. "We'd be outraged. We don't expect *him* to take the war seriously."

"Nephi takes everything seriously," Mellie muttered. As if in agreement, the Packard shuddered and went silent.

"Well now, you're a sight for sore eyes, Mellie." Duett pulled open the passenger door and Mellie climbed out, brushing down the folds of her cotton skirt. "I'm telling you the mortal truth."

With a furtive glance, Lyman rounded the front end of the auto and kissed Duett's cheek. She tucked a hand into the pocket of his tweed vest and smiled. "Torito's up the mountain with Shadi Lace," she said, winking at Lyman. "Step on in, the both of you, and I'll fetch the little tyke and Granny Bee. They're up the hill a piece where Press is fixin' to burn off some cholla for the stock. She likes to wander, that Shadi Lace. Granny Bee and Torito just go along natural-like."

"I'll go on up with you," Lyman said. "Press could probably use a hand. You're all right in the house, Mellie?"

"Oh, I'd be fine, I'm sure…but I'll walk along with you if it's all right."

"Of course," Duett answered. "Work like that makes you hotter than a boiled owl." She poked Lyman playfully in the chest. "You're warned now."

"The cottonseed cake is gone then?" Lyman asked as they started around the side of the house.

"Oh, no. We just want to have something set aside for when the winter rain *does* finally come. Even when the grass is up, you need forty, maybe fifty acres for one animal, and that's in a *good* year."

An odd livestock enclosure sagged under a cottonwood tree next to the main house, and to the right stood several crumbled mud-brick walls. Such a country, Mellie thought. You could see further but still see less than any place she could imagine. Emptiness closed around her as they passed these structures and began to climb.

"I could get a bit more with little trouble," Lyman was saying.

With her high-topped boots and divided skirt, Duett kept pace with Lyman up the steep hillside. "Press and Granny Bee would have none of it," she said. "He's a bit on the shy side about handouts. And besides, what else do I work for?"

"Handouts from us evil-hearted Mormons in particular, eh?" Lyman turned back to Mellie. Her high-laced black shoes and gathered skirt made the climb up the steep slope seem eternal. Lyman winked and offered her a steadying hand.

Duett laughed and stopped to catch her breath. "Burning all this cactus gives us something to do with our time," she said. "This time of year is as close as we get to a holiday. But what with mending gates and fences and harnesses and card playing, Press is about full up on free time. And Granny Bee and me, we've hooked so many rugs and braided so many mats we can't hardly see straight. Come early February we'll be weaning calves, and that means running all day every which way – taking slick ears from their mamas so the old cows can dry up before they drop their new calves." She started up the hill again. "The yearlings are gathered together over ten days to two weeks, and then we let them loose on another part of the range where they can't find their mamas at all. That way they learn to look out for themselves. We'll be busier than a one-armed paper-hanger then. And after that, of course, there's spring roundup."

A cow path s-curved up the hillside, pockmarked with cattle dung and the craters of dried hoof-prints. They were above and behind the house now, and Mellie stopped to glance down at the flattened tract where the ranch buildings stood. A stab of anxiety washed over her as she gazed across the emptiness. Identical grizzled hills rose up beyond an unpeopled stretch of sand and rock, open space and spindly vegetation. A corner of Lyman's black Packard – the sole hint of civilization and safety in Mellie's eyes – was visible at the front of the house. Looking down the hillside, she noticed that the cow path veered off to the right in the direction of a small mud-hole banked with dirt, probably to hold runoff from a nearby canyon. Pounded on all sides by animal hooves and drought, the spot had been reduced to a fringe of dried mud compressed between a line of brittle scrub and a circle of silted water. Mellie shaded her eyes and pursed her lips.

Just above her, Duett had stopped to rest in the umbrella shade of a pinyon pine, and Lyman doubled back to help

Mellie. They'd reached a short, narrow slope that marked the top of the mesa, and shreds of straw-colored grass, rocks and boulders were strewn over the baked earth. Stunted cliffs that flanked the left side of the tableland shot up in the sunlight, pale pink and gouged with afternoon shadows. The worn path they'd been following meandered off in all directions. At the far end of the plateau, where they could see Press working, a pitiful knot of white-faced cattle stood around him, their dusty heads bowed.

"That handful of scallywag stock, they follow Press around like a troop of baby chicks after an old hen," Duett said, as Mellie stopped again to adjust the laces of her shoes.

"They really eat that stuff?" Lyman asked as Press dropped a stack of cactus onto a pile of twigs and dried weeds.

"If this was your regular January, with snow on the ground maybe a few days at a time, they'd be out browsing on oak, mountain mahogany and Apache plume. Down below, we chopped up palo verde and they ate off the tops. Poor critters are starved for a good rain and a fistful of alfalfa. But they'll go for this feed like a fox on a henhouse if they get hungry enough. Over by Tucson, they're breaking open the saguaros and letting the stock eat out the insides."

Press struck a match as Shadi Lace bounded into the open from a cluster of boulders. Granny Bee and an enormous black bull lumbered along behind them. Mellie watched, spellbound, as blotches of red flames shot out from the heap of vegetation, and plumes of smoke floated skyward.

"Cows can make themselves eat or drink most anything when they're short on food and water," Duett explained.

"When times are hot and dry, they'll eat cholla, prickly pear… both. Even the spines. Sometimes, the stickers swell up their tongues so much they can't drink."

They started off again but Mellie caught her heel in the dirt. Only the big-eyed cattle were aware of them – Press tending to the fire and Granny Bee to Shadi Lace.

"Some stockmen burn green mesquite or palo verde," Duett went on. "Or they tie on old rags dipped in kerosene to singe the cholla where it stands. Those little stickers whip the flames right along. But when animals browse a cactus fired like that, they feed so close they kill the whole plant. Most folks cut up the forage parts instead – like Press is doing now – and throw them on a pile of lit weeds."

They set off again across the flat, where a wind devil was rising up along the edge of the parched ground. The thin spiral twisted toward Shadi Lace and scooped up dust and debris from the desert floor, tossing it skyward. The little girl tugged up her coveralls and ran after it with a squeal.

"I suppose a high wind up here would spread a fire like that pretty quick," Lyman said.

"Not so much as one down below," Duett answered. "These short canyons hereabouts, with their floors jammed with dried seedlings and other young growth, they draw just like a chimney, straight up the sides. A fire goes more slowly downhill, carried along by dropped branches and, in the high country, by rolling pine cones."

They were still too far from Duett's kin to be heard. Hard of hearing anyway, the old woman rested an arm on the black bull's rump while Shadi Lace dipped in and out of the dust devil's errant path. The crackling fire occupied Press' complete attention. He prodded the blaze with a forked branch, and splashes of firebrands exploded in the air like tiny skyrockets.

Unnoticed, Shadi Lace slipped in behind him just as he jerked the stick out of the flames to add more fuel. The limb slapped against the little girl's back and broke. Tatters of ash and glowing twigs adhered to the thick fabric of her coveralls, and she began to scream. Throwing the stick into the fire, Press spun around and reached out for Shadi Lace. But she had already run off.

Lyman and Duett tore off after the terrified little girl. Mellie gasped and put a hand to her mouth as Shadi Lace veered off into a patch of clear ground that allowed her to pick up speed. As the child's wispy hair caught fire and began to curl, Mellie stumbled forward, unable to secure her footing. Again, just as Lyman and Press closed in on her, Shadi Lace shifted course, and a tail of flame whipped up from her back. She was running directly for a scraggly incline, just below and to the right of where Mellie stood. Tearing her hands and skirt on the ragged terrain, Mellie clamored down the rocky hillside, turning her ankles repeatedly. Reaching the base of the slope, she rushed up at the child with her skirts unfurled, and Shadi Lace slammed into her head-on. Mellie wrapped the skirt around the screaming child and they dropped together to the ground.

# BOOK FOUR
## Duett

# CHAPTER NINETEEN
# Friday, January 18, 1918

After Shadi Lace had been taken off the mountain and tended to at the house, Lyman had driven the family into Safford, where a doctor with the whiskers of a he-goat and the disposition to match, said Granny Bee had done right by Shadi Lace with her salt potions and aloe jelly. Annoyed at the weekend disruption, he'd hustled them on home again with little fuss.

The child's thick coveralls and her roll in the dust with Mellie had kept the fire from doing more harm, and Shadi Lace suffered only minor blistering down the middle of her back and along the tops of her shoulders. Her straw-colored hair had been trimmed to a short bob, and with her round pink cheeks, she looked like a cherub. To give Duett the time to care for her daughter, Mellie had run herself ragged the past week, going out to the farm day and night to help Lela. Edna and Lyman had filled in whenever they could. Granny Bee would step in for Shadi Lace on Sunday evening when Lyman would bring Duett back to work at the farm.

But two days earlier, Mellie had shown up at the ranch unannounced, driving out in her daddy's auto. Near tears, she had pleaded with Duett to come in to Pima to look after Sarah this afternoon. At three-thirty, there was to be a Church sponsored baseball game there between some of the older Academy students and some young people from the nearby Valley town of Central. The Soreheads against the Tenderfoots, Mellie said. And Sarah, a Tenderfoot, meant to play. Something – whether it be wild-eyed terror, hope, or plain old-fashioned stubbornness – had left her disinclined to accept or even believe the gravity of her circumstances, and there was no talking the child out of such reckless behavior. Lessons had been cancelled for the afternoon so that students could attend the game. But Mellie had a school meeting in Thatcher to attend, and that left no one around wise to Sarah's condition, no one to lend a knowing hand if something went wrong.

If the Valley folks had helped the Brennicks break some land for alfalfa, or if they'd had enough feed for their stock, Press would not have lit a fire, and Shadi Lace would not have been burned. But that was not directly either Mellie's fault, or Sarah's, and Mellie had put herself at great risk to stifle the flames. With Shadi Lace well looked after by Granny Bee, Duett had agreed to help, and Mellie had come by just after noon to drive her into town with a promise that Lyman, whom she had consulted in the interim, would drive her back to the ranch early Saturday morning.

The game would likely be a short one. Even in the regular season, Mellie said, when the men played "Singles" against "Marrieds," the ball – a stone wound with strips of cloth and rubber and covered with shrunken leather – usually got knocked to pieces by the end of the third inning. There was further talk of a hayrack and a team of horses going up into the foothills for a picnic if the weather held. But Sarah *had* been persuaded to sit that out.

A stiff row of Lombardy poplars – "Mormon Candles," Granny Bee called them – reached out in a long and lean line toward the river and held off a cold wind from the balding western mountains. There, well apart from the others, Duett watched and waited.

Yesterday, the drought had broken a twenty-year record. Folks talked up a blizzard in the Midwest just last week. But the air in the Valley, under a pasty silver/white sky, hung as sapless as a salt flat. The smallest hint of normality had settled over Pima, as the winter fields took on a pale greening with irrigation sluiced in from the canals. But as dusty as the salt cedars standing along the far edge of the playing field were, they had a fine grayish green about them – telling Duett that water, though probably brackish and sparse, was at least near at hand. She couldn't help but harbor some resentment against a town – and maybe even a people – whose suffering could not possibly compare with the parched and crackling dry waterholes back on the dying Santa Teresa.

Out on the playing field, Angelina's feisty White Leghorn hen flopped around like a drunk at an Irish wedding. She'd scratch in the dust behind the batter, and when the ball singed the feathers along her neck, she'd shoot up into the air four feet or more. Best of all, whenever Angelina – who wasn't supposed to play at all – begged a turn and hit a single, the fat bird, full of flaps and struts, trotted off with the little girl to the rag-pile of first base.

On Sarah's first time up, Shotgun bounced around just

beyond the practice swipes of her bat. On her first swing, she smashed the ball solidly and flung the stick aside in a dead run. But the ball veered off past the foul line to the right, and she was called back to try again. This time the bat connected with a healthy crack, and the ball soared toward second base. Duett jumped to her feet. Angelina ran in from the sidelines and snatched Sarah's hand, and the two girls raced off together toward first base, Shotgun out front as though leading the way.

A chorus of shouts rose up from the tier of benches just down from Duett. On a blur of yellow legs, Shotgun whirled along, with Sarah and Angelina close behind. When Sarah pushed ahead, Angelina stopped. So did Shotgun, her plump body bunched up in the dirt. Sarah let out a shriek and stumbled over the old hen.

The player at the pitcher's mound had already sent the ball flying their way. As Sarah spun around and fell, the ball clapped into her body just below her ribcage. Shrieking in pain and surprise, she crumpled to the ground. In a great rush, the bleachers cleared, and the crowd surrounded her.

"Papa, where's Papa?" Sarah moaned. She pulled her knees into her chest as Duett elbowed her way through the throng and dropped down beside the distraught young girl.

"Give the child some room to breathe," Duett ordered. "And one of you fetch Mr. Beecham from the store." Sarah was shivering by now, and her forehead had become wet and cool to the touch. Duett covered the girl's upper body with her own woolen overcoat and cradled her hands around Sarah's face. "You'll be fine, Sarah," she said, hoping to calm the child. But she didn't quite believe it herself.

When Sarah lay at last in her own room above the Pima

store, Duett stripped her of her long-sleeved shirtwaist, chemise and lime green cotton shift. Parts of her clothing were spotted with brown-tinged blood, and her undergarments were stained bright red. Weakened and subdued, Sarah let Duett help her into a clean nightshirt and then back into bed.

Outside the room, Ira paced up and down in the hallway. When runners from the ball field had rushed in, he'd been ready for a sports injury. But the words "female trouble," which Duett had popped into her assessment to keep him at bay, clearly gave him great discomfort. He'd given Duett the run of the sick room.

Sarah's eyes were closed, her breathing labored. Duett sat on the edge of the bed and mopped the young girl's face with a damp cloth. "Mellie…Oh, Mellie," Sarah whimpered. As she rolled her head from side to side on the pillow, sweat-soaked amber curls clung to her cheeks. "I'll die for my sins now, I know I will."

"No one's a dyin' here," Duett said gently.

Sarah's long lashes fluttered open. "Oh…it's you, Miss Brennick," she said.

"And you're too much just a snip of a thing to have any dyin' for sins on your mind," Duett added.

"I'm sorry," Sarah said, curling into the covers. "I must have fallen asleep."

"That ball rapped you harder than a mule's kick." Duett squeezed the young girl's hand and stood up. "But you'll be fit as a fiddle and right soon."

Sarah's fingers fidgeted in the bedclothes. "What about…" She let one hand drop lightly to her abdomen.

"Had the wind knocked out of you is all." Duett moved to the foot of the bed and pulled up another cover from the blanket chest. "Your pa thinks you've been off your feed lately. Let's just leave it that way, why don't we." She shook the blanket out and looked Sarah in the eye. "Not enough good vittles in you by my reckoning either. You're way overdue for a hefty helping of my famous rosemary roasted chicken." She laughed as she flung the quilt – a blue and white patchwork design of Lela's making – across the bed and tucked in the ends. From behind the fall of her hair, she watched Sarah's face as she worked. "No matter how things air out," she suggested gently. "There might be some blame in putting off a wrong on a man who's passed on. A man not rightly situated to defend himself."

Sarah's eyes dulled to the color of a jaybird's wing.

"You know," Duett continued. "Sometimes the best a body can do in this old world is try to live a decent and God-fearing life. Whatever else he was, Billy Ben was a good boy. And he did his best with what the good Lord gave him. To saddle him up in the hereafter with something he had no hand in, why, that doesn't seem right, now does it?"

Sarah's eyes glistened with tears as they darted around the room. Avoiding Duett's face altogether, they settled on the lacy drapes at the bedroom window. "I didn't want Billy Ben to die," she said, her voice barely audible. "I swear I didn't, Miss Brennick. But I had to make him stay away from me, don't you see?" She closed her eyes, her voice barely a whisper. "I was just so scared."

"Scared of what?" Duett asked. But Sarah had fallen asleep.

# CHAPTER TWENTY

# Saturday, January 19, 1918

From the pantry in back of the Pima shop, Duett peered into the living room where Mellie was kneeling before her father. Ira stood in the middle of the room, his worn Bible in hand. With its pale green curtains closed against the early morning sunlight and a single candle flickering on top of the oak dining table, the balance of the room disappeared into the shadows.

Ira laid the Bible on an end table and placed his hands on Mellie's head. "Sister Malvina Beecham," Ira said. "By the authority of the holy priesthood, I seal upon thy head a father's blessing. Thou art a choice vine in the House of Israel, Mellie, and I pronounce blessings upon thee in connection with thy husband and thy posterity."

What with all the weeping and wailing about Nephi's

disappearance and the burden of Sarah's troubles, Duett thought Mellie herself ought to see the upshot of any blessing right off. Husband and posterity could wait.

"May thy children grow around thee like plants of renown," Ira went on. "May they rise up and call thee blessed. Be filled now with the light of revelation." The last thing Mellie needed was another revelation, Duett thought with a wry smile. The poor girl knew far too much already.

"Let goodness be thy constant guide, a light unto thy feet and a lamp unto thy path." Ira shifted his weight and took a deep breath. "In the name of Jesus Christ, I seal you up against the powers of darkness and seal upon you the blessings of holy resurrection and eternal life. Amen."

Had Duett been blessed in Mellie's place, she'd have passed on the posterity, the husband and the revelations and gone straight for the rain. She whisked a flour sack tea-towel from her shoulder and went back to dry up the last of the breakfast dishes. Her plans to get back to Shadi Lace and the Santa Teresa had come none too soon, she thought, as Lyman's auto chugged to a halt by the kitchen door. He would take her home for now and then come back for her late Sunday evening, when she'd return to care for Lela at the farmhouse.

Noah's latest ravings there only came when Mellie stopped by, it seemed. They were always out of Lela's earshot, thank the good Lord, but Noah cut such a blowzy figure, so slack in mind, that Duett wondered how much longer she could keep to that old house. In this stifling family, Lyman was her breath of fresh air, and she rushed out to meet him on the side staircase.

As she and Lyman set off down the Pima Road, the mountaintops turned dove-colored, their peaks indistinct under low, cold, black clouds. They talked through Shadi

Lace's ordeal on the mountain and her steady recovery. They touched on Lyman's missing plates, Nephi's disappearance, and Sarah's mishap on the ball field which had troubled everyone, especially those wise to her true state of mind *and* body.

"News like that travels fast," Lyman said. "She's not out of the woods by a long shot, in my view." He turned off the Pima Road onto the long, rutted track that led out to the Brennick Ranch.

"You got that right," Duett agreed, sweeping in her wind-blown hair. The fix poor Sarah was trapped in was deeper and darker than any mesquite bosque Lyman could ever imagine.

"Edna's dropping by the store later this morning so Pop and Mellie can visit with Mama an hour or so," Lyman added.

"You know," Duett went on after a time, "Mellie begged your daddy for his blessing just before you came. He barely had time to set one fine foot on the staircase. God's truth, she's as jumpy as a hop-toad these days."

"I'm worried about her myself," Lyman said. "We've all tried to help out. But Mellie tends to go it alone for far too long."

The conversation soon shifted to the latest rumor brewing over in the Aravaipa country. Talk in the hills and over by Klondyke ran that some of the sheriff's men meant to haul the Power brothers out of Power's Garden with a bare hand. But they said, too, that no one would be fool enough to mess with those boys. Duett knew the Valley would fly off in all directions when something happened, and she believed, with many others, that it would. And soon.

The Packard churned up the last hill before the Brennick ranch house. And there, just as the engine died, the gray skies opened up like the windows of heaven. Great drops of water struck up the dust like smoke and hissed and splattered on the Packard's hood. A sudden burst of silver-gray rain beat in streaks against the house.

Duett jumped out of the auto and flung her arms up to the emptying sky, tears and rain mingling on her face. Lyman set the brake and joined her, reaching for her outstretched hand. Not aiming to miss a drop of precious rain, Granny Bee met them on the porch with a grin, two empty buckets in her hands. Deftly, she slung them under the canales roof drains at either side of the entrance before she joined Duett and Lyman in the yard, the three of them spinning around in the rain like madmen.

The storm hit on all four feet then. Bone dry soil, set like cement, turned from dust to muddy pools. Rain sluiced down, a great glut of water gushing in big snakes of runoff that zigzagged down the hillsides, grinding pebbles and then boulders in the creek bed below. It was a storm that would top the mountains with snow and wet the whole Valley; a rain that would bring back the winter feed. In a week, the green-up would climb all over the hills, slippery with shoots of filaree and grass. It would creep down the rutted road and beyond, out into the mesquite corrals and the alfalfa pasture, and then all along the flat of the Valley. A great glory of green.

# CHAPTER TWENTY-ONE

# Sunday, January 27, 1918

"Praise God that we're still blessed with Shadi Lace's young life," Lela said, taking a tentative seat at the dressing table. "You're a treasure yourself, Duett, to come back to us so soon. I'm so very grateful."

Duett brushed through the length of Lela's hair and then went out to fetch some mint tea from the kitchen stove. During the summer months, fresh mint was floated in cold water with vinegar and honey, a remedy Granny Bee used for stomach trouble. The winter tea was dried and steeped in hot water but soothed just as well.

Noah himself ministered to Lela regularly now. None of that handholding business Duett had heard so much about, but plasters and potions and the like. Still, by Duett's reckoning, Lela's condition only worsened.

"My pleasure," Duett called back from the kitchen. "As for Shadi Lace, she'll have her legs under her quicker than a butcher's dog." She sprinkled a pinch of dried, dull-green leaves into twin china cups and filled them with hot water from a pot that simmered at the back of the stove. A cloud of steam warmed her face, while, at the same time, a snap of coolness tickled the inside of her throat.

"Most children have such marvelous resilience," Lela said as Duett came back into the room, leaving the doorway open behind her by looping the faded yellow curtain ties over metal hooks on either side. "My poor Nephi has never faired well in that respect. He's been such a sickly child. Lung trouble again, Ira tells me. I don't remember now when I even saw him last."

Duett set the tea cups, a matching set in an old rose pattern, on the table and tried to smile. A mother ought to know the truth about her child, good or bad, she thought. But that was hardly her place. "Shadi Lace is a game girl," she said. "She'll come around. She's mighty weary of lyin' there, though. Has to keep off her back, you see. She's after Granny Bee like a pack of hornets. What's this? What's that? More questions than Saint Peter at the pearly gates." She took Edna's wooden horse and its snip of cotton cloth from the pocket of her apron and passed them on to Lela. See-ing as how she and Lela had grown quite close, Lyman had suggested that Duett find out what, if anything, his mother might recollect of the old toy.

"Oh, yes, this lovely piece." Lela spread the square on her dressing gown. Early afternoon sunlight touched the corner threads with pale gold. "Now, Mother Josephine was never called 'Josie,' at least not to my knowledge," she began. With a slight tremor, Lela's fingers traced the bright yellow letters. "The hand of a child, wouldn't you say?" She glanced up at

Duett. "Josephine would have been three or four years old in 1856. A woman of immense tribulation, so I've been told. Her mind had quite gone by the time I knew her." She lowered her voice. "There was a plural marriage, you see, and whispers of a lost child, Edna's twin sister. But Josie? No... no one named Josie was ever mentioned to me."

Duett nodded and set the lot of Lela's limp hair atop her head with a metal clip while Lela, letting the trinket and needlework lie in her lap, sipped her tea over a lengthy but comfortable silence. "There were two Spratt girls, you know," Lela said thoughtfully. "Josephine and her older sister, Adriana. They were adopted into the Spratt family as very small children, I've been told."

"Oh, the foolishness and vanity!" Noah Beecham appeared suddenly out of nowhere, a black specter in the doorway, and charged into the room from the kitchen. "'How quick to do iniquity are the children of men.'" Bent over his cane, the old man made for the women, reaching out for the cloth and the toy, but Duett snatched them both from Lela's lap.

"These ain't yours for the takin', Mr. Beecham," Duett said with great offense, as she dropped them back into her apron pocket. She was about to follow with a stampeded argument on gain and gifts when Mellie's voice shot through the room from the doorway.

"How are you feeling today, Mama?" Mellie asked, her voice tight and strained. Face ashen white, eyes puffed up and red, she moved past Noah and Duett. As she bent down to kiss her mother's cheek, she almost smiled.

"Oh, now, Mellie dear," Lela said with great alarm and brushed a frail hand along her daughter's arm. "You don't look well at all. You should be home in bed yourself. Perhaps you've Nephi's malady."

"I'm fine, Mama," Mellie answered, though nothing in her face or voice changed. "We'll visit in a short while. I've actually come to talk to Father Beecham." A terrible darkness touched Mellie's eyes as she turned to her grandfather, who had already begun to shuffle toward the open door. "Some news from the Church," she added.

"Lovely," Lela said, with obvious confusion.

Duett took Lela's arm and helped her to the bed, drawing the covers up over her wasted body. As Noah maneuvered himself through the doorway and out into the kitchen, Mellie trailed behind him. Duett folded another blanket across Lela's feet and listened as a scrap of paper was snatched up in the other room and slapped rhythmically in someone's hand. Footsteps followed.

The outside door had just closed behind Mellie and Noah when Duett left Lela's room. She closed the curtains and tiptoed across the kitchen to crack open the outside door, watching Mellie and Noah with both curiosity and dread. The blackness she'd heard in Mellie's voice inched along her spine like rattler venom.

"He's dead…" Mellie said and shook a note in the old man's face. He crumpled over his cane and began to sway.

Dead? Ephraim? Duett thought.

"Dead…," Mellie said again. "On his sixteenth birthday."

"Lord have mercy," Duett whispered. It was Nephi.

"Did you hear me? Nephi's lying dead in some cold, dusty shack." Tears streamed down Mellie's face, and Duett felt a sudden stinging in her own eyes. "And you! All of you pious old men in no danger of dying yourselves, you call up these young boys to some great adventure. You drag them into the game with all your talk about honor and glory and duty, all so some stupid munitions dealer can get rich." Mellie shook the paper in the old man's face again. He hung over his walking stick, trembling. One hand swiped under the silver rim of his spectacles and came away glistening. But he said nothing.

"I hate you," Mellie went on. "I hate all of you. At least Nephi's happier where he is now. God will take him into heaven, because he's already been in hell. You put stars in the eyes of children who haven't even seen their own shadows yet."

As Mellie turned back toward the house, Duett closed the door and darted back to the kitchen table. If Mellie had noticed any motion at the doorway, she never let on. She came into the kitchen alone, the paper held in her hand so tightly that her knuckles had gone white. "Could you come back to the shop with me, Duett, and watch over Sarah while Mama's asleep?" she asked. Her voice faltered, and she raised a hand to cover her eyes.

"Of course. Is there anything else I can do?" Duett asked.

"There's nothing anyone can do anymore," Mellie said, biting her lower lip. In painful silence, Duett followed her out to the auto.

\*    \*    \*

Back at the Pima store, there were two letters and a formal death notice lying on the dressing table in Mellie's room. Duett had not meant to read any of them. She'd only come into the room for another blanket for Sarah. With a profusion of apologies, Mellie had asked Duett to stay on at the Pima store for the afternoon, as the bleeding Sarah was suffering from her baseball accident had worsened over the past several days. Ira had closed the shop, and he and An-

213

gelina had left for Safford with Mellie to pass the news of Nephi's death on to Lyman and Edna.

The first letter Duett read came from Ephraim Heber:

> *December 28, 1917*
> *Le Mans, France*
> *My Dearest Malvina,*
>> *What a great and good sacrifice to come forward and pledge our service to God and country. The Lord God will not fail us. We must save the soul of the world.*
>> *I leave for an active sector in three days. I have talked to some who have been at the front for four days. What a wonderful and exhilarating time they had. In the tip of a strip of woods, the French guns are firing. Up in the sky, rings of smoke and in among them, specks of dust lit up by the sun. The aerial battles are wonderful. Planes climbing and dropping like a giant wheel rolling through the sky. Heroism, glory and poetry fill the heavens. We are the successors to King Arthur's knights. The men of one of our divisions had decorated their helmets, and they swept by us like plumed warriors. Everything is happening so fast. And I am in the midst of it.*
>> *With regards,*
>> *EH*

Duett carefully placed the letter back on the dressing table. Better Ephraim lost than Nephi. He already had his soul all laced up for the Lord. She knew there'd be no poetry in the loss of Nephi. Duett opened the second letter – penned in Mellie's younger brother's hand – and read:

> *Fort Bliss, Arkansas*
> *Dear Mellie,*
>> *It is so much colder here than I had thought. I miss you all. Some of us have the influenza but it is not deadly. I have chosen the rightful path and gone to the war. I didn't see the Three Nephites in Fort Thomas, but I know they were there for us. I went as a servant of the Lord to see that His will was done. But when I saw the wondrous*

*thing God wrought on that evil man who blasphemed
against the Church, my faith was strengthened. I knew
then that I must fulfill my vow to God and follow in the
footsteps of his servant, Ephraim.*

*Pray for me, Mellie. But do not fear. I put myself
in God's hands. I know you have kept your word about
my going as I have kept mine to God and Father Beecham. But it is so much colder here than I had thought
it would be.*

*Your brother,*
*Nephi*

Poor Mellie! She must have known that Nephi meant to go
to war. He must have sealed her to silence. How she must
be suffering now – her little brother dead in the training
camps. And poor Mellie drowning in the secret of how he
got there.

A moan from next door broke through Duett's thoughts.
She quickly folded the second letter and placed it back on
the table with the first.

When she entered Sarah's room, the girl sat hunched
at the end of her bed, her arms folded across her abdomen.
Bright red blood stained her bed-gown between her legs.
"Oh, God," she cried. "I'll die now, I know I will. I'm so afraid.
Will God forgive me, Miss Brennick?"

"Lie back now, Sarah." Duett pulled back the bedclothes
and rushed to Mellie's room for more coverlets and blankets.
She piled these on an incline and positioned Sarah's body
so the girl's legs and hips were raised above her head. She'd
often seen Granny Bee ease the bleeding of a birthing gone
wrong with stacked blankets and hoped the same measure
might work for Sarah. Taking the sheets off Angelina's bed,
she shredded these into long pads, removed Sarah's undergarments and began to sop up the smeared blood from the
young girl's thighs.

"I never meant to hurt him, Miss Brennick." Sarah's shallow breath came in gasps against the pillow.

"Never mind that now," Duett answered. She tucked a narrow strip of the torn fabric between Sarah's legs.

When she reached up to mop the girl's brow with another piece of cloth, Sarah, panic-stricken, snatched her wrist. "I swear it," Sarah said. "I never meant to hurt him, Miss Brennick. Please, help me!"

"Hurt who?" Duett asked, without stopping her work.

"Billy Ben," Sarah whispered. Duett froze. "It was me, Miss Brennick. I threw those firecrackers down from the cliff. But I only meant to scare him," she sobbed. "I wanted him to think Ephraim's threats had come true. He'd leave me alone then, even when I lied about him." She collapsed into Duett's arms. "It wasn't him that hurt me, Miss Brennick. It was Ephraim. Ephraim Heber."

# CHAPTER TWENTY-TWO

# Sunday, February 3, 1918

"**A** damn sight more she done to the boy than hurt him." Granny Bee slammed a fist on the tabletop and drew a gnarled hand across her thin, gray lips. "And that Ephraim Heber. Who'd a thought that fool hoe man would go sniffin' 'round one of his own? Set fire to their britches, everyone of 'em, I say." Duett gulped down the last of her coffee and drummed her fingertips against the cup.

"You tell 'em all what a hell-roarer that Heber fella turned out to be," Granny Bee went on. "Struttin' 'round like a damn saint when all he's lookin' for is to lay any she-stock that passes his way. Billy Ben weren't no lily man by a mile, but he was a good boy all the same."

Duett let her loosened hair fall over the back of her chair. A week full of Beechams and now this spat with Granny

Bee. Not that Duett could blame her. She picked her words with care before she answered. "If it was just that snake of a man Ephraim Heber, or that awful Noah Beecham, why there'd be no holdin' me back," she said. "You and me both know Billy Ben's high female fever. He was up to no good with that little girl. Would have acted the everlasting damn fool, I reckon, and gotten what he was after, if he'd of pushed just a little harder. Skittish as a jackrabbit, that Sarah is. We all know what she done." Duett pulled herself upright and eyed Granny Bee with conviction. "And I know she raised a lot more than a mortal scare out there in Fort Thomas. But I don't reckon she meant to hurt nobody. And that evil old man, why he'll have her hide nailed to the barn door when he finds out what she done and who she done it with. Her road's no picnic either."

"Them Beechams don't give a hoot in hell about any of us," Granny Bee spat back. "Cut and run while you still can, girl. That's what I say."

* * *

With folks calling in to both the Beecham farm and the Pima shop to pay their respects, the truth of Nephi's demise could not be kept from Lela, despite the great anguish it brought her. Everyone mourned for Nephi – the Beechams, the Brennicks…the whole Valley. A steady boy…a dreamer, they said – as if *they* knew. With the pain of Nephi's death so fresh upon them all, Duett settled on keeping Sarah's confession to herself – outside of Granny Bee – at least for the time being. One tragedy at a time, she thought.

Sarah, still with child so far as Duett could tell, would spend the weekend under Mellie's watchful eye, resting in her room above the Pima store. Though her bleeding had eased, Sarah had promised to stay in bed a full day, and Duett knew Mellie would hold her to her word.

As was their custom during bereavement, the women of the Relief Society brought by so much food that Duett's services wouldn't be required in the kitchen for days. Noah would look in on Lela for a few hours. So late in the morning, under a brilliant blue cloudless sky, Lyman drove to the ranch to fetch Duett out to Orin Harland's place, tasked with passing on word of Nephi's death.

Feeling the weight of their errand, they headed south toward the Cactus Flats, Lyman making small talk about his grandfather to lighten the heavy silence between them. "Orin Harland whips up as mean a brew as any that ever came out of an old Ozark still," he said. "Strange that in these days of sacrifice and shortage for the war, white lightning goes quicker than a flea to a dog. I wouldn't be surprised if the old man doesn't share a lick or two with that scrawny mutt of his, General Lee."

"Is your granddaddy of the Mormon persuasion?" Duett asked.

"Oh God, no," Lyman answered. "That he's disaffected from the Saints would be putting it mildly. You saw from the reunion that he scares the hell out of them with his corncob pipes and toothless grins. I mean, scares the living hell out of them!" Lyman gave Duett a wry smile. "His family did some sharecropping back in Arkansas," he continued. "My grandmother, Orin's wife, died when Mama was born. She was their only child, and was raised there in the South by her maternal grandmother until the old lady passed away. They were ripe for the picking, so to speak, as religions go, and Orin brought Lela out here in the 1880s as Mormon converts."

Lyman's automobile rattled through a spread of greasewood and crossed a shallow puddle in the middle of the hacked-out track-way that led to Orin's place. "Conversion is a sticky business," Lyman said. "But in Orin's case, it didn't stick at all. Never took much to religious dogma, all the rules and regulations and such. You know, he brews up something he calls 'Autumn Leaf.' One sip," Lyman laughed, "and you turn color and fall." Duett jabbed at his arm as the Packard came to a halt beside an odd hovel of corrugated tin, wooden planks, chicken wire, tar paper and adobe brick.

"What the hell..." Orin's bellow from the back of the building was followed in due time by the old man himself, in the company of a skeptical General Lee, who gave the auto a wary but disdainful sniff. Wild as a broomie's tail, Orin's hair climbed up the back of his head to splay out in all directions. The same grizzle spread down the sides of his face to the man's lower jaw and upper lip. Woolen trousers, black as a panther's pelt, puffed out like air balloons and hung by threadbare suspenders, fastened well above his waist. The pant-legs ended three or four inches above a pair of dust-colored miner's boots.

"Well, Lyman, you old fool son of a bitch." Orin slammed the axe he was carrying into a side beam of the front door. "I'd a knowed yer hide in a tan yard," he said.

As Lyman climbed out of the automobile, the old man plucked a felt hat from his head and wiped his brow with the cuff end of an empty red flannel shirt sleeve that dangled from where his left arm should have been. "Beggin' your pardon, ma'am," he said to Duett, his good right eye poking around her cheekbones. He'd lost the sight in his left eye to the War Between the States, Lyman had told her. "This here your gal, boy? A right good-lookin' woman she is too, by God." Orin fetched a corncob pipe from his shirt pocket, popped it a time or two against his knee and pinched the stem in his mouth. "Come on in here and rest your britches, damn you boy. You too, girl." Lyman stumbled forward with the sudden clap of the old man's hand on his back. He opened Duett's door and helped her from the Packard. "This is Duett Brennick," he said.

"Brennick...Brennick." Orin's good eye squinted in deep thought. "Pack of Brennicks out there in the Arkansas country tough enough to rub the hide off an alligator. Nary a one of 'em could write his name, but they was all fightin' bastards. But you'd be one of them Texas Brennicks over Fort Thomas way, I'd venture." Orin didn't wait for an answer. He cracked open the door to his cabin and stepped inside. "Now the place ain't much," he said. "But, by God, it suits me fine."

Duett ducked around the protruding axe handle in the doorpost and followed the old man through a slat-backed door that sagged on three leather hinges. By her eye, the place wasn't much at all. The dirt floor, maybe fifteen feet square, had a pile of rubble in the left rear corner where part of the tin roof had fallen in. Right of the door stood a home-made cupboard and a dry sink that showed a trace of having once been white. The open shelves held canned goods, tin dishes and eating irons of every size and sort. Above a square table littered with pots and pans was a window made of greased parchment. Halfway up the wall, lanterns and scraps of clothing hung from nails affixed to a pot-rack. On the other side of the sparse room, a cot covered with horse blankets and a heavy canvas tarp was pushed against the wall, and a kerosene lantern swung from the open rafters.

For seating, Orin motioned to a seedy wicker-bottomed chair, a three-legged stump-stool and a closed wooden bin, probably full of potatoes. Duett took the chair, Lyman the stool. His grandfather sat down on the wooden box and began to fill his pipe. In the midst of idle talk, Orin took off his outer shirt and snagged it on a nail. Lyman had explained to Duett on the way out that you could judge the rigor of a winter by the number of collars around the old man's neck. "For years, he was in the habit of two baths a year," Lyman had warned her. "One at Christmas. The other on the fourth of July. But he made himself sick one December, so he's given them up altogether." As Orin reached across Duett to ply the pot-bellied stove with fresh fuel, the point of Lyman's story became clear.

Orin had already heard tell of Nephi's death and was full of war torn tragedy himself. "Gettin' wind of that poor boy's passin' cut me to the quick." Orin shook his head. "It's tearin' your Mama's heart out, I'll wager. And only in his sixteenth year. Fifteen myself back in '62 when I put on that piece of work yonder and went straight to hell in the last damn war." He motioned to the back wall where Duett picked out a gray military jacket of the kind worn by the Confederate Army. "Smoke, boy?" Orin fished the makings for a wrap out of his shirt – Bull Durham and a greasy wad of rice paper. Lyman accepted. "My old man died when that damn General Steele took Little Rock in '63. You know…the wife used to say, 'By God, Hal, them damn wars took your ma, your pa, two baby sisters, a wing and an eyeball. And good Lord,' she says, 'You ain't got much of a mind left neither.'"

Orin laughed so loud and long then that he fell into a spasmodic cough. He fired up the pipe, tossed the spent match to the floor and spit after it.

"Your sisters died in the Civil War?" Lyman asked, lighting his smoke. "I didn't know that."

"Hell no, boy." Orin spit again and sucked on the pipe. "Them was Indian wars, by God. Redskins got 'em in '57. Me and the old man, we buggered off to them Californee goldfields. I was a snot-nosed kid. Maybe ten years old. But we picked up some work at some damn sawmill. They was to come out with a pack from Missouri, ma and the young'uns, Josie and Ariel. Must have been four or five years old at most, the two of them. Never did make it though. Redskins got 'em in '57. That's what we was told."

"Josie?" Duett glanced at Lyman.

"Yes ma'am. And by God, wasn't she a pretty little thing. I hated them savages for what they done." Orin pulled on the pipe again, his good eye fixed on Duett. Under his scrutiny, she began to fidget and pulled Shadi Lace's toy horse from her lap bag. Without looking down, she played her fingers along the sleek curves of the puzzling trinket.

If old Orin had had any teeth left, he'd have dropped them then and there. His snappy blue eye settled on Edna's wooden pony. "Christ, girl, how in hell did you come acrost that damn piece of work?" He reached over to take it from Duett's hand. "Cut that son-of-a-bitch myself for my baby sister, Josie, just before I took off with Pa for them goddamn goldfields."

# CHAPTER TWENTY-THREE

# Tuesday, February 12, 1918

The whole muddled mess had almost become too much for Duett. Lela's father, Orin Harland, and Ira's mother, Josephine Beecham – two of Lyman's own blood grandparents – had suddenly become brother and sister, making Lela and Ira first cousins! Just how that had transpired remained a mystery; though Duett and Lyman had a hunch old Noah Beecham had the answer.

Not to put too fine a point on it, but both Duett and Lyman had been thunderstruck by Orin's tale. They'd asked a lot of questions, but Orin had no answers. In the end, Lyman was not a man to be shamed by any circumstance over which his mother and father had had no control. But he was more determined than ever to learn the hows and the whys of it.

Duett had hesitated to saddle him with still more grief. At the same time, she reckoned that Lyman ought to have the whole goods on Sarah's predicament. On their drive back to town on Sunday, she'd told him the tangled truth, and they'd agreed to put Lyman's family tree on the back burner until Sarah was safe. Given her fragile state, Sarah would keep to her bed above the Pima shop for the week and then be taken out to the Brennick Ranch.

It was only a matter of time before the cat was let out of the bag and Noah and everyone else would know about the baby. Just how that cat was set free seemed like something they could still get a handle on. So Lyman and Duett had stopped at the Pima store that day to share their concerns with Mellie, the three of them agreeing to speak privately with Ira, and then Lyman had taken Duett to the farmhouse.

In the early afternoon, while Lyman looked after Sarah and Angelina at the Pima store, the rest of the family met at the farm to arrange Nephi's burial service. His remains had yet to be returned from Arkansas. They gathered in the parlor so as to spare Lela yet more devastating news, and when tentative plans had been laid, Noah went outside to take his customary turn around the orchard. Her face drawn, Mellie approached her father.

"What is it, Mellie?" he asked.

"How can I tell you this, Papa?" Mellie dropped her head in her hands. Ira made to get up from the couch and go to her, but Edna, standing beside him, laid a hand on his shoulder.

"Sarah's to have a child," Edna said simply.

There it is, Duett thought. She watched Ira slump, speechless, into the sofa.

"I should have known," Ira said after a time. "Maybe I

didn't want to…I don't know anymore. That Billy Ben…," he seethed and pulled himself upright on the couch, folding his hands and resting his elbows on his knees.

"All that doesn't matter now, Ira dear," Edna broke in. "But as a matter of fact, we need to spare the boy any more ill thought. Sarah says the baby's father is Ephraim Heber."

"Oh no, no," Ira moaned, raising one hand to his forehead. "Ephraim Heber? Can it be true? What next? My boy's gone. My poor Nephi's gone." He sank back into the sofa. "And now little Sarah? My God, Edna, what's to become of her? What about Father Beecham?"

"Now listen to me, Ira." Edna took a seat beside her brother. "You know I've always believed that Father Beecham took Mama away. And now young Nephi. Must we let him have Sarah, too?" She stopped to knead her brother's shoulder. "She'll go with me to Chicago as soon as possible, but Malvina and Duett are quite right. She needs to leave here *now*. The Brennick place is far safer for her than here in town. Noah *will* find out. You know he will. And he'll make a hateful, blustering example of her. Have her stand up before forums and counsels and whatnot. He'll *shame* her, Ira. Do you really want that to happen? And do you really think he'll fault Ephraim?"

"We're just like the Powers now," Ira stammered. "At each others' throats."

"That business in Aravaipa has nothing to do with us or with anything that's happened here," Edna insisted. "Our Sarah needs help, plain and simple. And thank God the Brennicks are willing to take her in."

"It's a black hole your Sarah's in just now, Mr. Beecham," Duett added. She and Lyman had already mulled over all the "business in Aravaipa" and, though they both knew it would have *everything* to do with the lot of them, she would force herself to concentrate only on Sarah for the present. When the girl was safe – away from Noah Beecham and off to Chicago with Edna Sutherland – Duett would cut and run just like Granny Bee had said. She'd be done with the whole Valley for good. But for Lyman, of course.

Just two days ago, on Sunday last, word had come out of the Aravaipa country that Sheriff McBride, the Mormon lawman from Safford, and Deputy U.S. Marshal Frank Haynes from Globe, along with two Mormon Graham County deputies, T. Kane Wootan and Martin Kempton, had gone into Power's Garden in the early morning. All of them but Marshal Haynes were dead now, and old man Power with them.

Without warning, the door of the Pima farmhouse flew open, and the parlor fell silent. Noah Beecham lumbered into the kitchen and pulled a quart of hand-pressed cider from the icebox. Brushing past him silently, Ira walked out the back door "for some air," he said.

"Tonight, then, girls," Edna whispered. Without a word to her father, she set off in the Hudson for Safford. She would return in the early evening with Lyman, bringing Sarah from the Pima store, and the lot of them would settle Sarah out at the Brennick Ranch.

Seated at the kitchen table, Noah shuffled the Safford newspaper noisily and began to read:

*"'The entire community was shocked at the news received here Sunday afternoon that Sheriff McBride, Chief Deputy Martin R. Kempton and Deputy Sheriff T. Kane Wootan had been killed in a battle with the Power boys in the Galiuro mountains shortly after 7 o'clock Sunday morning. The news was brought by Marshal Frank Haynes of Globe, the fourth member of the party which left here Saturday afternoon for the Powers' home to bring back John and Tom Power who were wanted by the*

*government on the charge of evading the selective draft. Old man Power came out of the door nearest to them carrying a gun. The officers called to him to throw up his hands. Placing his gun between his knees, he raised his hands and as he did this, the door behind him opened wide enough for a gun to be shoved through. The battle commenced. Some twenty-five shots were fired. Then the shooting stopped and everything was quiet. An inquest was held at the court house Tuesday afternoon and the jury brought in a verdict that McBride, Kempton and Wootan had died from gun shot wounds inflicted at the hands of John Power, Tom Power and Tom Sisson.'"*

Noah laid the paper on the tabletop and scowled. "Lurking about to murder innocent men," he grumbled.

For Sarah's sake and Mellie's, Duett struggled to stay calm. She busied herself at the kitchen sink while Mellie began to lay the table in advance of the evening meal. Noah stabbed the newspaper with one finger. "And to believe that their country had no claim on them. Godless traitors."

Duett sighed and put another wormy piece of wood into the bowels of Old Ironsides.

"Those murderers spilt the blood of good, just citizens. And for what reason? Our lawmen were only doing their job."

"It's hard to say what really happens in a hair-trigger deal like that, Mr. Beecham," Duett answered, but Noah only glowered.

"They believed they were outside the pale of the law and the authority of government, that's all there is to it."

Despite her best intentions, Duett had nearly taken her fill of this evil old man. "Some folks that should know say old man Power had his hands over his head when he was shot," she said.

"Some that should know…" Noah sneered and punched back his spectacles.

"They know from the path of the bullet that killed him," Duett said, her voice tight and deliberate. "People don't go out on an ambush in their long johns, do they?"

"I don't know what you people do," Noah muttered.

A wave of stifling anger rolled across Duett's chest, leaving a hot tingle in the palm of her hands. "Well, I'll tell you then," she answered, turning from the sink. "One of them lawmen took a hair-triggered rifle from the Upchurch place. Sunday morning was cold in them hills, not full light then either."

"It was an accident," Mellie snapped from the other side of the room.

"They were fine men of the Church," Noah said, ignoring Mellie altogether. "Had those murderers not had friends the likes of you Brennicks in the hills, they'd not be loose today."

"The only thing to blame is intolerance," Mellie insisted, facing the two of them. "And a cold winter morning. And one man not familiar with another man's gun."

"There's never been one good word spoken about the Powers, any of them," Noah said. He stood up, tucked the folded paper under his arm, and started for the dining room.

"Maybe you just ain't been listenin' to the right people," Duett called after him. "Kane Wootan was spreading his tail feathers over there in the Klondyke store about how a man could go into Power's Garden and bring them boys out with a lightning bug on a stick," she said. Noah stopped and turned back to face her. "And, Kane said, the man who did that would be sheriff next. That's the straight of it. Only they got more than they bargained for. John Power can shoot the eye out of a gnat."

"The devil rages in his heart," Noah mumbled, fixing his frosted blue eyes on Duett. "That's nothing but a filthy lie."

"Stop it. Both of you," Mellie demanded. "It was an accident. Do you hear me?"

"The devil it was." Duett came closer and laughed in the old man's face. "Neither of them boys was against the war. They'd of come out on their own when they finished work on that stamp mill in Kielberg."

"The slackers *they* were? I don't believe that for one minute."

"I don't care what you believe," Duett hissed. "It's the truth. But you just can't live with the notion that a man don't want nobody messin' with him."

"What about the notion of duty to God, duty to country?" Noah shouted back.

"Those boys were never any hands to mix much with anyone," Duett said. "And right away you people say there must be something wrong with 'em."

"Now there you have it." Noah wagged a finger in Duett's face. "Something *is* wrong with them. Something's wrong with the lot of you."

"Please. Don't do this," Mellie pleaded. From the corner of her eye, Duett saw her throw a frantic glance toward Lela's room.

"'A perverse and crooked people.'" Noah's face reddened with rage. "'Those who rebel against the light, the morning is to them as the shadow of death.'"

"You of all people should know about death, old man. You even brought it on your own grandson. Talkin' up war like it's some great adventure he's missin' out on. Some wild shindig God wants him to put his hands all over." Duett's own face flushed with anger. "You're all cut from the same cloth, you insufferable Mormons. You own everything worth having and then begrudge the rest of us what little's left."

"There's nothing you people could possibly have that's worth laying one clean hand on," Noah sneered, wagging his hoary head. His gnarled hands were cupped on the top of his cane.

"Well you'll not set one foot on the Santa Teresa. None of you. A tangle with one of you and sooner or later we gotta fight the whole damn pack."

"Leave my house! Now!" Noah roared.

"Those Power boys got in some Mormon's way, and now they're payin' the price."

"Get thee behind me Satan," Noah howled again, stabbing a shriveled finger at her.

"You're not the hand of God, Noah Beecham, however much you might think you are."

"I said get out!"

Duett stood her ground. "But you throw *His* words around like you owned *them* too. You're nothing but a half-dead, hypocritical, hateful old man." Duett spit her words into the old man's face. "*You're* the evil in this house. And you and me, we both know it. Did you know Sarah's to have a child?" She watched the old man's eyes widen. Somewhere in the thick air behind her, she heard Mellie stifle a sob. "And the father's not Billy Ben, much as you'd like it to be. It's your own black-hearted saint, Ephraim Heber."

"Curse the devil and his lies," Noah seethed, coming at Duett with his cane raised.

"That's *God's* truth," Duett taunted, stepping easily out of his path. She snatched the cane from his upraised hand and forced him into a chair at the table.

"Lies! Lies! All lies," Noah raved, clutching desperately at the yellow rose on his lapel.

Duett smiled as the butcher knife of her words sunk into the old man's chest. As she hovered over him, she gave the blade one final twist. "Blind as a bat with fear, she was already sniffing the rot your withered soul would heap on her, so she fingered Billy Ben instead." Duett smirked as the old man's face convulsed with hatred and disbelief. "And then she killed him."

# CHAPTER TWENTY-FOUR

# Wednesday, February 13, 1918

Late afternoon sunlight hung in a blank blue sky, paling as the sun slipped toward the horizon. Long shadows inched out over the brushy hillsides of the Santa Teresa, and the pale blush gloaming Duett always favored at sundown rose up from the hills and gentled the land. And yet the air seemed as thick and stagnant as the prospect of a gathering storm.

Inside the Brennick ranch house, Sarah slept fitfully, alone in the back room Duett shared with Shadi Lace. Assumed still to be with child, she'd been spirited there in Lyman's Packard the night before, as planned, along with Duett, Mellie and Edna, who had all stayed on at the ranch overnight.

Granny Bee rummaged about in the kitchen, on occasion meandering into the dining room, where everyone had gathered to await the inevitable arrival of Father Beecham and the other Mormon elders. Ira had been persuaded, with great reluctance, to take Lela and little Angelina to the shop, where they'd be spared any uproar.

Her nerves prickling, Granny Bee lolled about at the table, poked around in her mending box and then set off for the kitchen again. Shadi Lace played outside in the summerhouse, asked to keep a watchful eye out for the dust of Noah Beecham.

Along with Duett, who was patching the knee of one of Shadi Lace's coveralls, Press and Lyman sat around the table, the men cleaning a pair of battered Winchester rifles taken down from the gun rack in the corner of the room. Granny Bee eyed the pieces as she came back in from the kitchen, this time with a steaming pot of coffee. "Lordy be," she said. "We've gone to hell in a hand-basket, ain't we?"

Duett held up her cup to be refilled. "Hell's got nothin' on the likes of old Noah Beecham and his ilk." She glanced toward Mellie and Edna, who'd been planted at the front window from nigh on daybreak, it seemed. "Meanin' no disrespect to you and yours now, Mellie," Duett added. "Yours neither, Mrs. Sutherland." Both women looked back into the room and smiled weakly.

"No offense taken, my dear," Edna answered.

"Of course not," Mellie put in, as she and Edna turned back to the window.

"I can be a damn fire-eater up against a man as huffish and spleenful as old Noah Beecham," Duett went on, running a finger around the rim of her coffee cup. "Him pickin' on them Power boys when he don't know 'em from a plug nickel. I brought this whole kettle to a boil before its time, Mellie. And I'm sorrier for it than anyone. I wish I'd been just a tad less tempersome..." Her voice trailed off.

"Are we brewin' coffee here or just heatin' water?" Granny Bee demanded, before Mellie could respond. "This here's a boil that needs lancin', and the sooner it's done, the better off we'll be." She pounded a knotted fist on the table. "When you're sittin' on the can, you better do something and soon, 'else get the hell off."

"Right you are there, Mrs. Brennick," Lyman said with an uneasy laugh. "My grandfather would be hauling his hellfire out here one way or another, Duett. Better sooner than later, that's what I say. You got a few truths out in the open, that's all," he added. "There's not enough of that going around these days, in my opinion."

"You're absolutely right, Lyman," Mellie said. "Please don't trouble yourself anymore, Duett. These things had to be said. We all know the truth had to come out." She caught Press' eye, and he returned her faint smile. "Frankly," she added, still looking at Press, "I feel as though a terrible weight has been lifted from me, at least to some degree. I only regret that it's had to fall back on all of you."

Press had stopped working on the Winchester, and Duett could see from Mellie's face that the deep blue of his eyes had thoroughly flooded the space between them. She reckoned, though, that everything Mellie might once have hoped for between her and Press had slipped into a dismal sinkhole. With the trouble in the Aravaipa country and now with Noah Beecham to contend with, the slow dance Mellie and Press had shared over the past few months had come to a bitter end. Duett's heart flinched for both of them as she watched Mellie's eyes fill up with tears.

"I want to thank you again for taking Sarah in," Mellie managed. "I don't know what we'd have done without your help." When Mellie dropped her gaze from Press' and stared out the window again, Edna moved to wrap a plump arm around her niece's slumped shoulders.

"Poor child's a heap of raw nerves," Granny Bee said. "That damned evil-hearted Noah Beecham." She made a growling sound and spit back into the fireplace. "Fancy him backin' that polecat Ephraim Heber over his own grandbaby. And then layin' all the blame on her."

At the rattle of horse trappings, Mellie stepped back from the window. Press, who had been watching her, turned away and picked up his rifle.

"That'd be him then," Duett said. She stood up just as Shadi Lace bounded in.

"They're here, Mama," the little girl announced. "Two big buggies and a bunch of old men."

"Go on back now and stay with Sarah," Duett told her. But Shadi Lace hung about moon-eyed in the doorway.

"You heard your mama! Skedaddle!" Granny Bee eased the child back into the house before grabbing a shawl and starting outside with the others. All of them but Press stepped through the front door. His rifle barrel braced on his left shoulder, he leaned in the open doorway.

Four or five stout and bearded old men in inky wool homespuns – Noah Beecham among them – had climbed down from two equally black buggies, one pulled up close behind the other. Each driver held the reins of the coal-colored mares that had pulled them in.

"You people have my granddaughter," Noah called out from where he stood leaning on his cane right of the first rig. "We've come for Sarah Beecham."

Duett reached for Lyman's hand as a spine-chilling breeze swirled around the old man's grizzled face and dropped down to twirl in the dust at his feet.

"The Lord God delights in the chastity of women," Noah

bellowed. "He cannot look upon sin with the least degree of allowance. We must come forth, stand before Him and acknowledge our shame!"

"*I* brought Sarah here, Father Beecham," Mellie said as she stepped forward. Her slim fingers played nervously along the buttons of her dusty blue shirtwaist. "And she'll stay here. I'll not have her badgered or made a spectacle of."

"It's all settled," Edna called to her father. She stepped over to put a protective arm around Mellie's waist. "Sarah's going with me to Chicago."

"We've come for your sister, Malvina," Noah barked, ignoring his daughter altogether. He cleared his throat once or twice as though fixing to preach a sermon and then shuffled forward again.

Press ambled out from the shadowed doorway and let the rifle drop down into his left hand, the barrel pointed at the old man's feet. Noah stopped. "The girl stays here, Beecham," Press said. "Now get the hell off my land. And take them with you." He waved the rifle at the clutch of men at Noah's elbow, and they scurried to the back of the nearest buggy like squatty rats.

"He that contends against the Lord shall be accursed," Noah answered, undeterred. "We'll take the girl."

Press paced forward a step or two. "It ain't us contending," he said. "Only you."

"You've no business meddling in our affairs. You or your heathen people!" Noah slid a cold eye over to Duett and Granny Bee and then faced Press.

Duett dropped Lyman's hand and joined her brother. "I've about had my fill of your curses, old man," she said. "And it's long past table-turnin' time." Her voice rose, and she eyed Noah with a clear loathing. "I reckon accursed's something you're packin' along in your own saddlebags, Noah

Beecham. By my estimation, it was your people's selfishness that burned my little girl. Let's see you stand before the good Lord holdin' that piece of work in your bare hands."

"We had nothing to do with your daughter's misfortune," Noah sneered. He cast a glance over his shoulder for his cohorts. They skittered out from behind the buggies like roaches from a sideboard and clumped up behind him.

"Drove your poor boy Nephi mad to cover up your sins," Duett persisted. Noah's face puckered, and his eyes narrowed. Duett knew then that she'd snagged the right cat's tail. Damned if she wasn't going to sniff out every murky secret this old devil had hidden away. She sharpened her words, determined to cut the truth right out of him. "He died for them, too, you could say," she said. "Least whys I would, with you pumpin' him so full of your twisted hoo-haw in the name of patriotism."

All the color drained from the old man's face. "I don't know what you're talking about," he hissed. "We don't have to listen to this profanity." He looked over his shoulder again to the cluster of old men, but none of them made a move to defend him.

"You know, Mellie," Duett went on, keeping her eyes locked on Noah's. "Your granddaddy, Orin Harland, carved a toy horse for his little sister, Josie, just before the child disappeared. That same horse ended up right here in our hands. But then you know all about that, don't you, Mr. Beecham?"

"What?" Edna whispered to Mellie. "Do you know what this is all about?" Mellie's faced paled, and she shook her head.

"Josie Harland grew up as Josephine Spratt, your grandmother, Mellie," Duett continued. Noah's eyes widened, both hands gripping the tip of his cane. "And her sister, Adriana

Spratt...why that would be Ariel Harland." Duett's voice quieted and then rose again almost at once. "I'm sorry that it's me doin' the telling, Mellie, but this old man let his son, your father mind you, marry blood closer than a flea to a hound." She glowered at Noah, her hands planted on her hips. "Are you gonna tell us how that happened?"

"My God! Can this be true?" Edna demanded of her father.

"It can," Lyman answered grimly. Behind Duett, Mellie made a whimpering sound and steadied herself against the ranch house wall.

The men with Noah began to mumble among themselves until the old man's piercing stare stunned them into silence. "These people don't know anything," he snapped. "How could they?"

"Where did you get those two babes, Mr. Beecham?" Duett asked. Noah said nothing. "Stole them, didn't you? You were too young to skulk out and do it yourself. But not old Solomon Heber. Must have been quite the gent in '57. Nineteen, maybe twenty years old?"

Noah's head dropped to his chest, and his breathing became shallow and rapid. The old men behind him threw uneasy glances to each other.

"They say Orin Harland's little sisters, Josie and Ariel, were murdered by Redmen in 1857," Duett went on. "Josie was just a snip of a thing, barely four years old. Orin told me and Lyman himself. They were on their way to California with a Missouri wagon train. But that's not really what happened to them, is it?" She challenged the old man with a pointed stare. "They weren't really murdered, were they?"

Noah looked up again, a terrifying shroud of darkness cast over his face.

"They were stolen by Solomon Heber after John Lee's

slaughter of innocents in that campground at Mountain Meadows," Duett announced, pulling gasps and muffled curses from nearly everyone present. "Only you thought Josie's little trinket – that horse your good wife Josephine gave to Edna – had melted away with all the other spoilage from that day. But you were wrong."

The old men with Noah muttered anew and exchanged restless glances. Mellie and Edna had both clapped a hand over their opened mouths, and Granny Bee spit with fervor into a rose bush.

"What a corker to have the thing pop up in your very own orchard," Duett added. Lyman stepped up beside her. "No wonder you sent Nephi to eradicate any record of it," he said. "Burning Pop's calendar. And yours. And then breaking in to steal my glass-plate negatives, all of it to hide a kidnapping. Solomon Heber's blood is all over this mess. Yours, too."

"It wasn't kidnapping!" Noah roared. He pulled himself erect with renewed defiance. "Brother Heber took those children by the will of God and for the glory of the Church. He *saved them* from a band of infidels."

So Solomon Heber *had* gone to Mountain Meadows in 1857, just like the Valley rumors implied. And old Noah Beecham knew he'd been part of the massacre – a hundred and twenty innocent men, women and children murdered in their camp on the Virgin River by Mormon dissidents masquerading as Red Indians. A handful of children spared but stolen, with Mellie and Lyman's grandmother among them.

"Those loud-mouthed Missourians, they tore down our fences!" Noah shouted. Clenched on the tip of his cane, his hands began to shake. He glanced again at the men gathered at his elbow, who were by now whispering feverishly among themselves. "They abused our women," he shouted above them. "Called them whores. Poisoned our wells. Gave their oxen our names and then laughed as they beat them. And you call them innocent!"

Shadi Lace darted into the silence that followed and tugged at her mother's skirt. "She's gone, Mama!"

"Not now, baby," Duett whispered, taking the child's hand.

"Evil lies, the lot of it!" Noah pulled himself upright and stumbled forward toward the house. "Make way, for the judgment of the Lord is at hand." He pushed past Duett like a madman, waving his cane wildly. "I've come for Sarah Beecham." With the sudden snap of gunfire, he froze. Another snap followed. And another. The dust shot up around Noah's feet, and he dropped to his knees.

A ribbon of smoke trailed upward from the muzzle of Lyman's rifle. "Someone should have knocked you down years ago." He nodded to Press and put up the rifle.

"She's gone, Mama," Shadi Lace announced again into the stunned silence. "That girl in my room...she's gone."

Like barn owls, Noah and the Church elders eyed the others. With barely a whisper, Shadi Lace spoke up again. "That girl in my room, Mama, she's gone."

Noah dragged himself up from the dirt and started for the house once more.

"Hold on there, Beecham." Press dropped his rifle barrel into his hand with a clap. "I'm a hell of a better shot than Lyman is," he warned. "Duett, you go on in and check on the girl. We'll just wait right here, won't we, Mr. Beecham? Gentlemen?" He tipped his hat to the gathered Elders.

Duett found the room where Sarah had been sleeping empty, just as Shadi Lace had said. Her rumpled cot was cold to the touch. In a panic, Duett swung around through the room until her eyes fell on the open door of the store-room across the back courtyard. When she stepped inside, she felt the suffocation of despair long before her eyes could adjust to the darkness. And then she saw Sarah. The girl's lifeless body lay crumpled on the floor in a wine-colored pool of blood. Her wrists bore the unmistakable marks of her anguish.

# CHAPTER TWENTY-FIVE

# Saturday, February 16, 1918

Ephraim Heber got himself killed in the "great adventure" that was the war, a skull of death grinning behind the unsmiling face of his life. His last letter to Mellie came out of the trenches, Lyman said. "If death should come to one whose cause is just, it will be honorable," the letter read.

The churchmen gave Ephraim a fine farewell, saying he had passed on with dignity to his "Celestial reward." An official notice from his brigade commander extolled Ephraim for "defending the liberties of mankind as a true American," and the British soldier in whose arms Ephraim had died sent the family a note about "distressing bombardments" and strips of flesh that rolled off with the socks of the men in the trenches, their feet being wet "for bloody years."

After a simple memorial service for Sarah in Pima, Lyman brought Duett back to the farmhouse one last time in the old black Packard so she could fetch out the rest of her belongings. The fading scars on Shadi Lace's back were nothing compared to those etched in the hearts of the Texan and Mormon families, or on the cold, lifeless wrists of poor Sarah Beecham. Lyman and Duett came and went with not so much as a "howdy-do" to Noah, gathering Duett's things and loading them into the auto.

Lela, of course, worsened when she learned of Sarah's death, another precious child taken from her long before Nephi's grave had grown cold. Her eyes turned glassy, and she rambled much of the time, broken with grief like Mother Josephine before her. Ira did his best to console her, but Lela was lost in sorrow. Where little Angelina, Lyman or Mellie might bring a flickering smile to her face, it died all too soon.

Her fondness for Lyman's mother undimmed, Duett trusted that Lela could be spared the tangled web that tainted her marriage. By a 1901 statute, all marriages between first cousins had been proclaimed "void and incestuous." Though the law only applied to unions in which both parties were aware of their blood relationship, there seemed no need to trouble Lela with any of that now. Lyman and Duett had stopped by the shop earlier to say goodbye, but Lela had barely acknowledged them.

As for Noah Beecham, he spoke to no one. But then again, there was no one left to listen.

"Mellie's going to Chicago with Edna the first of next week," Lyman said as they drove on toward the Santa Teresa. "Marry me, Duett," he added without a pause, as the barren landscape slipped past Duett's window. "We can go to Tucson. We can…"

"I told your granddaddy I'd not leave the place," Duett

246

said softly. "And I won't. These are my people, Lyman. This is my home."

"I'll take Billy Ben's place then," Lyman answered. "Work the studio as I can. It's just you and me in the end anyway, isn't it?" He turned to her with hopeful eyes. "You've always said I'd make a fine sally man," he laughed.

"Yes, Lyman, it is." Duett smiled and reached for his hand. "And yes, you will."

# Epilogue

A posse of over three thousand men took part in the search for Tom Power, John Power and their hired hand, Tom Sisson. The group included civilians, sheriffs' posses from Graham, Pima, Gila and Cochise counties, and soldiers from Fort Huachuca. After twenty-nine days on the run, the fugitives surrendered on March 18, 1918, just south of Hachita, New Mexico, eight miles below the international border.

At the time, claims were made that the lawmen who rode into Power's Garden had arrest warrants for John and Tom Power for draft evasion, as well as warrants to question Tom Sisson and Jeff Power about the death of Ola May. There is no record, however, of any warrants being issued, or of any charges ever being filed against the brothers. They denied receiving draft registration notices, and no evidence was ever produced to the contrary. In fact, no documentary evidence regarding the Power's Garden shootout has survived beyond contemporary newspaper accounts and a transcript of the inquest held on the lawmen's deaths.

As early as 1921, the transcript of the trial had mysteriously disappeared from the county courthouse. Roderick J. Roberts Jr., a PhD candidate in the Department of Folklore at Indiana University in 1974, collected historical interviews for a doctoral thesis called "The Powers Boys." These documents substantiate marked cultural differences in the interpretation of the Kielberg Canyon incident.

Threatened with lynching, the three accused men were brought to trial in Clifton, in Greenlee County, on Monday, May 13, 1918, charged with murder in the first degree. The proceedings lasted for seven days. Witnesses later reported that, in their opinion, only one side of the story – the lawmen's – was told at the trial, and that the Powers' attorney was frequently inebriated. There were later allegations, never proven, that he had been bought off by the Gila Valley Mormon community. A guilty verdict was returned in twenty-five minutes, and the three men were sentenced to life in Arizona's state prison in Florence. (Arizona had outlawed the death penalty in 1916, but it was reinstated on July 3, 1918, not two months after the trial.) Tom Sisson died in prison on March 23, 1957, at the age of eighty-six.

The Powers' first parole hearing was held in 1952, when relatives of the deceased lawmen managed to keep them imprisoned. A second hearing for clemency was held on April 20, 1960. According to newspaper accounts, Lorenzo Wright, an ex-warden and a former stake president of the Mormon Church, "tongue-whipped" the brothers into asking for forgiveness, a move which apparently swayed the prison board into releasing them. The day after parole was recommended, Governor Paul Fannin signed an official commutation of their sentence. Both brothers went to live with an old friend, Lee Solomon, foreman of the AC Ranch near Kirkland Junction.

In 1963, the brothers were released from their parole restrictions and they returned to the Galiuro Mountains area. On January 25, 1969, Arizona Governor Jack Williams accepted and signed a full and unconditional pardon for all three men. John was seventy-seven. Tom was seventy-five.

Tom Power died of a heart attack at age seventy-seven on the Joe Bull Ranch near the Powers' home on Friday, September 11, 1970 – John Power's seventy-ninth birthday. He had cast his first vote just two days earlier. Sixty-two people attended Tom's funeral, most of them from nearby ranching families. A dedicatory prayer was led by George Nelson, a Mormon Elder from Thatcher. John sat at the foot of his brother's casket with his first cousin, Verda Morgan Wootan, and her husband, Clyde Wootan, a first cousin of the slain deputy, Kane Wootan. Tom was buried in the Klondyke cemetery near his sister, Ola, and their grandmother. John Power succumbed to influenza in a trailer outside the Klondyke Post Office on April 6, 1976.

Marshal Haynes, the only surviving lawman, claimed that the Power cabin had been surrounded just after 7 A.M. on the day of the shootout. No identification was given to the men inside. When Jeff Power stepped out, he was ordered to throw up his hands. According to Haynes, the old man either dropped his hands to grab his shotgun, or someone behind the cabin door began firing. When the shooting stopped a short time later, Haynes said he went up to the cabin and looked in the window. He saw and heard nothing. He rode up the trail some distance and looked down on the Power cabin until 10:30 A.M., when he set off for Klondyke.

This post-shooting scenario is improbable, as the Murdocks and Henry Allen, neighbors of the Powers, arrived on the scene well before 10:30. The Power boys also brought their wounded father inside much earlier.

The Power boys always claimed self-defense in the shootings. They had just gotten up and were lighting a fire, they said, when one of their belled mares ran down past the cabin. Jeff Power stepped outside with his shotgun to see if a mountain lion was threatening his livestock. The men he encountered outside never identified themselves as lawmen, the brothers said, and when their father was ordered to throw his hands up, he put down his weapon and did so. He was then shot point-blank, and a battle ensued. As he was dying, old man Power identified Kane Wootan as the shooter.

The controversy over what really happened in Kielberg Canyon continues to this day. Contradictions and inconsistencies are legion in the recollections of contemporaries, yet this difference in accounts is hardly surprising. There are likely as many versions of *any* event in history as there are cultures – or perhaps people – to record it. Belief does not live by logic alone, but by the consuming need it fills.

# Book Club Discussion Questions

1. Do you think the conflict between the Mormon settlers and Texas ranchers in Arizona's Gila Valley was primarily about religious differences, or was it more about economic disparity? What role did the area's persistent drought play in the conflict?

2. Mellie and Duett are both resilient women who face considerable life challenges. Discuss the development of their characters and why you think they were able to maintain a strong friendship despite having such different backgrounds.

**3.** The narration of *Power's Garden* switches between Mellie's perspective and Duett's. How are their voices different? What commonalities do they share?

**4.** What challenges do you think Lyman and Duett will face as they attempt to build a new life together? If Lyman and Duett could make a relationship work, why couldn't Mellie and Press?

**5.** Why do you think Mellie chose not to press charges against Ephraim Heber when she was sexually assaulted? Do you think she made the right decision? How might the situation have been handled differently today?

**6.** Do you think Mellie would have married Ephraim had he returned from the war? Did Mellie have the opportunity to self-govern her life, or were her choices limited?

**7.** Edna is a strong, level-headed and compassionate woman. How did she emerge from her childhood so seemingly unscathed emotionally?

**8.** Is the fact that *Power's Garden* takes place during wwi an integral part of the story? What thematic elements does the war bring into the plot?

**9.** How might the story have ended if Edna had never given Shadi Lace her mother's wooden toy horse?

**10.** Why was Noah so deeply involved in covering up Josie's true identity? What consequences might he have faced if the truth had been revealed earlier? Is the "Mormon Church" responsible for the Mountain Meadows Massacre?

**11.** According to Arizona statute, marriages between first cousins were deemed "incestuous and void" in 1901. Do you think Noah wrestled with the moral ramifications of Ira's marriage to Lela?

**12.** Is Noah Beecham an inherently evil man, an abusive man, or is he simply blinded by religion or 'set in his ways'? Do you think he adheres to the doctrine of his Mormon faith, or do you think he has developed overzealous views that are contrary to the tenets of his church? How do his interactions with the members of his family impact the development of their own religious views?

**13.** What ultimately drove Sarah to take her own life, despite having been safely spirited away to the Brennick ranch? Why do people resort to such drastic measures when problems arise in their lives? Do you think pregnant teenagers face the same kind of desperation today?

**14.** Who do you think was the father of Sarah's baby? Do you believe that Sarah truly intended Billy Ben no harm when she threw the firecrackers toward him during the horse race? Why did she point a finger at Billy Ben before recanting and blaming Ephraim for her pregnancy? Who do you feel is ultimately responsible for the death of Billy Ben?

**15.** How much do you think Lela's failing health was impacted by the emotional dynamics within her family? Do you think consistently withholding information from her was justified?

**16.** Nephi confided in Mellie more than once about having heard voices or seen visions. Do you think he was receiving some personal revelation, or do you think these occurrences were manifestations of an emotional imbalance? How does Noah maintain such power over Nephi? The others? Why was Duett able to stand up to Father Beecham when no one else could?

17. How do you feel the Beecham family dynamics will change with Noah's loss of influence and control? Do you think Ira could emerge as the patriarch of his family? Will Lela's emotional distress be alleviated? What kind of future do you envision for Angelina?

18. In 1969, the Governor of Arizona signed a full pardon for Tom Sisson, Tom Power and John Power. Why did it take so long for the judicial system to exonerate these men after they were falsely accused and wrongly imprisoned for their roles in the Kielburg Canyon shootout?

19. How does keeping secrets impact families? What kind of secrets should be kept, and which should be exposed?

20. Talk about some other examples in history that involve deeply rooted clashes in culture. How do these circumstances evolve, and what can we learn from them to improve our own relationships with others?